CAFE KINSHASA

CAFE KINSHASA

A Twelve Bar Blues

Nick Wray

First published in 2011 by:
Mam Tor Publishing Ltd.
PO Box 6785
Derby DE22 1XT
email: mamtor@mac.com

Cover Photograph by Linda Swanson
Cover Design by Liam Sharp
Rick Rogers as ZB

CAFE KINSHASA

This novel is a work of fiction. Names and characters are the product of the author's imagination and any resemblance to actual persons, living or dead, is entirely coincidental.

ISBN 978-0-9562925-1-3

Formatted by www.bookformatting.co.uk
Printed and bound in the European Community.

Nick Wray lives in Derbyshire, and plays the piano, flute and melodeon in various outfits. His first book was "*St Cyborg's*", a collection of science fiction stories, and his second the blues thriller "*A Tribute to Zed Beddington*". Both were published by Mam Tor.

www.wraymusic.co.uk
www.mamtor.com

Thanks to Cate for the support and the legal advice, to Gerald de G for the critique, and to Terence B for the encouragement.

Thanks to Liam and Chris for bringing Zed to life…

For Linda S, who went home from the gig far too early

Tuning Up

It's all thanks to the fans, bless 'em. It was the fans who kept the Zed Beddington Band going for all those years, the fans who paid for Zed's luxury flat, and his boozing and his smack habit. It was the fans who shelled out for each album, even the crappy Yuletide one made in a hurry when we needed to buy a new lighting rig, the one with the cover featuring a smirking Zed as the sleaziest-ever Father Christmas, one who'd never get a job in the Co-op grotto, even with a fistful of CRB checks, plus Danny as his goblin little helper, and Otto and me posing by the silver tinsel tree, wearing clip-on flashing LED reindeer antlers, Gawd help us. It was the fans who reached into their pockets to collectively provide the wad which Zed flashed about as he seduced other men's wives the length and breadth of Britain. The fans it was who laid out a tenner a pop to see us every time we played in their local, and who bought the merchandising from the trestle table by the bar – the Zed Beddington T-shirts, the miniature enamel badges of Ida May, Zed's legendary golden guitar, the ZB coffee mugs and beer tankards, and the branded condoms, with the slogan "*Real Bluesmen slip into a Zed Bed*".

The fans even wedged out for the 2000 Millenium Zed Beddington Band calendar, which featured me, Billy Silverthwaite, as Mr April, all thirty days of it, sexily fingering my bass, clad in black leather jacket whilst sitting astride my amp. Zed, of course, had the lion's share of the months, including all the thirty one day jobbies, leering out at his fanbase for the whole of January, March, May, July and so on. The calendar's now a collector's item – if you've got one mouldering in your attic, doing a reverse Dorian Grey, the photos staying ever-youthful whilst the band gets balder and paunchier, hang onto it for now – they're going on Ebay at the mome for a monkey a punt, but the price is creeping up at about a fiver a year.

I'll raise an amber pint of Olde Stoatfucker to the fans. The guys who turn up in their *homage* porkpie hats and shades, Ida May badge on the lapel, their ladies on their arms. They may be on their third marriage, can't see the kids except weekends for two hours at the contact centre, latest job coming to an end Friday and nothing more in sight, the jeans not fitting any more, but we are their real family. We belong to them, and they belong to us, all together in the great brotherhood of the blues men. And they mourned as brethren should when Zed had his neck broken by a falling amplifier during a crash in the band van on the way home from a gig.

At least, that's how the world and his civil partner think it happened. As www.bluespedia.co.uk says: "*Brian Alexander "Zed" Beddington, British Blues singer and guitarist, born Nottingham, July 19th 1947, died March 31st 2004 in a traffic accident on the M18 near Doncaster. Despite a career marred by alcoholism, rumoured drug abuse, and erratic behaviour both off and on stage, Beddington, a former miner, had an enormous influence on the British Blues scene, his band (Otto Anderson, drums, Matty Barker/Bill Silverthwaite bass, Danny McPhee, guitar) having several top twenty hits during the seventies and eighties....*"

But you've bought this book, or borrowed it, or nicked it, so I'll tell you something – it wasn't so. Zed had really died a year earlier, killed in a jealous rage by the former friend and workmate, Mitch Mitchison, whose songs he'd stolen and made his own, and whom he'd then cuckolded, to boot. Mitch, who'd been down the pit with Zed in their salad days, was now the landlord at the Grey Swan, the Derbyshire pub where Zed had had his first break years before, and it was in the yard at the Swan that I'd found Zed's body in the back of the van. Otto, Danny and I, without then knowing that Mitch had bumped Zed off, had buried Zed's body in secret, realising that without him we had no jobs and no income. We had called in a Zed lookalike, Bob Thompkins from Rotherham, who had been eking out a miserable living as a one-man tribute act. And with Bob we carried on as if nothing had happened, as if Zed were still alive. It had been a plan born of desperation, but, to our astonishment, it had worked. For months we had zigzagged the country with Bob in the lead role. The fans, despite their adulation, and their obsession, never cottoned on that the man shambling on and off stage, singing into the centre mike and strumming Ida May was no longer Zed Beddington.

In the crash it had been Bob who had snuffed it. The fans and the journos and Zed's ex-colleagues from the shut-down mines had turned out in their hundreds to pay their last respects at the funeral, but I had breathed a sigh of relief when I had seen the plume of smoke going up from the crematorium tower, which meant that Bob had gone for good. Nevertheless, things had started to unravel. Danny had been driving the van when we'd crashed. At first he'd tried to claim that it had been me who had been at the wheel, but he got pulled for drink-driving and perverting the course of justice *etcetera etcetera*, and he had been looking at going down. He'd been in such a state that he'd started blabbing to all and sundry at gigs about what had really gone on.

And so Otto, with no greater qualm that if he had been squashing a fly, had strangled Danny, after we'd played a gig at the Grey Swan. I'd sussed out by then that Mitch it was who had bumped off Zed, and in a *quid pro quo* to keep my mouth shut and keep the band on the road, we'd buried Danny's body in the Grey Swan's cellar and Mitch, who, after all, had written all the songs which had made Zed famous, had joined the band as guitarist.

But dying, or ostensibly dying, had been Zed's best career move ever – CD sales went northwards at ninety degrees, and we had gone back through our personal tapes and MP3 recordings to glean every scrap and out-take we had been able to find from the interminable alcohol-fuelled sessions, and frankensteined them together to make a couple more top-selling discs. And it was because of the bereaved fans'subjunctive demand that the music be kept alive that we decided to carry on playing, even after the crash, when there was no more Zed, *ersatz* or *echt*. I had been going to call everything off, but every promoter and landlord and landlady at every venue said the same thing: "You've still got to come and play. Keep the music alive." So we added Tommo as an extra guitarist, because frankly Mitch was no longer up to it, loaded the van once more, and, in pubs and clubs from Thurso to Thanet, we went on gigging.

First Bar

Home Chord of A

"Dada fuuu. Dada fuuu!!" Friday morning, three o'clock, *ante* bloody *meridian*. I stumbled out of bed in the dark, and into James Albert Silverthwaite's room, groping by the door for the wipes and a nappy.

Jimmy was already standing up in his cot, his arms outstretched. In the dim light of his lamp, decorated with characters from children's television's *Right-On Railway* – Emin the Ethnic Minority Engine, Letitia the Lesbian Loco and Tracey the Transsexual Tender – I unpoppered his sleepsuit. I could see that it had been soiled by the toffee already squeezing out between the elasticated margin of his filled nappy and his plump thighs. I pulled off the fouled clothing, unpicked the nappy, and wiped his bum clean. He gazed up at me with serious big eyes. "Baba fuuu."

I propped up his bottom, slid a clean nappy underneath and velcro'd it shut, then reached into the drawer and pulled out a new sleepsuit. By the time I had this on him he was wide awake, and trying to stand up again. I put the dirty nappy into a plastic bag and carried Jimmy downstairs, where I put the bag into the bin, and shoved the old sleepsuit into the open porthole of the washing machine, to await a full load. We had been on recyclable washable eco-bunny cottons but they had made Jimmy's delicate *derrière* so sore that we'd had to go for landfill instead. He was sucking his thumb in a suggestive fashion, so out of the fridge I got one of the bottles of formula I'd made up the night before. With Jimmy on my knee, his mouth clamped onto the bottle in my left hand, I fired up the laptop with my right. Let's see what the word was on *www.britishbluesgoss.co.uk*:

harpmouth, *beermonster37* and *nakedblueslady* are in the room

harpmouth: any1 going 2 brustle's 2 c tribyute 2 zeebee?

beermonster37: no i been 2 holland b4 ale way 2 xpensiv

nakedblueslady: i am naked in zees memmory

harpmouth: i liv right by m1 i mite go down to bridge 2 watch van go by n wish lad's good luck

beermonster37: wot duz there new van look like?

harpmouth: its lite blu transit 1374 cc reg is sumthing like ZB 101 FU2

nakedblueslady: now zee is dead i am naked 4 bill

beermonster37: how much gig's they playing in brustle's?

harpmouth: 3 awl @ same venu first time they been abrord sinse zee died

nakedblueslady: i woz naked awl thru zees funerul

bluesfiend666 is in the room

bluesfiend666: fuk off nakedblueslady i woz there and didnt c no naked lady ☺

beermonster37: nakedblueslady is a man we all kno that

nakedblueslady: fuk off i am lady

beermonster37: u going 2 b naked @ zeestok?

nakedblueslady: not 4 u

Didn't these people have nice comfy warm beds to get into? Didn't they have families, or lovers, or jobs to have to get up for in the morning? Maybe they were all on night shift in call centres, or perhaps they all had insomniac eleven-month-olds like I did.

harpmouth: u kno they going as 3peice tommo not going 2

brustle's

beermonster37: y that?

harpmouth: his wife going 2 giv berth soon

bluesfiend666: did u kno that mitchs wife has left him again?

beermonster37: thort he woz looking even more mizerabl than normle

bluesfiend666: wurd is that bill and his missus not 2 happy eether

nakedblueslady: i want 2 hav bills baby i am naked

bluesfiend666: fuk off nbl men cant do that u r man

beermonster37: anyway bill has baby already ☺

harpmouth: hes 2 knackrd 2 play proply i saw him fawl asleep on stage @ northamptn last week

bluesfiend666: no wunder his wife not happy lol

beermonster37: yeh well his missus onely married him 2 get baby shes pushing fourty

Jimmy stopped sucking, went cross-eyed and moaned. I sat him upright and patted his back gently, to be rewarded with a cathartic burp. He grabbed the bottle and resumed pulling at the teat. I logged in myself.

<u>*wurzelman* is in the room</u>

wurzelman: Shouldn't we be interested in the music, rather than the colour of the band van or whether they're having kids or relationship problems?

bluesfiend666: fuk off wurzelman blue's is our life and our relijon

beermonster37: blue's and beer

bluesfiend666: zee is our god wurzelman u r heretik u will die

nakedblueslady: i woz naked 4 zee but now i am naked 4 bill

With Jimmy crooked in my elbow, I got up and one-handedly

made myself a cup of tea. When, at five, it was time to load up, I inserted Jimmy into his sling, podgy legs dangling down each side and face and arms pressed against my chest. Van keys between my teeth I picked up a PA speaker which I could just about carry with Jimmy's feet an inch or so above it. I stumbled out through the front door into the morning chill, set the speaker down, opened the van at the rear, and, by leaning back so that my spine felt like it was about to snap, manoeuvred the speaker in. Jimmy twisted his head round to watch what I was doing. "Ah fuuu…" he said contentedly. I clambered into the van and shoved the speaker to the back. I was making a lot of noise, and I'd already had complaints from the neighbours, threatened Asbos, injunctions, control orders, *etcetera etcetera*.

I got the rest of the stuff loaded without crushing Jimmy to death, although it took twice as long as usual, and at one point a microphone stand caught against a doorframe, and as it came free it whacked Master James from behind. Fortunately it struck his well-padded bottom, and not the back of his not yet fully knitted-together skull.

As the clock in the living room struck six I took Petra a cuppa and put Jimmy into bed with her. Instead of getting up to see me off, Petra turned drowsily, the lad yawned and stretched, and the two of them went snugly back to sleep.

First stop was for Otto, cockney exile Mr June in the calendar, pictured louring in his standard black T-shirt behind his drum kit, muscular arms grasping his sticks. As I drew up outside his flat a car swerved across the way, trying to take my parking slot. I got in first and the other guy had to idle in the road. Otto's door opened up and out trotted a young blond woman in the shortest miniskirt I'd seen for a long time. Without looking back she slid into the car and it roared off, the driver giving me the finger as they went past. I looked at Otto as he pulled himself into the van. "Let me guess, she's an ethnic Russian from Kazakhstan and you're helping her with her English?"

"Fuck off." Otto settled into the middle seat, reached down to his bag and pulled out a can of lager. "Drive."

We trundled out of Nottingham, over the M1 and on into

Derbyshire, the grotty industrial bit with endless trading estates and hypermarkets, not the nice bit with the Bakewell puddings. In Coatstall, Mitch was peering out through the Grey Swan's door. Mitch hadn't been in the calendar as he hadn't been in the band then, which was just as well, as with his beergut and the suitcases under his bloodshot eyes he wouldn't exactly have been the housewives' choice. Zed had been a plug-ugly fucker as well, but at least the horse had kept him skinny. Mitch staggered over and clambered in. "Morning."

Otto said nothing. I nodded. As I put us into gear, Mitch produced a bottle of Guinness. "I thought you were going to do some driving," I said.

"I need summat." Mitch levered off the top with a bottle-opener. "Just the one."

Rock and roll, I thought, sighing, me and two beer-sodden murderers heading down the M1. I felt groggy from lack of sleep and no breakfast, and every time a car zoomed past us I was scared that I might accidentally swing out. Despite what he had said, after twenty minutes or so or rolling along in silence Mitch opened a second bottle. He shrugged apologetically. "Sorry. I need it. I can still drive." Otto was well into his third or fourth can. He wasn't going to be behind the wheel; years before, after a 2*a.m.* shunt into a shopfront, the culmination of a drink-driving career, he had been banned for life. My head drooped and I had a momentary nodding-off sensation. I indicated left and pulled over onto the hard shoulder, with the hazards going. Mitch looked blearily at me. "What's up?"

"I can't drive any further. I'm bolloxed. I've been up all night. It's not safe."

"Okay, I'll take over." Mitch put down his bottle and made to open his door.

"No way," I said. "I'll take us to the next services. You have a coffee and then do it." I nosed us out into the slow lane during a nanosecond in which nothing was lightspeeding by. A minute later we passed under a slim footbridge, and up top I saw a figure semaphoring frantically at us. Tied to the railings was a banner: "*Good Luck ZB lads!*" It had to be *harpmouth*, as good as his online word. Craning forward in my seat I waved back as we passed underneath.

We got to Toddington services and whilst Mitch and Otto stomped off to the café I stretched out on the strip of manky carpet between all the gear. I shut my eyes and tried to think about Jimmy and the lovely fluff on the back of his head. In the night I would curl up round him, protecting his little bones from harm, from cries and shouts and the birds which were screaming and swooping…

***

I could hear seagulls. The engine was switched off. I sat up and cautiously opened the door. I could see lines of lorries and cars, and massive ships looming over them. We were at Dover.

On the ferry Otto and Mitch settled themselves in the bar. Leaning on the deck railings, I tried to convince myself that the swell wasn't making me feel ill. Look at me, son of Albion, Devon-born heir to Drake and Raleigh, feeling seasick when we hadn't even left the harbour yet. I was hungry, that was all. I watched the grey cliffs and the ugly buildings of the ferry terminal slide away. Sat near me were a family, a handsome thirty-something couple with a pair of tow-haired kids. They were all chattering and laughing, the two children careering round excitedly. The parents didn't seem perpetually exhausted, tetchy and ready to kill each other. Maybe fatherhood at forty eight was leaving it a bit late, but that wasn't the cause of our problems. Petra had devoted herself at the hospital to working her way up the medical foodchain, and, when she wasn't working, to her son – our son – and I felt ignored and marginalised, an inferior contributor to the whole show, even though I did the bloody graveyard shifts, so that she wasn't so exhausted that she gave someone 100 *ml* of morphine instead of 10 and found herself up before the GMC.

We'd met at a gig, and she'd told me then that she had been my greatest fan, and at that time she really had liked the music, and being in the tow of the great Zed Beddington, as she, like the rest of the world, thought Bob really was. But over the years, her attitude to the music had changed. Maybe she'd thought that I'd be a global superstar by now, wearing mirror shades and flying by private jet to stadia in LA, my every need met by teams of obsequious roadies, instead of still rumbling up and down the British motorway network in the Transit. "Why don't you do some new stuff? You can write good songs, Billy."

I *had* written some good stuff – and at home I sometimes played through them – but that's not what the punters wanted to hear. They only wanted to be in the comfort zone of the familiar two dozen hits which Mitch had written three decades earlier, the songs which Zed had then stolen and claimed as his own. I was treading water musically, it was true, but someone had to look after the child she'd wanted, when she was on night shifts, and likely *beermonster* was right about her only getting together with me to have that child. She wouldn't have met a fellow medic who'd have been willing to sacrifice his career for childcare. And what also didn't help was coming back in from gigs at some unearthly hour to find her sat up with Jimmy in the sitting room, resentful and unspeaking, handing me the squirming bundle before going off to sleep on her own in what had once been our bed.

Grunting to myself, I went below to the cafeteria, got myself a late breakfast with a cup of tea and read the paper, sitting at the far end of the boat from the other two, so that we wouldn't run into each other in the toilets. I was just finishing my toast, hoping that it would subdue the queasy feeling, when a voice interrupted my thoughts.

"Bill!"

I looked up. Two squirrel-like faces, male and female, were grinning at me. "Bill!" the man said again, enthusiastically. Both of them were wearing Zed Beddington T-shirts, he over his beer paunch, and she over her ample bosom.

"I'm sorry..." I said hesitantly. "I think you have the advantage of me?"

"Skipton," said the woman. "We spoke to you after the gig. We told you how we're coming to Zedstock. You signed our CDs."

We had played in Skipton a couple of months earlier but I still couldn't recall anything about these two. "I'm sorry," I said, "I think you're muddling me up with someone else. CDs?"

The man looked sheepish. “I’m terribly sorry,” he said, in embarrassment twisting his hands around, the right one of which had been held out for me to shake. “I’m sorry, I thought you were... I’m sorry.” He turned away, ushering his wife before him. I felt suddenly guilty for blanking them, but I could almost script the bloody conversation, about how great Zed had been, how tragic it had been that he’d died like that, and how fabbo it was that we were still carrying on *etcetera etcetera*. Then, when they’d cleared off, I thought, Beelzebub’s bollocks, I hope they’re not travelling to see us, because then I’ll really be in it when they see me on stage. Then I’d have to pretend that it hadn’t been me whom they’d met on the ferry. I sipped moodily at my tea, but it had gone cold.

From Oostende we rolled inland. Some friend of a friend of Otto’s ran a bar in Brussels and wanted three nights of A Tribute to Zed Beddington, even with just the current trio, and at three o’clock, *post* bloody *meridian*, exactly twelve hours after I’d been woken up by the fruit of my loins, having not hit anything, despite being on the wrong bloody side of the road the whole way from the coast, we were grumbling through the inner city. Mitch, who was leafing his way through a French phrase-book, looked out of the window at the thronging pavements. “Fuck me, they eat donkey here.”

“What do you mean?”

“Look.” Mitch gestured with the book. “Mule and *Frites*. That’s chips, isn’t it, *frites*?”

As we were stationary, waiting at a red, I was able to look at the sign, chalked outside a café. “*Moules et frites*.”

I snorted. “Local delicacy. Donkey, chips and mayonnaise.” The lights went to green and I had to concentrate on following the map on the dashboard before me. No point in asking either Otto or Mitch to cope with all the foreign names. Anyway, a couple of minutes later we poled up with a sharp handbrake stop outside *Le Mannekin Pis*, a microphone’s throw from the Midi Station. I knew I had the right place as there was a huge placard above the door announcing: “*Trois soirées de Zed Beddington*!! *Vive sa musique*!!”, and, knock me down with a guitar stand, there was also a shop window dummy standing outside the bar, dressed as Zed, complete with mohair suit, porkpie hat and brothel-creepers. Slung over its back it had a gold spray-painted guitar, and its two immobile hands reached forward to copy the pose of the famous little boy's statue. Somehow, someone had rigged up a stream of yellow water which emerged from between the plastic hands and arc'ed down away through a drain. The posters with our mugshots, including Tommo's, unfortunately, were plastered all over the outside of the café. I looked expectantly at Otto, who had been jolted out of his slumbers.

"You go in and do the intros," I said. "We'll unload."

"Fuck off, Wurzel," said Otto. "Rabbit's always your job."

"Normally, yeah, but he's your mate."

"Mate of a mate."

"And?"

Otto took a draught from his can. "Fuck off, Wurzel, just do it." He turned his face away to stare out of the passenger window.

"He doesn't speak English," said Mitch. "The guy who runs the bar."

"I see. So how the fuck did you arrange the gigs then?"

Otto crushed his now empty can in his fist. "Through my mate who's a fuckin' Moroccan. Alright? Now do one."

"Okay. Okay. What's the fucker's name again?"

"Armand." He pronounced it to rhyme with *arm* and Cockney *hand.* I got out and went into the gloomy bar. Although the doors were open the windows were still shuttered and all the stools were stacked on the tables. Despite all the razzmatazz outside it was quiet and still, just a clicking sound and Francophone cursing – it came from two guys who were playing table-football by the counter.

I went over. "*Er... 'Scuse me. I'm looking for Armand.*"

A chap my own age, reddish moustache like a walrus, stopped thrusting the rods and stood up. "*That's me.*"

"*I'm Bill. Zed Beddington band... We're playing here.*"

He nodded and stretched out a hand. We went out to the van – there was space round the back where we could park up and unload, and leave the Tranny overnight, which was great as Armand very kindly presented all three of us with some bottles of beer, and I could have one without getting my collar felt for drink-driving by *les flics*, or whatever the Sprout equivalent was. We set up – I'd even remembered to bring the continental adaptors – sound-checked, and then strolled via a *patisserie* to the *pension* where we were stopping.

Flopped onto my bed I chewed my way through a portion of *brick*. My mobile beeped. I knew it would be Petra. I should have texted her first thing, saying that we had got here OK, but every time I thought about contacting her I put it off. If I were too curt in my message I might piss her off even more, and if I were too lavish she might take the hump at that, at my presuming things that just weren't there at the moment. Whichever way, I was stuffed. After a couple of minutes moodily studying the ceiling rose I flicked open the phone.

boy 9lb 11oz all well

That was from Tommo. Baby was a big chappy, I thought, but Suzy's problem, not his. Or mine. I sent back congrats and then immediately texted Petra.

got here ok seems good place hope you and j well x

I decided one **x** was about right. I imagined Tommo sitting proudly by the hospital bed, cradling his new-born giant son, his wife smiling exhaustedly but indulgently at them. I wanted Petra to answer, but the phone was silent.

There was a knock on my door. "Come in, *entrez*. It's not locked. *Ce n'est pas...*" Locked? What was that? Anyhow it was Mitch, so my bilingual effort was wasted. "Alright?" I asked warily.

"Yeah." He leant against the wall by the door, looking down at me. "Can you get British telly?" he asked, gesturing at the set on a bracket.

"Haven't tried."

"Can't get anything but French and Dutch, I think."

"Dunno. You can probably get some porn if you're feeling desperate."

"Fuck off." He must have thought this a sly reference to Alison's departure.

"Can't help you, then. Tommo's missus has sprogged, by the way. All well."

Mitch said nothing, but just stood there, longer than was needful.

"What the fuck is it, Mitch?"

"I'm sorry. There's a problem."

I assumed he meant something to do with the gear. "What?"

"Otto and me, we've got to go back to London as soon as we finish the last gig. On the train."

"What?" I hadn't taken it in – my mind was still half on Tommo and Suzy and the new one, and Petra and Jimmy.

"Yeah, we've got to see someone. Just had a call."

I sat up. "Mr Big's just rung, has he? And you've got to nip on the old midnight Eurostar. And I've got, what, to load up and drive all the gear back on my tod?"

"Yeah. It's business."

"I see. Nice one. You two fuck off and leave me to do all the work… Oh yeah, and get me to drive back to Blighty with half a weight of Henry stashed somewhere in the back."

Mitch was shaking his head. "No, no way."

"You're damned right, no. No fucking chance. Why the fuck are you still doing this Mitch? You don't need to. You've got the band now."

Mitch wrung his hands. "I can't just stop… There's people who'd… You know."

Otto was pushing his way into the cramped room. "Will you two shut the fuck up? Half the fucking hotel can hear you." He shut the door. "Mitch told you?"

"Yeah," I said, "And I'm telling *you*, no fucking way. Funny that, isn't it, first time we happen to come abroad since Zed copped it, and suddenly you two have got to fuck off and leave me carrying the can? I tell you what, I'll leave the gear and the van here and come back on the train myself. You can come back and pick it up. If I get pulled over, whilst you two are swallowing oysters in the bar at St Pancras International with Don Bollockeoni it's me looking at ten years swallowing dick."

Otto took a step over to me and laid his massive hairy hand over my mouth. It was horrible and humiliating, but, as I knew from past experience, he was so strong that there was nothing that I could do. "I said, shut the fuck up, Wurzel. Anyway, you're flattering yourself. They like the young pretty ones inside." He leered at me as he sat down heavily on the bed and motioned to Mitch to take a pew in the split leather chair by the *en suite* door. "Now you just fucking listen to me, Wurzel. Right?"

I nodded. Otto took his hand away, but put it into onto my thigh which he started to squeeze in an unpleasant fashion. "Now," he went on, "It's business, we've had a call, we agreed that you'd be kept out of it all, and we're keeping our side of the deal. You know *nurthing*." Otto had never been able to do accents "Anybody asks, which they won't, we went back after the gig on the train, you've no fucking idea why but as you were the only one sober enough to drive you didn't object to a peaceful little pootle back on your own through the lovely French countryside."

"Belgian," I said. "And get your fucking hand off my leg."

It was all too glib, a sudden phone call just after we'd got here. They had to be plotting something. On the other hand, Otto was right; they had been – I suppose scrupulous was the right word, but odd in the context – careful to do whatever sordid deals they were still carrying out well away from me, and from Tommo, who, in any case, knew absolutely tiddly-squat about what they had been and were up to. I leant back against the wall. "Okay," I said slowly, "I want your word, from both of you, individually, that there's not going to be any smack, or any other fucking illegal substance going back with me." I looked across at Mitch, whom I reckoned I could trust marginally more.

"My oath, Billy. You'll know everything that's in the van."

"On Alison's life?" I knew that Mitch was desperate to have her back, although not desperate enough to stop the drinking which had driven her away.

He nodded. "Yeah." I knew that was about as serious as I could get him to be.

No use asking Otto like that – he'd happily perjure himself on whichever former Soviet citizenness had been his last half-hour stand. He had stopped kneading my thigh, and was staring at me. "Have I ever let you down, Billy Wurzel?"

"No."

"Then I'm not fucking starting now." He carried on staring at me, unblinking, for longer than I could endure, and I looked away. "Anyway, Wurzel, let's go to work."

I glanced at my mobile. "It's only half past six."

"Half seven. Frog time."

I'd forgotten about that. We ambled up from the hotel. It was a warm sunny evening, and the good burghers were out letting their dogs shit in the gutter, doing the evening shopping or sitting outside the zinc bars. That kip I'd had in the back of the van had been the longest stretch I'd had in months. My mood of hostility and being fucked-over began to lift. Hearing the chatter of French and Arabic and Turkish around me I felt re-energised, cosmopolitan, interesting, a bit more attractive maybe. I should text Petra again, with something humorous and affectionate. As we filed into *Le Mannikin Pis* I slapped the dummy Zed's cheek. Its sunglasses slipped and I had to stop and adjust them. Inside the bar there was now a decent crowd, sipping away at their weeny continental-sized beer glasses.

We did the final set-up, checking the connections and levels. When I tried to pay Armand for a drink he waved me away; I hoped for his financial sake that he wasn't going to be subbing Mitch and Otto all night. Leaning against a speaker I texted Petra. **Ça va? Tout va bien ici il ya du monde je t'aime bill x baise J pour moi** By pressing the button about seven times I'd found the *c* with the cedilla.

There was no reply by the time we got on stage. From my vantage point I scanned the crowd warily for my friends from the ferry, but they hadn't shown. Must have just been a chance meeting. Unless, of course, they were going to show up tomorrow night, or the night after. We were on for eight hundred euros a show and Otto would break legs if there were any attempt to weasel out of paying. Three profitable evenings of ZB Tribute on the trot seemed a tad *optimistique* on Armand's part, but there were already quite a few guys dressed as *Monsieur* Beddington in the audience, so it looked like they had the same set of saddoes here as we did at home. Maybe the anoraks'd all come for all three nights.

Armand gave me an enthusiastic double thumbs-up from behind the mixing-desk, which was conveniently positioned on the counter, next to the taps. He'd volunteered for the job – he said that he did it for all the bands. I'd explained as well as I could how our desk worked, and after that we were going to have to hope for the best. He seemed to think that he could multitask without dripping beer into the slider tracks.

I tapped my mike. A thump from the monitors told me that it was working "*Ah... Hello, ladies and gentlemen, welcome to Le Mannekin Pis. We are the Zed Beddington Band, and we're keeping the music alive...*"

Someone shouted: "Bravo! You're doing good!"

Fuck I thought, do I switch to English? No. Fuck them; if they wanted to speak American to me, they could fuck off. "*Okay, allons-y, here we go!*" I turned to face Otto, who had a row of opened bottles like a line of penguins curled round his cymbal stand.

Otto lifted his sticks. "One, two, three, four..." No French for him. And we were away. The monitor sound seemed okay, and judging by the happy expressions on the punters' faces it was alright out front. Mitch sang the first song and then I did the second, "*Green Turtle Blues*", a number on the off-beat where I could fit the vocal lines between bass runs. It was one of the few songs which Zed had actually written, and which had been added to our set after I'd joined the band. And the audience knew it – with heavily accented voices they were singing along. One of the Zed lookalikes was already boogieing back and forth at the front of the crowd, air-guitaring on his Ida May replica. A photographer was prowling to and fro, taking shots, the flash flaring out of the corner of my eye. At the end there was a thunder of applause. I felt emboldened to talk a bit more; I usually did a bit of jaw-jaw after the first couple of tunes.

"*Thanks, thankyou. You probably know that usually there's four of us, but our guitarist, Tommo, well, his wife's had a baby this afternoon, back in England!*" I could see Mitch making a get-on-with-it face at me, but the audience understood and whooped and cheered. "*So,*" I went on, "*This next song, it's for Tommo and family. On y va, Otto!*"

Hearing his name, Otto launched us away. It was Mitch's turn to sing. By now there were three Zed clones doing their thing on the floor. I was concentrating and looking down at my fingers when I began to hear something strange, a big cheer, and then some pulsing sound, an alien noise over the racket that we were making. I saw, to my astonishment, that some big African guy had climbed onto the stage, had somehow managed to plug in a spare mike and direct it onto a couple of those big upright drums which have roped-down skins over the top. He was playing along, in perfect time, in complex cross-rhythms that fit in perfectly. How the hell had he known where to get one of the mikes from, and which socket in the desk to put it into? I looked over at Armand, but he just grinned and shrugged; maybe he had set it up. I turned round to face Otto – the guy was straying onto his turf, after all, but, as ever when he was playing, Otto's expression was unreadable. Mitch was still singing. Things like this occasionally happened – I recalled a beer festival in Milton Keynes where I'd literally had to throw a drunken fuckwit off the stage. He had kept trying to climb on with his saxophone, yelling that he was here for the jam session and who the fuck were we to say that he couldn't play? – but three of the rules for a professional band are that you never let anyone onto stage with you unless *a*)you know them and their competence, *b*)they're someone whom you know your audience will want to hear and *c*)you've worked out *exactly* what you're going to play beforehand. You don't just let Joe or Josephine Public stroll on and guest for slice of free glory.

Mitch reached the last verse, and I concentrated on trying to make eye-contact with the bloke – I wanted us to have a clean finish at least. He saw me and nodded as I made a chopping gesture with my hand, and we all ended as neatly and tidily as if we'd rehearsed it a dozen times. Whoever this fucker was, he was good.

The applause was huge. "*Merci! Merci!*" I bellowed into the mike. "*Thanks to our friend there!*" I pointed and the clapping redoubled. Now I was in a bind. I didn't want to cause an international incident by stopping the drummer chappy, but should I be encouraging him to carry on? I looked over to Mitch for guidance, but he was turned away, dicking about with his amp. No point in going to Otto. When in Rome, or Brussels, rather, I thought... I looked across at our new friend. "*Okay, are you carrying on?*"

He shouted something which I didn't understand at all. Fuck it, I thought, just see what happens. I was to sing now, on a track with a bass lead in, so I started the run. Our new colleague joined in, watching for cues and stops. At the end of the song, when we'd all arrived at the home chord, he went off on an intricate improvisation, four beats in the left hand and something like threes over them, tighter than the Standard Atomic Clock thing they have in Paris or wherever it is that provides the universal time unit for everyone, *x*-trillion oscillations of a krypton atom per second. The crowd were clapping along on the main beat, and the drummer's hands moved in an ever faster blur as he wove the rhythms. I looked at Otto again, and, maybe for the first time in all the years I'd ever known him, I thought I saw something like a trace of resentment, or anger, in his expression. He knew that he was being blown away and he disliked it so much that for once he couldn't hide his feelings. Fuck him, I thought. I waited for the right moment and joined in with the drums, barring octave chords on my bass and running triplets up and down. This was more like it; let's show the fuckers out there what Billy Silverthwaite could really do when he wasn't trammelled by his sad sack band mates. Mitch was looking daggers at me, but he was lost – no way could he get in. I caught the drummer's eye and he grinned, nodded and we took the improv round again. The crowd were loving it, the Zeds down the front standing in a line and jiving back and forth. The drummer momentarily held up four fingers – four more times round the block, three, two, one, and we were out to a perfect stop. They were screaming for more, but I knew that I should stick by the old entertainer's rule – always leave them wanting more, so I yelled a few "*Merci*!"s into the mike, then we scrambled off. I suddenly just wanted to talk to Petra. I felt buoyed up and confident, and I knew that this was the moment to grasp the nettle, talk to her whilst I had it in me not to read bad things into every hesitation or ambiguous remark. As I tried to slip out of the stage door a figure loomed up, and a light flashed again. "What the fuck?"

"Sorry, my friend, I am press. You give me an interview?" It was the guy who had been taking photos during the set.

"No. *Pardon. Non.*" I couldn't afford to let my mood dissipate – I pushed past him to go outside. It was getting dark. I opened up the back of the van, sat on the tailgate and dialled our home number. The phone rang, and rang until the answering machine kicked in, my own voice saying: "Sorry, neither Petra nor Bill are available at the moment but if you want to leave a message..." I switched my mobile off before it got to the recording bit. Petra should be at home – it was nearly half eight o'clock in England and Jimmy should be down by now. My mood was ebbing; I should try her on her own mobile but now I felt frightened of another stilted conversation. I rang the landline again and was almost relieved when I got the recorded message once more. This time I did speak.

"Hi, it's me. Hope you're OK and the boy is too. It's the break – they love us, and we've got some local guy joining in as well. Maybe I'll speak to you later. *Je t'adore, je vous adore, tous les deux...*" I clicked my phone off again. Was I trying too hard, leaving texts and messages without anything back? Where the fuck was she? Had she gone out, round to one of her NCT femfriends with Jimmy tucked up to fall asleep in the pushchair or the rear of the runabout on the way back? Should I text? No, wait until she answered me in some form.

Armand was awaiting me at the door. "*Hey, matey, that was fantastic! They love you!*" He pressed another open bottle into my hand. "*If you want any more, just say, okay?*"

"*Okay. Thanks... Who's that bloke with the drums? You know him?*"

"*No. I though he was a pal of yours.*"

Otto was still sat at his kit, eyes invisible behind wraparound shades, a bottle tilted into his mouth. He hadn't stirred from his position the whole break, as if he needed to keep hold of his territory, both literally and metaphorically. I got onstage to check the tuning on my bass. Otto leant across. "Who the fuck is he, then?" he asked, pointing to the drummer, who was chatting to a couple of punters at the bar.

"I've no idea."

"Well, tell him to fuck off, tout bloody sweet."

"You do it." We started the second set. The drummer sat out the first couple of numbers, perhaps sensing that it'd be more dramatic to come in later. Once he was in the whole place was rocking, the Zed *doppelgänger* strutting their stuff beneath us, couples dancing, the men leading their ladies with an arm around the waist and the other hand clasped, the old-fashioned way which we never saw at gigs in England. During the last song of the set a light flashed in my eyes – I looked up to see the photographer crouching down at the foot of the stage, taking more pics. At once our drummer friend sprang down, and tried to seize the camera. A furious argument broke out as, in bemusement, we three *rosbifs* carried on playing. I saw Armand come out and try to intervene – abruptly the drummer climbed back on stage, unplugged his drums as quickly as he could, and pulled them off towards the door. But the crowd were all shouting "*Bis*! *Bis*!", so we had to dredge a couple of oldies out of retirement.

I got off stage at last, and was just about to get another drink when a large arm was wrapped round my neck. It was Otto. "I need you." He dragged me though the crowd to a table where an attractive thirty-something woman was sat alone with a glass of wine.

Otto released me. "Ask her whether she wants another drink."

I shook my head. "Fuck off."

"Translate," said Otto. "Does she want another?"

I leant down to the woman, who smiled expectantly. "*Sorry to tell you this,"* I said, "*But my mate here's a fucking psycho and if I were you I'd fuck off out of it as quickly as possible.*"

She got to her feet and I backed off before Otto could grab me again. I slipped outside, thrusting the doors open, racing my way through the people on the pavements, expecting any moment to feel a heavy paw clamping down onto my shoulder. I hurtled along the neon-yellow streets and made it back to the *pension*. The main door was open, and I tore through that, up the short flight of steps and fumbled my room key into the latch.

Second Bar

Fourth Chord of D

I was woken by a ping on my mobile. **glad all well j and i fine**

As messages went it could scarcely have been terser, and there was no **x** at the end, but at least she was still talking to me. It was light outside. Eight fifteen, frog time, as Otto would have put it. I stared blearily at the phone, unsure of what level of commitment and passion to show, particularly at this hour of the morning with the remnants of a head full of Flemish lager. In the end I wrote:

Had good night had fabbo african drummer onstage with us

Too much, I thought then. It sounded like I was trying too hard, telling her how marvellous the music was, despite everything. I deleted the last seven words. **Had good night bit hacked off got to drive back on my own as O and M taking train for some reason Tommo and Suzy hav new sprog all ok x**

That seemed suitably non-committally informative about things that didn't really matter without being too offhand. Having decided to avoid Otto and Mitch and the hotel's six euro breakfast, I bumbled along one of the main throughfares. I bought a French language newspaper and opened it at random, and, blow me, there we were on the centre pages, a big pic of me and Mitch standing feet apart, wielding our axes, with Otto caught in a blur of sticks behind his kit. In the foreground the Zeds were dancing and to the side our drummer guest was captured in profile. The headline read: "*Chez Armand la musique de Zed vive*!". I needed to settle down and read this properly. I had just spied a suitable-looking café when someone grabbed my arm.

"*Hey, salut*!"

It was a big black guy, between me and the sun. I squinted at him. "*Pardon*?"

"*Hey, remember me*?"

I smiled in as friendly a way as I could. "*Yeah, yeah, drums. Last night*."

He hadn't let go of my arm, and he shook it enthusiastically. "*That was fab, last night.*" He started to drag me off; he was as strong as Otto and I found myself being unwillingly towed along. "*Come and have a beer.*"

I didn't want to be rude, but it was a bit early and I needed something to eat. "*Sorry, but I need some breakfast, coffee, you know*."

"*No problem*." The next thing I knew, he was pulling me in a life-threatening weave through the Alice-through-the-Looking-Glass traffic, down an alley and into a little bar. He waved me onto a stool at the counter, gabbled a mixture of French and some other language to *le patron*, another African, and after we had seated ourselves on two stools a couple of croissants was placed in front of me, together with a steaming bowl of coffee.

"*Okay? I'm Maurice, by the way*." He had a pull on a bottle of beer.

"*Bill*," I said, opening up the paper, and pointing to our photo. "*You seen that?*"

Maurice studied the photo. "*I don't want to be in the papers*." Shaking his head, he said something, again in a melange which I didn't understand at all, to the bloke behind the counter, who looked at me with interest. I was the only white guy in the place. On one wall was a big clock of an irregular shape – it looked vaguely familiar, a rough square with a kind of panhandle sticking out on the left. Written above it in neon tubes were the words "*Café Kinshasa*".

Maurice followed my eyes. "*You know what that is*?"

"*Congo? You from there?*"

"*Yes*." I detected a slight change of mood. "*I am. Are you married?"*

Oddly abrupt question I thought, but maybe a kind of Congolese ice-breaker. "*Yeah.*"

"*You got kids*?"

"*Yeah. A boy. He's only little.*"

"*Look at this.*" From out of his jacket pocket Maurice pulled something square. A CD case. He handed it to me.

"*Is that you?*"

Maurice nodded. There was a picture of him with a set of drums, just like the ones I'd seen him playing the night before, and a couple of other guys, one holding a bass and one holding a guitar. I opened up the case and looked at the track listings. It took me a moment to realise that a couple of them were our tracks – Zed Bed tracks – translated into French. They even had my song, "*La Maison aux Reptiles.*" at number four.

"*I had no idea we were big in Congo*."

Maurice laughed and pulled at his beer. "*Zed got everywhere.*" He was right, I thought, although, recalling Zed's insatiable and cosmopolitan sexual appetite, maybe not in the sense he meant. Maurice took the CD from me and clicked his fingers at *le patron*, who put the disc into the little player above the bar. And then I heard the weirdest thing – those tracks, which were so familiar to me, one of which I'd even written, played back with a lively jit-jive guitar and a fluid percussion which was both infectious and disturbing. I couldn't understand any of the words, though – they were neither French nor English. Maurice was watching my expression. "*What do you reckon?*"

I nodded. "*I like it.*" Something was touching about this – somehow these guys thousands of miles away in some remote corner of Africa had heard our music and had paid us the compliment – awesome from such players – of reinterpreting it. Maurice seemed pleased at my comment.

Le patron turned the volume down on a gesture from Maurice, who took another mouthful of his beer and then swivelled to look at me. He hesitated for a moment. "*My daughter.*" From out of his pocket he drew something else – a photo, which he held it up to me.

The kid must have been about fourteen. She was smiling with big beautiful eyes into the camera. "*She's very pretty. What's her name?*"

"*Oh... Laure.*" Maurice was studying the photo himself. "*My wife's name was Marianne... She's dead.*" He looked at me challengingly, seeing what my reaction would be.

"*I'm sorry,*" I said evenly. What can you say when you're told of the death someone whom you never knew? "*How did... What happened?*"

"*You've heard of Mobutu?*"

"*Of course.*"

"Not everyone has. But, you know, Mobutu and his mates looted the whole country. We had petroleum, diamonds, minerals, but that crew of thieves took the lot. We just wanted fair play and to be able to keep what was ours, but they put down any rebellions. And when Kabila came on the scene we thought things would be different, but then the Tutsis came from Rwanda and burnt everything along the route to Kinshasa. They came to our village and they shot Marianne in front of me. The soldiers wanted to take her.. I tried to stop them, but..."

The momentum of his speech petered out. I sat there in silence. Around us cutlery clattered and voices chattered. Maurice was drinking at his beer, calmly, just as if he'd not said anything. Then he looked sideways at me. "*They killed my wife, and I couldn't do anything, and they chased after us, and we fled into the forest. We were there three days, then we went back into the village. Nothing was moving, there was nothing but bodies everywhere."* He took another swig of his beer. "*Bill, you know, down there in Congo, it's not like here, in Belgium or in Europe. We inherited your frontiers, your lines on the maps, and everyone's been fighting ever since. I was all alone in my village, I had to leave, I went to the capital, I didn't have enough money for both of us but I got hold of papers and tickets for Laure to fly here, to Brussels.*" He paused again in his narrative. " *You're not eating."*

I took another bite of croissant. Whilst chewing I said: "*And where's Laure? Still in Brussels?*"

Maurice shook his head. "*She didn't get here. I saw her get onto the plane, but... It didn't crash or anything. It landed here. My sister went to the airport to meet her, but she never came out of the gates.*" He put the beer-bottle to his lips. "*After three months, I got the money to follow, but we never found her. There was no trace of her.*"

Why was he telling me this? I said nothing, taking another mouthful of croissant, but then I felt something pushed into my hand as it lay on my leg. It was a roll of papers. I looked at Maurice, who motioned me with his own hand to be discreet. The papers were scruffy hundred euro notes, rolled together with an elastic band.

"*What's that*?"

Maurice tapped my hand with a lithe finger. "*You can help me. You can take me to England.*"

"*What*?"

"*In your van. I've seen it. You can hide me behind the gear in the back.*"

I squeezed the roll of banknotes. "*Sorry, why? Why do you want to go in the van? Why don't you just go by train? You've got the money here.*"

"*I haven't got a passport. I'm here illegally.*"

"*How did you get into Belgium then? From Congo I mean?*"

"*They gave me a passport. The people who sorted my flight. Then they took it off me, to use it again.*"

"*Why don't you get those people to get you to England?*"

Maurice smiled sadly. "*That money's not enough, and it's all I have.*"

"*Okay, but why do you want to go to England? There you'd be...*" I couldn't think of a way of saying "more conspicuous". "*Here you speak the language, you've already said you don't want to be noticed. But in England... You don't speak English, do you?*"

Maurice shook his head. "*No. Okay, Bill, I'll tell you why.*" He looked around. No-one seemed interested in us; the initial curiosity I had caused had waned. *Le patron* was chatting to someone at the other end of the counter and everyone else was talking, eating and drinking at their tables. "*I think that my daughter's in England.*"

"*In England*?" I echoed. "*How come?*"

Once again Maurice produced something from a back pocket. It was something else creased and crumpled, and when I held it in my hand – in the other I was still grasping the bankroll – I saw that it was a postcard, with, of all things, a photo of a Beefeater on one side.

"*Read it.*" said Maurice.

I turned the card over. The address was printed neatly on the right: *Maurice Habayarama, Café Kinshasa, Bruxelles, Belgium/Belgique.* On the left was written: *Papa, je suis en Angleterre L.*

Maurice said: "*It came about a month ago. They kept it here for me.*"

I looked at the card carefully. It was dog-eared and smudged, but the stamp and the postmark, although the date and place of posting were illegible, looked genuine enough. "*How did she know to send it here?*"

"*My sister had said that if we had problems we should meet up at the Café* "

I handed back the card, together with the money. "*Maurice, I'm really sorry. I can't do it. I can make some enquiries for you in England but that's it... There's no room in the back, anyway, with all the gear. And it won't be just me in the van – there'll be the others, the other two...* " Of course this wasn't true, but what could I say? "*And, besides, there's checks, infra-red, dogs, all those things...*"

"*For the artics, yeah,*" said Maurice, "*But they don't check cars and vans and things very often. We'd have a good chance.*"

I wondered how he knew this. I shook my head. "*Sorry*" I repeated. "*If you'd got papers you could hitch a ride with me up front. But not in the back, like that. Sorry,*" I'd just told him that there was no room a moment before, but he didn't pick up on this.

"*If we got stopped, you could say that you didn't know I was there...*"

"Fuck," I said out loud, in English. Heads turned at the unexpected sounds and for a moment I was the uncomfortable focus of attention once more. "Fuck. Fuck. I'm sorry. *Desolé. Non.*" I stared at the plate. Ten minutes ago I'd been enjoying being in the cafe, thinking this was it, linking up with the locals whilst

Mitch and Otto were struggling with the hotel TV, and now this.

"*There's a thousand euros there*."

"*It's not about money*." I slid the roll back to him and fumbled in my pocket for my own dosh. "*I'm off. Sorry*." I pulled out a twenty euro note, far too much, I was sure, but I plonked it down on the counter, grabbed the paper – I'd keep that article for our band archives – and got off the stool. Maurice didn't try to stop me.

I walked out of the bar and back along the main street. I couldn't take him. It could be some kind of trap. What would a Congolese teenager be doing on her own in England? And why the fuck didn't Maurice try to get her to come to Belgium? Surely it was far easier to smuggle someone from England into Belgium, rather than the other way round? But then he didn't know where she was. Said he didn't, at any rate. My feet were taking me towards the station. Without my making any conscious decision I walked between two of the pillars of the concourse and found myself in the vast hall. There were long snaking queues of people buying tickets and exhausted-looking children asleep in their parents' arms, cradled amongst luggage, or even just lying on a thin coat on the hard floor.

On my phone I had a picture of Jimmy asleep, one that I'd taken a fortnight or so before. I brought it up onto the screen. His fat cheeks grinned earnestly at me. What were the penalties for smuggling someone? I was sure that if there were people hidden in a vehicle the responsibility was on the driver – you couldn't just say that you hadn't known that there was someone there. I'd read that in the papers.

I paced up and down. Some of the travellers had nothing but those tatty cross-patterned plastic travel bags, overstuffed with cheap clothing which was spilling out. A young woman breastfed a scrawny baby – she looked up at me as I sloped past and held out a thin hand. I fumbled in my pocket, found a few coins, I wasn't sure what, and dropped them into her palm.

I could get on the next train, the boat, go where the fuck I liked, thanks to the burgundy passport in my jacket pocket. It was just an accident of birth that meant that I had that, and that Maurice, who must have been about the same age as me, had had to flee as a *sans-papiers*, and wind up here, fearing deportation at any instant, and not even knowing where the fuck his daughter was. I tried to imagine knowing that Jimmy was lost somewhere in Belgium, that someone had told me he was somewhere, needing me but without my having any more info than that. How would I feel? I'd be terrified that someone would be hurting him, that he would have an accident without my being there to guide him, that he could just starve or fall out of a window or tumble into canal or any one of a hundred horrors…

I turned and went back out of the station, trying to retrace my steps, but I'd been so deep in thought that I hadn't registered where I had been going and now I couldn't find the bloody bar again. I asked a couple of likely looking types, Africans, who might know: "*Café Kinshasa? Do you know it?*" but just got blank looks. In the end, by a fluke, I recognised a brightly coloured shopfront and knew where I was. I slipped down the noisome alley and into the café. *Le patron* looked at me curiously. Maurice was not there.

"*Maurice*?" I asked. "*Do you know where he is?*" *Le patron* shook his head. "Fuck. *Merde*. Fuck. *Okay, here's my mobile number. Will you pass it on*?"

A nod. I scribbled down my number on a napkin, remembering to put the code for England onto it. As I gave it to *le patron* he passed me Maurice's CD. "*It's for you*." I made my way back to the hotel and went up to my room, where I lay on my bed, with the pillow over my head, wishing that the whole world would go away. Now I'd given the bloody phone number to the café-owner there was no backing out. Maurice would know that there could be no other reason apart from agreeing to take him for my having done so.

Someone was knocking at my door. "*Entrez*, come in." And it was Mitch again. "Yeah?"

"What are you doing?"

"Nothing, thinking."

"We've got a problem again… Not anything like yesterday," he added hastily. "With the hotel I mean. The guy downstairs is asking us for money or something. We don't what he's on about. I tried, but I can't make him understand."

I sighed. It turned out that Otto and Mitch hadn't paid for a beer in the little bar downstairs, thinking that it would be put on their tab. I sorted that out without too much aggro on either side, and then strolled out onto the pavement. Mitch followed me. "Do you fancy a drink?"

"Alright." I was still annoyed and suspicious about their travel plans, but I wanted to do something rather than fester in my room. We sat at a table on one of the thoroughfares, Mitch sprawled in his seat, his beer gut protruding from his denim jacket. He pulled out his phrase book and clicked his fingers at the waiter.

"*Messieurs*?"

"*Bee-air, si voo play.*" said Mitch. He held up two fingers in a V-sign. "*Duh.*"

"*Not for me*," I said hurriedly. "*I don't want beer. I'll have a black coffee, please.*"

"*Monsieur.*"

"That guy, the drummer," said Mitch. "If he turns up tonight, tell him to fuck off."

"He was fantastic. Kept the crowd going."

"We don't need him. It's our gig. We get paid whether there's a crowd or not."

"It's Armand's bar. If he's happy…" The waiter brought us our drinks. Mitch reached over-eagerly with clumsy paws for the beer and swallowed half the glass in one draught.

I unwrapped a sugar cube and stirred it into my coffee, looking away, up and down the street. "Billy…" said Mitch.

"What?"

"Alison. You're happily hitched-up. What the fuck do I do?"

If only you knew, pal, I thought, recalling what those arses on the net had been saying about my marriage. Clearly Mitch never logged onto the *britishbluesgoss* site. I tried to look sympathetic and thoughtful, coming across as the candid friend. "She'll never come back if you carry on drinking like this."

Mitch paused, with his beer under his lips. For a moment I thought that he was going to become angry, but he sighed and put his glass down. "I can't help it, Billy. I can't stop."

"Fuck it, Mitch. Look at you. You were a shit-hot guitarist. You wrote all those songs. That's what she wanted. Not a fucking soak.

Or a fucking drug-runner. Why the fuck are you still doing all that?"

"I can't stop. I can't. You don't know, Billy. You can't just bale out."

"Is it Otto? You've got too much on him to have to be scared of him."

"It's not him. There's people behind him, and people behind them and…" At that point my mobile rang, and Mitch paused in his jeremiad.

I fished the phone out of my pocket. It had to be Petra. "Hello?"

"*Bill? It's Maurice.*"

For a moment I was going to tell him, sorry, I can't do it, *desolé*, but I'd looked across at Mitch, who had picked up his glass again and was draining it down to the froth. God, I pitied him, but underneath that I loathed him too, and Otto. They were always laughing at me, and yet as soon as we crossed the Channel they were like a couple of helpless babies. And I knew what I was capable of, and it wasn't underpinning Mitch's plodding guitar strums. If I took Maurice to England maybe we could do more of what we'd done last night… I didn't even need to decamp to talk, as Mitch, for all his pathetic attempts with the phrasebook, wouldn't know what the fuck I was on about.

"*Okay, okay, I can't talk for long, but what the fuck, okay, I'll do it. I'll take you.*"

There was a moment's pause and then Maurice said. "*Hey... Thanks. Thanks. I don't know what to say. I've got the money still.*"

"*Fuck the money,*" I said. "*You'll need it in England, anyway.*"

There was a silence at the other end of the line. Mitch was looking at me curiously. He had signalled for another beer.

I went on: "*Are you coming to play again tonight?*"

"*No. Not if you're... I'll see you at the Kinshasa tomorrow morning. Ten o'clock?*"

"*Eleven.*" I said. "*See you tomorrow.*" I snapped my phone shut.

"Who the fuck was that?" asked Mitch.

"Didn't I tell you? King Albert wants to see me at the *Palais* fucking *Royale*. Wants some bass tuition." I got up. "I'm going for a walk. I'll see you at Armand's." I felt guilty; Mitch needed my help, really. I walked off to the Metro station I'd seen earlier, and went out to the Atomium. After an hour or so of wandering around my phone rang again.

"Hiya." This time it was Petra's voice.

"Hello," I said, already wondering what I should say, and how I should say it.

"You alright?"

"Yeah. How's you? And Jimmy Riddle?"

"We are fine. Listen, Bill, listen…" She hesitated. "Look, it's been difficult, I know, but I do love you and…" She sounded a little like she was reading from a script. She must have been feeling as awkward as I was, and have rehearsed this little speech beforehand. "I got your text."

"Sorry?"

"Saying that you'd be coming back on your own." I'd forgotten about that. "Listen, I've arranged a couple of days off. Jimmy and I can catch the train down to London, and come over, and we can have a couple of days in Brussels, and then all drive back together in the van."

Hell on a moto, I thought. In the van. Part of me was elated that she wanted me still, and part was already whirring away – what the fuck was I going to do about my promise to Maurice?

"Is it safe to put Jimmy in the van? He'll have to go in the cab."

"He goes in his seat in the front of the car," she said. "It's no different, as long as you don't tear along. Remember you're on the wrong side."

I could scarcely tell her not to come. Petra must have detected the hesitation in my voice. She sounded a little sharp. "Is there a problem? You'd better say if there is."

"No, no," I muttered hurriedly. "Sorry, I was taken a bit by surprise. No, it'd be great. When are you getting here? Do I need to rearrange the ferry back?"

"No need. We'll be there about ten o'clock tonight. We'll come to where you're playing. Text me the address."

"I'll need to get a better hotel. I've just got a single bed in a small room."

"Do that then." She said something indistinct, and I realised that she was talking to Jimmy. "We're going to see Daddy. Do you want to talk to him?" Back to me she said: "He's too interested in his rusk. We'll see you later."

"That's fantastic," I said. "I'm really glad that you're coming. I really felt..."

"Billy." She cut me off. "Now's not the time. I want to see you – that's what's important. We'll talk when I get there."

"Okay."

"Bye."

"Bye."

And that was it. "Fuck. Fuck. Fuckity fuck," I said to myself. A couple walking past looked at me curiously. It was my own fault. I'd bought bloody Maurice's bloody sob story and now I really was going to have to tell him that it was no dice. I had his number in my phone registry. I got it up, and stared at the digits, willing myself to make the call.

I wanted to see Petra, and even more I wanted to see Jimmy and dandle him and nuzzle the hair on the back of his head. And Maurice wanted his kid. And had she really sent him that card? With a fucking beefeater on the front. That was taking the piss, though presumably that little touch was wasted on Maurice. How the hell had his daughter got on a plane and wound up in the wrong bloody country?

I pressed dial. The number rang and rang, but no-one answered. I tried again. Still no answer. I waited a minute, and tried for a third time. A French voice told me to leave a message. "*Maurice, it's Bill. I'm sorry. There's a problem – my wife's coming over to Brussels with our son. She wants to go back to England in the van. So you see, it's impossible. I'm really sorry, but it's all fucked-up... But in England I'll make some enquiries, like I said. I'll ring when I'm home. Good luck. Sorry.*"

I clicked the phone to. Now all I had to do was find a better hotel. I caught the Metro back into the city centre and checked out of the *pension*, trying not to think about the money I was forfeiting. Neither Otto nor Mitch were around. Moseying along I came to a grand-looking place, *Hotel du Duc*, where I handed over an eye-watering sum for a double with *en-suite* and a cot. I went up to look the room over, whence I texted Petra the hotel's name and address and the street where *Le Mannekin Pis* was. I garlanded the message with one **x**.

Now it was time to go back to Armand's, so I stepped out of my posh room, locked the door, and turned, to find a knife held to my throat.

Third Bar

Home Chord of A

The knife-wielder was shorter than me, holding his arm up, curly brown hair flowing over an Arabic shawl. His hazel eyes looked coldly at me. Despite my bemusement I realised that I'd seen him somewhere before, and part of my mind was now spinning away, trying to place him, even whilst he held the tip of the knife jabbed against my Adam's apple. I backed away a tad to the door, and the knifepoint followed me. I couldn't go anywhere – the wooden panelling was behind me and I couldn't be sure that I'd be quick enough to slip away to the side. I tried to speak but my mouth was suddenly dry. The knifeman narrowed his eyes and slid the blade down to the hollow above my breast-bone.

"*Wanker. You're taking the African.*"

I shook my head as if I didn't understand. "Sorry… I don't… *non comprendez*"

"*Shut it. I know you speak French. You take the African with you… Otherwise, any more fucking about, your bird and kid get it. Capish?*"

I nodded, awkwardly, trying to keep my throat away from the blade. The guy backed away slowly, still holding the knife up. "*You'll get a phone call. Okay?*"

He reached the lift, groped for the switch, his eyes watching me for the least movement, the doors slid open and he was gone. My legs abruptly gave way under me and I sank to the floor, shaking and feeling very cold, as if I were next to an open window. I massaged my windpipe, still feeling where he had thrust the point. My limbs were trembling and I was sweating now. I imagined Petra telling me that these were the symptoms of shock… Petra.

With hands quivering I pulled out my mobile, but all I got was her answering service. She must have the phone switched off, maybe because she didn't want to risk getting any messages from me until she'd actually arrived, or maybe they were already in the Tunnel. And I had to go. I had a gig to do.

I was already getting to my feet before I'd made a conscious decision. It was the old performer's instinct – the show had to go on, no matter what had happened. I had a brief flicker of panic, wanting to get back inside my room and bolt the door, stay there, keep ringing Petra and tell her to turn back, but I smothered that. Mitch and Otto would be waiting. Armand would be waiting. The audience would be waiting. I stumbled over to the lift doors, was about to press the button… No. The guy could be by the doors at the bottom, waiting for me. I didn't want to be helpless in the metal box of the lift, sliding down, not able to see what was going on. There must be emergency stairs. I made my way down the corridor, passing anonymous blond ash doorways, all alike save for the numbers, and found a turn at the end. Here were two functional metal and frosted glass panels. "*Escalier*"

I pushed them open and clattered down, now running. I was going to be late, the others would be angry at me, Otto would… Otto. Otto wouldn't be scared of that guy with the knife. I could tell him. He'd sort it. He'd think I was a right bleeding-heart wanker for getting involved with Maurice and everything, and he'd laugh at me and tell me to my face what a tosser I was, but he'd sort it. I knew that.

At the bottom were more doors. I cautiously pushed them open. I was at the side of the lobby, a large room with a grand piano; it was a proper hotel, not like that rat-hole of a *pension*. There was a uniformed receptionist behind the counter and a couple enjoying a drink at one of the tables, but no sign of the guy with the knife. Should I check out, find somewhere else? But whoever was behind the knifeman was probably watching me – they'd simply follow me to anywhere new. And also, I'd booked two nights at an exorbitant cost, and I didn't have enough funds to get somewhere else of the standard which Petra was entitled to. I went over to hand in my keys at the desk, but thought better of it. Don't let anyone know whether you're there or not. I might want to get back into the room in a hurry. I walked out through the doors as nonch as I could manage.

The Zed dummy was still posing outside *Le Mannekin Pis,* its expression inscrutable behind the sunglasses. Armand was furtling round behind the bar. Otto was sat at a table, drinking, whilst Mitch was buggering about with the mixing desk.

"You're late," growled Otto.

"Whatever." I ought to be more emollient if I wanted him to deal with the knifeman. I was just about to open my mouth again to apologise, when Otto grasped my shirt, pulling it tight around my throat, round the very spot where the knife prick was still smarting. Discreetly, he pulled me over the table and said in a low voice: "Don't fuck with me again."

"What the fuck…" I could scarcely get the last guttural consonant out, the fabric was so tight around my neck.

"That little stunt with that chick last night."

"What do you mean?" So much was buzzing round my brain that I genuinely didn't know what he meant.

"That bird last night. You told her to fuck off."

Fuck me, I'd forgotten all about that. "No, I didn't." I strove to make my voice as injuredly innocent as I could. "I just asked her whether she wanted a drink, like you said, and…" I couldn't say any more as at that point Otto pulled my shirt collar so tight that I began to gag. He listened to the noise I was making with satisfaction.

"Don't lie to me, Wurzel. You've got no fucking talent for it." Blue spots were swimming before my eyes and my neck felt as if it were being sliced in two. "Don't fuck with me again. You understand me, Wurzel? Fucking *comprennay*?"

Unable to speak, I managed a feeble nod, and after a couple more seconds during which I thought that blood vessels were going to burst through into my brain and eyeballs Otto suddenly let go. I coughed and sagged onto the tabletop. Fucking hell, the second time in less than an hour. I tried to smooth my shirt with as much dignity as I could whilst glancing round the café. No-one seemed to have noticed what had happened.

Then Otto grabbed my shirtfront again. "Oh, yeah, nearly forgot. That drumfucker tries get on stage with us again, you tell him, *pissez-vous* off."

I croaked out: "He's not coming tonight."

Otto let go of my shirt and looked at me curiously. "You know that?"

"Armand told me, just now." Otto was satisfied and turned away. What a fuck-up – he wasn't going to help me get shot of *Monsieur Coupe-Gorge*. I got my bass out of the cupboard at the back of the stage, stuck the electronic tuner gizmo that I'd recently bought onto it and busied myself with making sure that I had G, D, A and E.

Folk were coming in through the doors, but fortunately, again, not the couple from the boat. They must have been *en route* to somewhere else. Petra and Jimmy had to be pretty close by now, and, of course, what was to stop the knifeman or whoever was behind him coming in tonight? They knew where I would be.

Armand put a bottle down beside me. "*You ready?*"

I nodded and had a pull at the beer, hoping it would sooth my bruised throat. Mitch and Otto took their places, and we were off. Whenever I made contact with Otto's eyes, to keep time, he glowered at me.

Halfway through the fifth number in walked Petra, with Jimmy behind her in the backpack. In one hand she had his favourite teddy. She saw me immediately, and smiled, and then reached round to direct Jimmy's attention towards me. I saw him gazing around with curiosity in his big eyes, but I don't think that he actually spotted me. I had to restrain myself, at the end of the song, from putting my bass down, climbing offstage to greet them, and make sure that they stayed put, didn't go off anywhere where they could be in danger, but, like I said, I'm a professional, and I knew that Petra would understand that I couldn't come straight to them then, even if she didn't understand a lot of other things about how I was. At least here they should be safe enough, with loads of people around. But later, when we left, how was I going to say: "Lovely to see you and the boy, darling, however there's a teensy little local difficulty – a homicidal Arab held a blade to my throat a couple of hours ago and he's going to slit yours if I don't do what he wants…"?

I waved a hand at her, and saw her take a seat, settling Jimmy on her lap. I hoped that the music wasn't too loud for him. As soon as we took the break I scrambled down to sit beside her, our thighs just touching. "Can I take him?" I asked. It was easiest to do things through Jimmy. As I lifted him up he grinned, showing his Nosferatu-style front fangs, which had come through a few weeks before, and stretched out his little arms. "Dada fuuu…"

"He slept on the train," she said, "And then woke up when we got off."

I cuddled Jimmy against me. He was snuggling himself against his much-worn teddy bear. I had a sudden chilling vision of the knifeman holding a blade to Jimmy's throat and then slicing through the flesh as casually as I might cut up a boiled egg. Something of this must have shown in my face, because Petra took my hand. "It's okay, Bill."

I stroked the lovely fluff on the back of his head and felt his compact little body in my arms. "Do you want a drink?"

She did, so I reluctantly handed Jimmy back and went to the bar, glancing over nervously all the time to make sure that they were all right. Petra caught my eye and smiled across at me, pointing out to Jimmy where I was. She was trying hard herself, I realised. It wasn't coming naturally to her, either. I wasn't sure whether it was quite ethical to get buckshee bottles from Armand for Petra but before I could say anything he'd handed me two, nodding over at her.

I took Petra's hand, as tentatively as I might have done on a first date. "Are you going to wait? Where's your stuff?"

"I went to the hotel first. Dropped it off."

The knifeman could have still been hanging around there. "Look, I'd really like you to stay until I've finished. Then we can go back all together."

"Lovely." She said nothing more, and as I couldn't think of

anything interesting to say I kept quiet as well, contenting myself with bouncing Jimmy up and down on my knee, my hands under his armpits. He was waving his arms around, pointing at the lights and the people.

The second half was more subdued that it had been the night before, when Maurice had been inspiring me, and we only did the usual couple of encores. I stowed my bass away, switched off my gear and the PA, and thirty seconds later Petra and I were walking hand in hand through the Brussels evening to the hotel, Jimmy on my back. I kept looking around to make sure that we were not being followed. Petra noticed. “What’s up?”

“Nothing… Nothing.” I stopped her and we kissed, James Albert gurgling happily on my back. But I had to break off, to check that no-one was sneaking up on us whilst my attention was distracted, and Petra looked up at me quizzically. Did she think that I found her repellent, as if she had bad breath or something? I pulled her towards me again to kiss her once more to show that I wanted her and our teeth chipped against each other’s.

“Ow,” she said, recoiling.

“Sorry…Oh, God, I’m sorry,” I gabbled. “Sorry. It’s just been exhausting, all the driving and sorting everything. Those other two have been useless, leaving everything up to me.” I sounded whiney. “Let’s go.” Without waiting for her to say anything more I grabbed her arm and pulled her through the streets. I wanted us out of the open. When we got to the big glass doors of the *Hotel du Duc* I went on nervously: “I hope this’ll do. It’s the poshest place in the city, according to Armand.” I hadn’t actually asked him; I just said it so as not to have to think of anything else. “You like it?” I was being far too anxious.

Petra looked round the minimalist lobby, with the Bechstein in the middle of the floor and a few smartly clad guests deep in important and whispered conversations. “Looks wonderful.”

“Come on.” In the lift I could see Jimmy on my back in the mirror. When Petra and I caught each other’s eyes we smiled vaguely, like two strangers having to endure intimacy for the length of the climb. I shepherded Petra down the corridor to the safety of our room, fishing the card out of my pocket and putting it in the slot the wrong way round, cursing as I turned it. The red light wouldn't go to green.

"Let me try." Petra slid the card out and back in, and something clicked. She pushed the door open, and flicked on the light. As far as I could see there was no-one awaiting us. "Lovely," she said again. "Let me get Jimmy out." I pushed the door to and tugged on it. It seemed to be locked. Petra got behind me and lifted Jimmy out of the carryframe. I wondered whether she would put a hand on me, but she didn't. She put Jimmy on the bed, opening up her case. "I need to change him."

"I'll do it," I said.

"Okay." She disappeared into the bathroom. I hadn't checked in there. Too late now. As I pulled Jimmy's trews down I half-expected to hear a scream, but all that came was the sound of the shower being turned on.

For once, Jimmy hadn't done his eveningtide superdump – the nappy was just wet. I cleaned the clefts between his little bollock bag and his thighs, put on a new nappy and inserted him into a sleepsuit. The cot was under the window – I dimmed the lights and put him down. I wondered whether anyone outside could see my silhouette against the blinds. Maybe someone was aiming a telescopic sight at me right now. Petra seemed to be spending a long time in the bathroom. I could still hear the shower. Jimmy snuggled down, rolling onto his side with his thumb in his gob. Was he hungry? I'd seen a couple of bottles of formula in the bag, but if they'd been out at room temperature for a while they could be full of deadly *campilobacter* by now. I patted Jimmy's stomach, but he suddenly sat up. "Baba fuuu…"

"Are you hungry? Bottle?"

He nodded gravely. I'd have to risk feeding him, otherwise he'd never sleep and Petra and I would get even more stressed, so I lifted him just over the bars, making sure that his outline wouldn't appear against the window, groped around for a bottle, and stuck the teat into his mouth. He sucked greedily, and after a couple of minutes he'd drifted off. I laid him back in the cot, again passing him low over the bars, and tucked him in. He looked so peaceful. How could anyone threaten an innocent child? The shower was still running.

Fuck me, she'd been in there for ages. Of course, the fucking knifeman was in there – he'd used the noise as cover to slit her throat, letting the blood gush down to the floor… I sprang up and wrenched the door open. I could see Petra's naked form indistinctly behind a condensation fuzzed plastic door.

"You alright?" I asked, as neutrally as I could.

"Yeah. Of course." She had her back to me.

"Sorry. I didn't mean to barge in. It was just I thought I heard you slip, fall over or something."

"I'm fine." She was soaping her upper arms.

"Jimmy's down." I started to retreat, closing the door. Should I take the initiative and pull off my clothes, get into the shower with her? Her body language didn't seem to be inviting me.

I went back out, and, having kicked off my shoes, lay on the bed, with the TV on, a report about Chinese business activity in Congo. I didn't really want the telly, because I wanted to think, and also be able to hear if there were any strange noises from outside in the corridor, but I couldn't face the thought of the silence and my not having any distraction when Petra eventually came out of the bathroom. And when she did finally emerge, combing her hair, she was wrapped in a big fluffy white towelling robe. She sat down a foot or so away from me on the bed, looking up at the television.

"What's this?"

"Just the news."

She lay back on the pillows, out of contact, feigning interest in the telly. I had to do something. It wouldn't be the rock and roll lifestyle, or my lack of ambition, or the sleepless nights with the kiddio, no, that fucking psycho with the knife was going to be the one to destroy my marriage if I didn't look out. I awkwardly shuffled over to Petra and put my hand around her waist, sitting up. She placed her hand over mine, and turned to me, and then we did kiss, properly, and undressed and got into bed. But it was no good. I couldn't… Well, okay, I couldn't get it up. I was too tired, too shocked by what had happened, too scared of where things were going wrong with Petra, too fucked-over generally to be able to relax. I was watching myself too much.

"I'm sorry," I said. "It's not you. It's…" Petra said nothing. I thought she might try something, but she just lay against me. I went on. “I think… I think I don’t feel close enough to you. That’s what it is.”

“Maybe,” she muttered. She sounded angry and disappointed. We lay there watching some crappy American cop show with Dutch subtitles, a low twanging babble of oaths and orders. Petra was breathing gently – she was asleep. I couldn’t drop off, both from fear and sexual frustration. We were safe in this room, I reckoned, and in the hotel lobby, but not between them, and not outside.

A patrol car flashed by on the screen. That was a thought – I could go to the police here. I could leave out the bit about my offering to take Maurice, just tell them some criminal gang had spotted a chance with the van of smuggling someone into England and that they had threatened me and my family. Even if they came into contact with Maurice, which was unlikely, what was he going to say? I could ask the police to keep an eye on us, and maybe escort us back to England. It was no good ringing – I wasn’t sure that I could explain well or convincingly enough over the phone, but if I went downstairs into the street I could flag down a police car. It was a risk. Could I leave my wife and child asleep in the room, whilst I sought help? Despite knowing that there was no-one there I opened the bathroom door, closing it before putting the light on so as not to wake Petra, half-expecting some nameless, shapeless thing to come leaping out of the dark onto me… But there was nothing, of course. In the bedroom I checked in the wardrobe and under the bed. I used to do that when I was eight, scared that a cyberman might be lurking there.

I pulled on my clothes as quietly as I could, found the keycard where Petra had left it on the dressing table, slipped out of the door and made sure that it was locked. The corridor was empty, save for elegant glass vases holding dried willow twigs at regular intervals. I padded down the stairs. The lobby was deserted – only a doorman dozing behind the desk. I went out onto the street, where it was quiet and cool, and stood outside the big glass doors with the hotel’s name etched into them. The occasional car glid past. I kept glancing back into the lobby, keeping half an eye on the lifts. How long it would take me to find the police? Maybe I should go onto the main thoroughfare, just up the way? As I stood irresolutely my phone rang. Who the fuck was that at half-past one?

I put it to my ear. "Hello?"

"I think you must go back to your room." The voice spoke in English, but with a strong accent.

"Who the fuck's this?"

There was a short silence, and then the voice spoke again. "I think you must go back to your woman and your child." The accent was Eastern European, maybe.

I looked around me. I could see no-one out on the street, nor in any of the parked cars. "Where the fuck are you? Who is this?"

"Bill, I will not say again. Go back in." The phone went dead. My reaction was a feeling of outrage at some fucker trying to boss me around. And using my name like that. If I wanted to walk around the streets of Brussels at night I'd damned well do it. But of course, I'd left Petra and Jimmy asleep, and now, considering that they could obviously see me, I wasn't at all sure that whoever it was wouldn't be able to get into the room. Still I wasn't going to submit just like that, so I stood outside the hotel doors, not going any further, but not going in either. I could see the lift shafts, and the stairs inside. No-one there. I checked the number which had just rung me. It was not the same as the one Maurice had called me on.

I wished that I had a fag, but of course that all belonged to another life, the one which had ended when Zed's had. I'd forsworn smoking for Petra and hadn't had even so much as a crafty puff on someone else's ciggy for thirty months. I kept my eyes on the lobby. Still no-one... Unless they were already in the hotel. Of course, they could be watching from another room. Hell's carillon. I sprinted back through the doors and pressed the button to call the lift, but it was on the top floor. The caretaker glanced up from behind the desk. I hurtled up the stairs. It was just as well that I'd given up the tabs as by the time I reached our floor my heart was pounding as if it were going to explode. I tore down the corridor. Our door was shut. I got out the key, and, despite shaking hands, managed to let myself in. All was well. Petra was asleep – and breathing – on the bed, and Jimmy stirred as I closed the door. I quickly checked the bathroom. No-one. I sat on the toilet lid and slowly got my breath back. I couldn't ring the police. I'd been foolish to go outside to try to find them. I had nothing to show.

I dialled the number which had called me in the street. After a couple of rings someone picked up, and I said, straight off: "I don't know who the fuck you are, pal, but what the fuck do you want from me?"

Again there was a silence for a few seconds, and then the voice said: "Okay Bill, you are good. Day after tomorrow you go to carpark behind Midi station, seven o'clock morning. You bring forgon."

"Forgon? What the fuck's that?"

"*Camion*. Car."

"The van?"

"Yes. Van. Wait there."

"Wait for what? Is this to do with Maurice?"

"You wait. You do this, no problem with wife or little one." The line clicked dead again. After a minute or so I tried Maurice's number. Just the answerphone again.

In the bedroom I stripped off my clothes and lay down beside Petra, moulding myself to her body again. But she shifted, still asleep, I think, and wormed away from me. I didn't even feel randy any more. Just empty and flat, and desolate and hollow... We are the hollow men… We are the cybermen…

***

I was woken by Jimmy. He was sitting up in his cot, looking at us. "Ah fuuu." The clock said half seven, which was half six at home.

Petra muttered something. "What?" I said.

"He's saying father. He wants you."

I lifted the lad out of his cot and put him into our bed. Then I filled the kettle on the table and made two cups of tea, using those horrible insipid Lipton bags which the Continentals always foist on us Anglos. I actually had some proper bags in the van's glove compartment, I recalled. As I passed a cup over to Petra Jimmy suddenly flung an arm up, and half the hot liquid spilt onto her. She leapt up. "What the hell…?"

"Sorry," I said, miserably. "I was just giving you your tea."

But she was up, running into the bathroom and holding her arm under the cold tap. She came back in, rubbing it. "Looks alright. You should never do that. Carrying hot liquids over a child."

"I know." My head was thumping through lack of sleep, and tension. The knifeman was waiting out there for us, but I had to act normally.

"Mama fuuu…" said Jimmy, who was sitting upright on the bed, glancing puzzedly back and forth. His face went red. I burrowed into the bag and found clean clothes and a new nappy. Petra went back into the bathroom to get dressed, scooping up her stuff, which had spilt out of the bag. I pulled on my own things, and then we went down to breakfast, not speaking. I had no appetite, but I forced myself to eat a couple of rolls, and drink some coffee. I was paying through the nose for it, after all. Petra concentrated on feeding Jimmy finger-sized bits of croissant.

There wasn't a right moment to utter suggestions, but I said: "Okay, what shall we do?" more or less at random. I'd have liked to just stay in the hotel lobby, where it was unlikely we'd be attacked, but Petra was hardly going to go for that.

"I've always wanted to see that Atomium thing," she said. I didn't tell her that I'd been there the day before. We walked out of the hotel into the sunshine, my head pounding. I took Petra's hand, and she at least interlaced her fingers into mine. Jimmy was on my back again. Petra wasn't going to leave me as long as Jimmy was attached to me. On the Metro I kept scanning the faces of the commuters, looking for Polish hitmen.

In the Atomium park Petra and I sat on a bench in the sun whilst Jimmy tottered around, chasing after pigeons and falling over every thirty seconds. "I know I'm not great company," I said. "I just feel tired, and sick of it all."

Petra's face brightened. "Sick of the band?"

"Yeah." I threw a bit of bread from breakfast that I'd secreted in my pockets to the pigeons.

"Then leave," she said. "Look at you. Look at us. It's killing you, and it's destroying us."

"Okay. Look, let me just do these two dates, now we're here, and then… Then when we get home…"

At that moment Jimmy yelled – he'd tripped over, and lay writhing and screaming on the floor. Passing respectable Brussels *bourgeois* looked at us with a mixture of contempt and pity as I leapt up and ran over to him. "Baba fuu!!!" Jimmy yelled. We comforted him, and although we didn't speak any more about it, the brief discussion about my leaving the band had somehow broken the ice between Petra and me. We walked back towards the Metro station, really holding hands now, and although I was still scrutinising every passer-by for hidden weapons, I managed to hide my wariness. Back in town we first-off took Jimmy to meet his soul brother, *le Mannekin Pis*, the statue, not Armand's bar, that is. Jimmy stared up at the little stone boy with grave eyes. He pointed excitedly, "Baba fuuu!"and then his face turned puce as he concentrated on filling his own nappy.

We hurried off to to *la Grand Place* to bag a restaurant table and make use of the toilet facilities. I made sure that we were by a wall, so that I could see anyone approaching us. Petra ordered the dishes, fluently. Master James was provided with a highchair by the staff, who cooed and fussed over him, and he spent a happy hour spooning food onto his face. I took Jimmy back into the loos to change him once more and put him into his pyjamas. I had to lay him on the window sill, and as I was busying myself with him the door burst open. I whirled round in terror, but it was just some guy who'd had a bit too much to drink and needed a slash urgently. He grinned alcoholically at Jimmy and said something I didn't catch.

We walked up to Armand's in the dusk. I had wanted to show Petra the Zed dummy, but it had gone. Perhaps Armand had tired of the novelty, or had forgotten to put it out. Otto and Mitch were inside drinking. Mitch made a bit of an effort when he saw Petra. "How's the old Duke's Hotel?" he asked her. My body went onstage to play the bass, but my mind was on tomorrow morning. Seven o'clock. I would have to come back here from the hotel, and take the van back round to the station. How the hell was I going to square this with Petra?

As soon as we'd finished the other two packed up their kits.

"Don't forget to get the wedge from Armand," said Mitch. Otto hadn't spoken to me since the night before. The two of them strolled out of the bar with half an hour before the train check-in closed, not a care in the bloody world – well, Mitch was as fucked-up as could be, but at least no-one was threatening to slit his wife's and childrens' throats – and no gear to pack away either, thanks to Muggins.

Petra had Jimmy in the sling around her chest, and was sitting at the bar, talking to Armand. I had a sudden panic that he would mention Maurice's being there the first night, so I went over and dragged her away as quickly as possible. Armand gave me some odd looks – maybe he thought that I was madly jealous, and Petra wasn't too happy either, but I couldn't take the risk. I ushered wife and child out of the door, and on the way back to the *Hotel du Duc* I said, as cazh as I could, to Petra: "Tomorrow morning I'm going to get up nice and early, nip back to Armand's and load up. You sleep in."

"Okay.". She didn't seem to attach any significance to that. Jimmy was already snoozing so I lifted him out of the frame and laid him in the cot. As if I didn't already have enough on my mind I was already worrying what I should do in ten seconds' time when I'd tucked him in -- should I turn round, just take Petra in my arms and kiss her masterfully, undress her on the spot and make love to her there and then, always assuming that the half-hearted erection that I'd somehow started to acquire would spring into the real thing? But I heard the bathroom door shutting. I quickly pulled off my outdoor clothes, and pulled on my light summer pyjamas. Petra seemed to be taking ages. My semi-stiffy had limped off, and I lay there, watching the telly without taking in anything. And I must have dropped off, because the next thing I knew, the bedside lamps and the TV had been switched off and Petra was snoring genteely beside me. I could see her shoulders – she was not naked but had her cotton nightshirt on.

In my mind's eye I saw Mitch and Otto, clutching their beers, safely ensconced in their seats on the 23.57 back home. Presumably they had to stop off in London and meet someone, whoever was next up the feeding pyramid, in the wee small hours, in some dodgy club or casino. Otto had been right though – the less I knew about it the better. But I didn't know about what was happening this side of the Channel either. Who the hell was going to be waiting behind the Gare Midi? Maurice?

Maurice. I got out my phone and tried his number again. No answer. It was two o'clock, Belgian time. God, I never got any sleep these days. I'd thought a few days away would give me the chance to catch up, but no, even that was denied me. I might have dozed for an hour but now I had never felt less sleepy in my life. Jimmy snuffled and stirred in his cot. I got up quietly and went over, looking down at him, cosy in his one-piece sleepsuit, silhouetted by the dim light percolating through the hotel curtain. Jimmy stirred again. "Dada fuuu…" he muttered. Then there was a farting noise, followed by an ominously liquid spurting sound. As quickly as I could I scooped him up. The changing mat was under the cot – one-handedly I pulled it out, laid a towel over it and put Jimmy down. It must have been whatever he'd eaten in the restaurant, or maybe the water being a bit different, as streams of diarrhoea had run down his legs and soaked into his sleepsuit. He lay there quite placidly though, so I stripped him off and as quietly as I could took him into the bathroom, where, standing him with one hand in the sink, I washed him down with a flannel. He watched himself in the mirror with interest. "Jimma fuu…" I slung the poo-soaked clothing and the towel from the mat into the shower. I'd worry about that in the morning. I could just leave the stuff behind in fact. We had some formula bottles in the little fridge, so I sat by the window, feeding him, the curtain a fraction open, staring down into the street. The occasional car went past, but I could see nothing amiss.

I could wake Petra and we could slip away, get the van, leave the gear (apart from my bass, which was in the corner of our room) drive over the border to France, or Holland or Germany, and get a ferry back from there. Or just leave the van. We could get a cab to the airport, get on the next flight over the water, even if it were to somewhere like Edinburgh or Dublin, just get away from whomever was out there. Mitch could come back to get the van. Or not. I could do what Petra wanted and leave the band, so then the bloody thing could rust away behind Armand's until Judgement Day as far as I would be concerned.

Jimmy was still now, his thumb lodged in his mouth, curled up on my knee. Carefully I put him back in his cot without waking him. I lay back down on the double bed. But if we did flee, that wouldn't be an end to it. They knew about the van so they knew about the band. They must know who I was. One look at the Internet and they'd have the next gig, and even if I quit they'd be able to find me, and through me Petra and Jimmy. Even if we never left England again none of us would be safe. And how the hell could I wake Petra up at half two *ack emma* and tell her that we had to skiddadle like thieves in the night? She want explanations – explanations which I wouldn't have time for. And even if I did try to explain, she'd think me such a fuckwit that that'd end things, and things that would end would end would wend…

Fourth Bar

Home Chord of A

The alarm on my mobile was going. I reached out in a panic – I couldn't afford to have Petra or Jimmy roused now – and switched it off. Half six. I pulled on my clothes and got out of the room without waking them.

Pigeons were boldly strut-strutting along the pavements, picking at titbits from between the cracks, and the early-risers were walking with that purposeful on-the-way-to-work gait which you only see first thing, and I, being a musician who worked late, hardly ever saw unless I hadn't been to bed at all. I passed a *boulangerie* and went in to buy a couple of croissants. As I groped in my trousers for coins, I had a horrid thought – had I got the van keys? I'd forgotten to check for them in the hotel and the thought of having to go back, rushing to avoid being late and having to find the keys without waking P and J was almost unbearable. I rummaged frantically in my pockets – not left, not right, no, there they were. Thank whomever for that little relief.

Armand's place was all shut. I didn't know whether he slept on the premises, but I avoided revving the van up overmuch as I eased it round from the rear. Then it was back the way I'd walked, making sure I was on the right side of the road at junctions, past the hotel, to the Gare Midi. There was a big white P on a blue background directing me behind the main building. At the machines, which were designed for left-hand drives, of course, I had to lean across to the passenger side, struggle the window down, and stretch out to pull off the ticket, having pulled up too far over, whilst a short queue of impatient Belgian commuters formed behind me.

When the barrier went up I drove into a large car park, maybe a quarter full. I stopped in a space from where I could watch the main entrance, and sat, eating my second croissant, glancing at the clock in the dashboard. Six minutes past six. What the hell? Then I remembered – I'd not changed it from England. My mobile said four minutes past seven. I swallowed the last of the croissant and wished I'd bought a coffee in one of those lidded paper cups to go with it.

There was a sharp rap at the van's passenger window. I jumped and looked round. A man, someone I didn't recognise, was gesturing at me. He had a round face, a cigarette in his mouth, and swept-back blond hair under a woollen cap. I leant across and wound the window down.

"Not here," he said. It was his voice from the phone.. "Camera. I get in." Without asking my say-so he reached inside, pulled up the knob to unlock the door, and climbed into the passenger seat. He tapped the end of the cigarette against the dashboard and the ash fell onto the floor. He pointed to a corner of the car park overshadowed by high buildings. "Go to there."

My hands shaking, I took the van over to where he had indicated, narrowly missing a car coming the other way as I turned a corner. He indicated free three spaces, and I was about to go nose into one when the guy stopped me with a raise of the hand. "No, you go other."

"What do you mean?"

"Your arse." He saw my expression. "*Nazad. Reculer.*"

He wanted me to reverse in, so carefully, I did, jerked up the handbrake, hesitated, then turned the engine off.

"Out," said my passenger.

"Okay." I dropped out of the driver's side and went round the back. The guy was stocky, about forty, dressed in blue denim with a black leather jacket. He lit another cigarette as he glanced round nervously.

"Open door," he said.

"What? Back, front, what?"

He said nothing for a moment, waiting for a guy in railman's uniform driving one of those little trucks full of luggage to go past, then pointed to the rear. "This doors." I opened up. "Okay." The guy looked around again, then gestured to someone to come over. A grey saloon drove slowly up, and reversed into one of the spaces alongside the van. Driving it was my acquaintance the knifeman, from the hotel, and in the back were two figures.

When the car was level with the van it stopped and someone pushed open the back door of the saloon. It was Maurice. He looked scared and apologetic. "*Salut, Bill.*" He pulled out a pair of drums, the ones which he had been playing at our gig.

"*Merde. Non.*"

I tried to stop him putting them into the van but the blond man grabbed my arm. He wagged an admonitory finger in my face. "He musikant, like you. It his work." Maurice scrambled quickly into the back of the van after his drums, pulling them further in. A second figure got out of the car. It was a young black woman, yet another someone I'd never seen before.

"What the fuck's going on?" I said. The blond guy ignored me. He seized the woman roughly – she was wearing a long, loose-fitting skirt -- and pushed her into the back of the van. The driver, who was chewing with half-open mouth, made a cutthroat gesture at me through the open window.

"What the fuck's this?" I repeated. "Maurice, yeah, but who the fuck's that?" I could see Maurice and the woman sitting together by the bulkhead. The blond guy started to close the van doors. I took hold of the edge of one to stop him. "I said, what the fuck is going on?"

The blond guy pulled the door out of my hand and slammed it to. "*Yop tvoyu mat'*."

"*Connard,*" said the knifeman from the car. "*Nique ta mère.*"

The blond guy put a stubby finger on my chest. "You take all two. You drive to England, no question. When you will be in England end of story. No problem with wife and baby." Then he stepped round to the passenger side of the grey saloon and off they went, the knifeman giving me the finger over the wheel.

I climbed into the front of the van. In the bulkhead, behind me, was a wooden panel, which I slid aside. Through the grille which was revealed I could hear gentle breathing. "*You okay, Maurice?*"

"*Yeah.*"

"*No-one said anything about anyone else.*"

There was silence from the back.

"*Who the fuck is she?*"

"*My sister.*"

It was my turn to be silent. I sat there, watching the car park slowly fill up. It was half-past seven. I'd actually arranged with Armand to load up at nine. I was going to have to text Petra and make up some bull about Armand unexpectedly not being around until then.

"*Bill?*"

"*Yeah?*"

"*I'm really sorry.*"

I wasn't sure whether he meant he was sorry that he was in the back of my van, or whether it was because of his (was she really?) sister being there, or whether he knew about all the threats *etcetera* and was sorry about that. I recycled knifeman's expression. "*Nique ta mère... Sorry, Maurice. What's her name?*"

"*Who? Our mum?*" That at least suggested that that the woman was who he claimed her to be.

"*No, for fuck's sake. Your sister.*"

"*My name's Clothilde,*" said a quiet voice.

I didn't answer. I slid the panel back, turned the ignition and drove us out of the car park. Again I had to stop at the barrier, lean across to the passenger side, get the window down, slide the ticket into the slot and furtle around in my pocket for change, but we hadn't been there long, so it only cost me a euro. When we got to *Le Mannekin Pis* I stopped the engine, and got out, went round to the back and slid in through the back door, opening it as little as I could. The daylight let me see the pair of them huddled like frightened children in a corner, but when I pulled the door to it was all dark inside. I turned on the interior light. Maurice and Clothilde stared at me, and I stared back.

"*What the fuck's going on*?" Neither of them said a thing, but just watched me, with big wary eyes. "*If you don't tell me what's going on you can get out now.*"

Maurice shook his head. "*Bill, they are dangerous. Just do what they say and take us to England, please.*"

"*Yeah, sure. Just like that. I offered to take you because I felt sorry for you. What the fuck have that pair of clowns got to do with it*?"

Maurice and Clothilde exchanged looks, then Maurice said: "*I'm sorry Bill. Bogdan told me to go to the bar, take the drums.*"

"*Bogdan*?"

"*That guy. The Ukrainian. He said there was a good chance I could talk you into it.*"

"*And why the fuck would he do that? What the fuck's in it for him*?"

But Maurice wouldn't say any more. I could see the fear on his face. I turned my attention to Clothilde. "*So what about you*?" As soon as I had said the words I knew that my tone had been too harsh. Clothilde shook her head and stared at the floor. Even in the twenty watt light I could see that she was weeping. "Fuck," I said in English. "Fuck. Fuck you. Fuck that Slav fucker."

I could throw them out. I sensed that their condition was so fragile that if I told them to get out, they would, even the burly Maurice. They couldn't make me drive back to England after all, and all I had to do was get out myself and threaten to find the nearest gendarme. But I had sort of sussed out what had happened – somehow Boris, Bogdan, or whatever the fuck he was called, who must run some kind of smuggling operation, had seen the van and us, the band, and realised that this was a nice little opportunity to make some money. He tells Maurice where to find me, and lets Maurice tell me his story, having made damned sure that Maurice had paid him for his introduction. And it would have been alright if Petra hadn't decided to come over.

Despite the danger I slammed my fist against the metal panelling, making the space boom. Maurice and Clothilde shrank even further back in terror. "Fuckety fuck fuck fuck." Reaching behind me I found the catch to the door, pulled it down, switched the light off and scrambled out. The cab clock said it was quarter to eight. I walked back to the *boulangerie* and bought more croissants, bread and, this time, coffees. After checking that no-one was about I opened the van's rear door as narrowly as I could once more, slid in, shut the door and turned on the interior light again. The two of them were still huddled together in a corner.

"*Voilà,*" I said, and held out the food and drink.

Clothilde's face was anxious and drawn, but a ghost of a smile passed across it. After a moment's hesitation, glancing at her brother, she reached slowly for a croissant. "*Merci.*"

I leant back against the doors and sipped at a coffee. Neither of them touched their cups. "*Look, I'll find a bucket or something. Have the drinks, please.*" Maurice and then Clothilde reached out at that and took their coffees.

We ate and drank without saying anything. I peeked at my mobile. Half eight. I might as well text Petra now. **Problem Armand not here yet you ok? Have breakfast I have x**

I was back in that state of angsting about the textual subtleties of what I was sending. Should I have used proper English? Or French again? My bladder was full. I had to have a discreet slash behind the van, wondering whether Maurice and Clothilde could hear me. Actually, why the fuck were they, and me, cowering inside? Why hadn't we just all got out and strolled to a café and had a nice brekky together? They were no likelier to get picked up here and now than they had been for all the time since their arrival from Congo. But they, and I for that matter, were scared of that Bogdan bloke, and the knifeman, who might well be watching the van. If we all got out, they might think that they were being double-crossed or grassed-up. And maybe Maurice and Clothilde were scared of me also, scared that if they got out I might drive off and leave them. I zipped up my trousers. I definitely needed to get some toilet arrangement sorted. What the hell did people do who spent days in the back of a lorry? At least these two should be out by nightfall. Or in custody by then. And I could be, as well.

I paced around the tarmac'd area behind *chez Armand*, and, amazingly, at one minute past nine the eponymous *patron* appeared, to unlock. "*How's your wife*?" he asked cheerily. "*Her*

French is fantastic."

"*Fine. She's waiting for me at the hotel.*" With that we went in, and straightaway I began to cart stuff out.

"*I'll give you a hand,*" said Armand.

Last thing I needed. "*No, don't bother. I know how everything fits in.*"

With a speaker in my hands I opened up the van doors, and humped it in, nodding to my two passengers. I explained in a whisper that I would build a little wall, giving them a foot or so of space. When Armand's back was turned I nicked an ice bucket, and on a later trip swiped some soap and a stash of paper towels from the loos. Maurice and Clothilde were well hidden behind the gear. Everything was a little nearer the doors than normal, but we always had a bit of spare space and it looked fine.

Armand had the moolah ready, a thick envelope of euros. We chatted – he wanted us back next year – I said fine, *etcetera etcetera*, thinking, hurry up you Asterix lookalike fucker, let me go… We shook hands and then I left for the last time. They'd need some water in the back, so I pulled into a garage and got a couple of bottles. I had to lean over everything and reach it across to Maurice's groping hand.

It was ten past ten when I took the van into the hotel car park. Petra was sat in the lobby with James Albert bouncing excitedly on her knee, but first I went over to the desk and explained that the van was mine, before they clamped it or had it towed away. "*Pas de problème, m'sieur.*" Bloody shouldn't be, at what this place cost, I thought as I went over to wife and child.

Jimmy held out his arms, and as I picked him up Petra wrinkled her nose. "You've got the same shirt on that you were wearing at last night's gig. What the hell have you been doing? And what was all that stuff in the shower? Has he got diarrhoea?"

"He seemed to, then," I said. "But he's fine, now."

Petra lifted up the curls on the back of Jimmy's head as I held him, and examined the nape of his neck. "I'll be the judge of that." She was a little sharp, reminding me of what she did for a living. I ran upstairs and got under the shower myself. Once acceptable, and having brought our stuff down, I settled up with some of Armand's money, which more or less wiped out my share.

"So where have you been?" asked Petra again.

"Armand fucked me about. Didn't turn up when he said he would. But it's all sorted. Where's the child seat?"

Petra had brought it with her. I had to be careful. "You put it in. I'll put the things in the back."

She handed me a plastic bag with wet clothes in it, Jimmy's pyjamas from last night, then leant into the cab to thread the belt through the child seat. "It smells of cigarettes."

"Mitch," I said. "I've asked him not to, but he just does it."

"Hmmm." She didn't seem convinced, but strapped Jimmy in. He gurgled and waved his teddy about.

Then with Daddy on his right, and Mummy on his left we headed home. In two hours we were at Oostende, and in the tail of vehicles curling round the docks. Maurice had been right. They had a separate lane for lorries, and as we queued with the holiday makers' cars and the guys with Transits full of cheap continental grog we saw a couple of lithe, dark-skinned youths climb over a fence. They looked about them, then dashed to the back of the nearest lorry, maybe thirty feet from us, trying to unhitch the canvas covers.

I pointed. "See that? Where do you think they're from?"

"Afghans, probably."

With a blast on a whistle a dozen gendarmes ran past us to the lorry and pulled the two guys off. They were frogmarched, wriggling and protesting, past us. "What do you think," I asked. "Poor sods, or scroungers trying to abuse our over-generous welfare system?"

"I don't blame them," said Petra. "Who could?"

We were waved through Belgian customs, and their guy in the glass booth gave our passports just a cursory glance. James Albert Silverthwaite had his own documents of course, but the picture, taken at three weeks, could have been of any prune-faced infant from any ethnic group in the world. Next we rolled up to the British controls. The queue edged forward. "Give us the passports," I said. Petra handed them to me and in my agitation I dropped them at my feet, and had to scrabble about for them. Two vehicles to go. The passport control didn't seem very stringent – just a handover of papers and a swift peruse. The car in front was Croatian, not even EU, but it was no different – thirty seconds and then they were away. I pulled up to the glass booth.

"Good day, sir," said the chap, from under his peaked cap. He looked at me with narrowed eyes. "Your passports?"

I handed them across, luckily this time not dropping them, though I left a huge clammy perspiration mark on the covers. He looked at Petra's and Jimmy's, shutting them both *tout* bloody *suite*, and then seemed to spend an eternity looking at mine.

"What have you got in the van, sir?"

Wasn't that more a question for customs? I thought vaguely. "Er… Music equipment." Should I say more? No. Less suspicious not to.

"Musician, sir?"

"Yeah." I nodded, a bit too vigorously.

"And the lady, sir?"

"She's my wife. She's a doctor. No, the other band members went back to England on the train. I'm just driving the gear back."

"I see." He looked interestedly at my passport. He'd already scanned it though the computer and I hadn't seen any red lights start flashing, or any sirens start honking. Anyway, why should they? I hadn't jumped bail, or got any parking tickets outstanding, as far as I knew. Still studying my picture, the official smiled. "I know."

"Sorry?"

"Zee Beddington. You were his bass player weren't you? I thought I recognised the name."

"That's right." I was unsure of how friendly to be. I could hear, or sense, that Petra was giggling. Laugh on darling, I thought, when this dickhead wants to open up the back to see the gear that the great Zed used to play with.

The bloke was shaking his head. "I loved Zee's stuff," he said. "Such a waste, the way he died. Crushed by his own gear in the back of the van."

"Yeah. It was a shock to us all."

"It's great that you're still on the road. Keeping the music alive." And at the point he reached down. The passports I thought. Nope.

He was handing me a CD. "I'd like you to take this," he said. "Me and my mates did it."

A Tribute to a Tribute to Zed Beddington was the title. "We've got our own tribute band, based back over the water in Dover," said the bloke. "That's me as Mitch… Look." He pointed to the cover where I could just about recognise him with a grey wig and what had to be an artificial beer belly rammed under his T-shirt. "That's Modger as ZeeBee." I was looking at yet another Zed wannabee, mohair suit, porkpie hat *etcetera etcetera.* "People love him," went on Mr Passports. "He looks and sounds just like Zee – you know, that's what you lot should have done, got in a Zee lookalike as a frontman. Did you never think of that?"

I shook my head. "No. Never occurred to us." I wanted to get away from this topic, so I pointed at the Otto clone, a balding chap in shades clutching two drumsticks. "Who's that?"

"That's Wally from the customs shed… And our mate Potter is you!" Staring out from the left of the group photo was a guy clutching a bass, with a carrot-like nose, wild cross-eyes and a receding hairline only highlighted by his combover.

"Let's see," said Petra, grabbing the CD. "Holy moly… Jimmy, do you think that's Daddy?"

She was practically choking with mirth, holding the CD up for Jimmy to inspect. He regarded it gravely, then shook his head. "No fuuu dada."

"We play all the Kent pubs…" said Mr Passport, adding hastily: "We've registered with Performing Rights. We do pay royalties. Please have it."

"My pleasure," I said. "Thanks."

"Please," he said. "Hey, do you think we could have a gig at Zeestock?"

"Zedstock? Er… Possibly. I'd have to listen to the CD first, of course." Fuck me, the last thing I wanted to do was piss this twerp off and have him pay closer attention to the van. I'd been biting my tongue every time he referred to Zed as "Zee". "Are your contacts on there?"

"Yeah. Give us a ring or email if you like it. We've always always dreamt of coming up and doing a spot." Then he did give me the bloody passports back, grinning. "No bodies in the back this time, eh?"

"Hope not." I handed the passports over to Petra, who was still sniggering.

Mr Bluesfan spoke into a microphone and then leant across to me. "Told Wally and the lads ahead who you are. A couple of them want autographs so don't worry when they come out." He grinned at me, pressed a button and the barrier went up. "See you at Zeestock. Can't wait to see that bloke from Jordan, as well."

"Georgia. See you there."

I thought that was the okay moment to clear off, so I put the van into gear and away we trundled. My whole body was pinging and trembling, but I couldn't show a trace of it to Petra, who was squirming with delight. "Hey, Bill, you've got friends everywhere. Fans of the great Zee Beddington." She knew of old how much that misnomer riled me.

"Yeah. Right." We were coming up to customs. Fuck me, through the loud-speaker system I heard a crackling, which I thought was going to turn into an order telling us to "Step out of the van now!!!" before a SWAT team blew off the back doors and dragged Maurice and Clothilde out in a fog of tear gas, but a moment later came the opening chords of *"Green Turtle Blues*", Zed's last hit before he copped it. A couple of guys came boogieing out of a door, porkpie hats on their heads, holding out copies of our last CD for me to sign. I recognised Wally, who in the flesh looked like Otto's sweet and innocent kid brother. I rolled down our window and autographed the CDs with a flourish. "See you at Zeestock," they said. "We've got all our own gear, and PA and stuff." Mr Passport must have tipped them the word about their gig from his booth.

"Will do." I eased us out of the shed. My hands were slipping on the wheel, they were so sweaty, but the blues gods had smiled on me, or maybe Zed himself in the Inferno had interceded with Satan or something, let Old Nick win a round of duelling guitar solo. We were guided into our berth in the bowels of the boat by one of those efficient chaps who wave and signal to you in a blokey, "Let's do this job properly" way.

As soon as the handbrake went up Petra was unstrapping Jimmy. “Don’t want him breathing fumes.”

“I’ll just get our bags.” I said.

I wanted to check on our passengers. I didn’t envy them being undulated back and forth for ninety minutes in the boat, but as I dropped down to the deck on my side Petra called out: “Come on, Bill, you don’t need anything.”

So I had to leave Maurice and Clothilde down below, whilst we went up and did the happy family thing in the café, sitting by the windows, Petra pointing out everything to Jimmy, who looked on with a bemused expression, before falling asleep on her lap during a feed. Petra and I sat side by side in two seats. I felt queasy again, although when we had been in the traffic queue the sea had looked as flat as the *x,y* Cartesian plane. Petra took my hand. “You okay?”

“Just tired. Lots to do, and it’s always me who has to do the doing.”

“So why did they have to go back early?”

I had spent a little time thinking out an answer to this one. “Otto’s got some elderly relative who’s at death’s door in London, and Mitch gets seasick. He was pretty ill on the boat coming over, anyway, so he wanted to go back on the train. And frankly I would have been quite happy coming back on my own.”

“You mean that you didn’t want us over?”

“No. No. You know I didn’t mean that. It’s those two, Mitch and Otto, I mean. They’re really getting on my nerves.”

Petra gazed at the seagulls following the ship, the birds hovering immobile outside the windows. “It’s time to move on.”

“Maybe.”

“Not maybe.” She leant round as much as she could without shifting Jimmy too much. “Listen, I forgot to tell you, I went and saw Doc Cridders the other day.”

“Oh yeah?” Dr Cridland was her superior, a pathologist with the bedside manner of a vampire. He fancied himself as Renaissance man reanimated, with his own French vineyard and his passion for Haydn. He’d actually invited me and Petra round one night to his flash gaff in Newark, where we had spent the evening tasting various wines in the company of some of his, and Petra’s colleagues. I kept looking out for Mrs Cridland, but when I eventually asked one of the other guests where she was, I was told that she had died a year or so before of some unbelievably rare disease. “Tragic,” the colleague had said, before spitting out his sample, a waste of good wine as far as I was concerned – I just kept swallowing. “I knew her. She seemed perfectly healthy, and then, a couple of weeks, and she was gone.”

“Tragic,” I’d repeated, refilling my glass. I could see Doc Cridland engaged in conversation with Petra. She was talking and listening far more attentively than she ever did nowadays with me, I remember thinking sourly.

Anyway, on the boat, Petra was going on. “I’ve got a new position. No more nights.”

“Just like that?”

“Yes.” Petra settled herself back in her seat. “We were killing ourselves with those shifts, so I told him that either I had to have more social hours, or I’d need to find a job elsewhere.”

“And he didn’t want to lose you?”

Petra looked at me with a vague suspicion in her eye, perhaps picking up something in my intonation. “Well, that’s my new thing. And yours is to move on from the tribute band. How long can you keep trading on past glories?”

“I dunno. People still shell out to see us. We get by. Anyway, you always said you were my biggest fan.”

Petra kissed me. “I am, but you can do better than this. You’ve got so much talent. You need to do something new.”

Jesus, love, I thought, if only you knew what new thing I was engaged on right then. As I tried to think of something suitable to say a booming voice through the tannoy told us in English, French and Dutch that we were approaching Dover, and that vehicle passengers should head back below. We joined the crush on the stairs, Jimmy awake now and staring intently at different people in turn. This was it, I thought. The next half hour or so would either see me out of the harbour complex and heading north, working out the last problem of getting M and C out undetected, or I’d be banged up in a cell awaiting God knows what. It’d kill my old mum and dad. Oh, and the end of my marriage and probably my relationship with Jimmy, so no fucking pressure then.

We settled back into the van. I hoped that neither of the two in the back had puked up or anything. The doors opened at the end, daylight streamed in, and on the signal from one of the efficient chaps in a boiler suit I pulled the van away, over the rattly metal bridge thing that the ferry was drawn up against, and followed the line of traffic past the weighbridges and security chicanes. We were coming up to the bit where they watch you on camera from a windowless building, with the raising ramp things in the road that stop you driving on if they want to check the vehicle. Surely someone on the boat had stuck a big fuck-off sign on the side of the van that said "Have a gander in here, boys, it's your lucky day"? Or maybe they had microphones so sensitive that they could pick up the thumps from my heart, let alone any noises from the back of the van. They had infra-red detectors that would pick up my sweating body, and they would wonder why someone innocent was so agitated. I cautiously looked across at Petra, who, of course, was as chilled out as an iceberg lettuce in liquid helium. She smiled at me. "You alright? Do you want me to drive?"

I shook my head. I still felt a bit blurgh from the swell, although we were now on dry land, but I felt even sicker at the notion that if Petra were at the wheel she might somehow be held responsible when they ripped the van open and found our two hideaways. "I'm fine. Just feel the boat moving still. Bit like Mitch, never been a good sailor."

"Okay." She gooed down at Jimmy. "Daddy doesn't feel too well."

Damn' right, Daddy is not a happy Daddy. Don't crash now, I muttered to myself, *sotto voce*, as I followed a Romanian lorry round the twisty exit roads. We went along by the harbour, up the hill, leaving the old off-White Bloody Cliffs behind, and then we were on the M2. Hades in a helicopter, I was shaking like the proverbial bloody foliage, and having to hide every trace of my agitation from my lady wife, who was trying to interest young Jimmy in our last sight of the sea.

Beforehand it had seemed too much like tempting fate to imagine anything past Dover, but I had to think now about how get shot of our stowaways, and also figure out a way of not letting Petra anywhere near the back of the van until I'd unloaded and cleared up. I needed to pull up somewhere, get Petra and Jimmy safely out of sight, open up and tell our guests to vamoose. After a quarter of an hour ruminating gloomily, seeing a sign for a services, I asked: "Do you want to stop?"

Petra shook her head, a bit surprised. After all we were only ten miles or so from the ferry. "Why, do you want to? Toilet?"

"No. Sorry. Just thought…" I let the words tail off. That had been silly. I should have waited an hour or so, when Petra was much likelier to need the loo or something. Now I was stuck with Maurice and Clothilde for much longer. We drove on. Jimmy dozed in his seat. Petra seemed to be asleep as well, but I was sure that she would wake if I stopped somewhere. I hoped that M and C hadn't suffocated like those poor Chinese bastards in that back of that lorry a few years before. But I had slept for several hours in the back without a problem. Unless they'd asphyxiated on the boat, what with the carbon monoxide on the car deck.

We reached the M25 and went anticlockwise, through the Dartford tunnel. Petra and the babe were still sleeping. When the fuck was I going to be able to stop? I couldn't use getting fuel as a reason – a row of pumps would be far too public to let them out at, though we would need some diesel before we got to Nottingham. When Petra woke surely she'd need a wee, or at least a leg-stretch? And what had happened to Jimmy's bowels? Normally I could have relied on him to need a change by now.

We circled round the north side of London to the M1. Toddington services was coming up. I'd pull off there. My mobile beeped. I'd look at it when we stopped. Then a minute or so later, I did hear something. A thump from behind. Hell and damnation.. Or not. They were still alive anyway. Or one of them, at least. What did they want? I could do nothing until we were off the motorway anyway – it'd be madness to pull up on the hard shoulder. There was another thump. Petra stirred and opened an eye. "What was that?"

"What was what?"

"Didn't you hear something?"

"No."

"Has something fallen over in the back?"

"Could have done, I s'pose. I'll check it when we stop."

Petra settled back to sleep. I cautiously eased my phone open and, half concentrating on steering, and half looking at the buttons, managed to get the message up. **arrete**

I swerved back onto the slow lane. I had to prevent their knocking – as carefully as I could I managed to tap **ok ne pas frapper**

We passed a sign: *Services 7*, and struggling to hold the van on a straight course I texted again: **on arrete 12 km**. Then, relieved that a passing police car hadn't seen my furtive and illegal movements I dropped the phone onto the floor and concentrated on weaving the van through the traffic as speedily and safely as I could. There were the blue signs with three, two and one dashes on as we came up to the services. I peeled us off and headed towards the remotest corner of the car park, as far away from the Happy Salmonella bar, or whatever it was called, as I could put us, and switched the engine off. At least they'd know in the back that we had stopped somewhere.

Petra stirred again. "Where are we?"

"Services. Sorry, I suddenly need a slash urgento. Must be all that coffee on the boat."

And Jimmy woke up at that moment, and rose to the occasion. His face was red as he strained. Petra unbuckled herself. "He needs changing." Normally, being *Monsieur* Right-On I'd have immediately said "I'll do it" and taken Jimbo off to the services, where I could get cross and demand to speak to the management when I found that the Baby Change facilities were only in the Ladies, but just then and there I wanted my wife and son out of it *asap*.

"You do that," I said. "I'll check the back."

Petra unstrapped Jimmy and felt around for the baby stuff bag. "You coming?" she asked.

"What?"

"I thought you wanted a waz."

"Yeah." So I had to traipse across the tarmac holding hands with

Petra, whilst Jimmy, in the papoose on her back, gazed around with big eyes at all the lorries and caravans. As soon as she had disappeared into the baby changing bit, which, perhaps disappointingly, wasn't attached to the Ladies but had its own door – in fact some bloke came out proudly holding his own sprog as P went in – I hared back to the van.

As I got the doors open Maurice's terrified face appeared over the wall of gear.

"*Bill, she's...*"

"*Is she dead*?"

"*No, but…*"

Maurice was shoving the amps aside. There was a sweet, sickly smell. Clothilde lay, her face streaming with sweat, breathing heavly, her robe pulled up to reveal her round belly. Fuck me, I thought, she's fucking pregnant. And her waters had broken.

"*Quick*," I said to Maurice. "*Get the fuck out, both of you. My wife's on her way back.*"

I scrambled onto the tailboard and started helping Clothilde out. "*Quickly*," I said again, "*You need to get a move on.*" Clothilde dropped down and, half holding her, half letting her stagger, I pulled her along, though a hedgerow and into the lorry park, where as gently as I could I helped her lie down on the grass verge, sheltered between two bushes. I kept glancing back through the gap over to the service station doors to see whether Petra had come out yet.

Clothilde was lying with her eyes shut, her breath coming in shallow gasps. I knelt down and took her hand; she raised her head a little. "*My wife…*" I said quickly, "*She's a doctor. She'll help you. You understand?*" Clothilde nodded weakly. I looked across at Maurice. He'd dragged his drums out of the van.

"*You knew about this*?"

"*What? About the baby*?"

I nodded.

"*Yeah. Yeah, but she's only seven months. Shouldn't be coming today.*"

"*Do you know the father*?"

"*Yeah. You do, as well.*"

"*What? Who the fuck is it?*"

"*It's Bogdan.*"

"*You're joking.*"

"*I wish I were.*" Maurice leant over, quietly saying that Clothilde had shagged Bogdan to get the money and contacts to get him, Maurice to Belgium.

"*And Laure*?" I asked.

"*Yeah, and Laure as well...*" He went on to say that when Bogdan had found out that Clothilde was up the duff he'd said no fucking way was he having a *nègre* baby. He'd threatened Clothilde, tried to get her to have an abortion, but when all his threats had failed he'd told her he'd send her to England, and she was so terrified that otherwise he'd resort to having her and her baby bumped off that she'd agreed.

"*Is she really your sister?*"

Maurice wiped his face. "*Yeah. Bogdan knows about the postcard, he knew that I wanted to go to England, so for him it was ideal, the whole thing.*"

"*Well congrats. You're going to be an uncle.*"

"*Fuck that.*"

At that moment I saw Petra appear. She was scanning the car park, wondering whether I was waiting for her by the buildings or by the van, and then, not seeing me, she started over towards the Transit.

"*Okay. She's coming. You don't know me, okay? I just found you by chance. Don't say anything about being in the van.*"

Maurice nodded. I didn't want to press Clothilde in her state but I had to. "*You understand, Clothilde? You don't know me.*" She nodded, moaning "*I'm going to get my wife. It'll all be fine, okay?*"

With that I ran back to the van and shut the doors. I had to make this convincing. Petra was just threading her way through the parked cars with a newly clean-arsed Jimmy. She saw my frantic expression, something I hadn't had to fake. "What's up?"

"You've got to come... I've just found... They only speak French..." I said, trying to ham up the surprise..

"Who? What are you on about?"

By this time I'd got us round our van. "There." I pointed and shooed her through the gap in the hedge, where Clothilde was visible.

Petra unhooked Jimmy from herself and handed him to me. “Take him. Quick.” Maurice – and his drums – had vanished. Kneeling at her side Petra ran her hand over Clothilde’s swollen belly, asking her in French how she was.

“*It hurts*,” groaned Clothilde. “*The baby…*”

Petra was holding her hand, telling her to breathe regularly. “*I’m a doctor. It’s all going okay.*”

Clothilde moaned and her body arched up in pain. Jimmy, still in my hands, pointed anxiously. “Mama fuuu...” Where the hell had Maurice run off to, the lairy fucker, leaving his sister like that? Despite my gaze continually being drawn back to the drama happening on the floor before me I was glancing between the lorries and the hedgerows, maybe expecting to see a figure haring off across the fields with a drum under each arm.

Petra interrupted my train of thought. “Got your phone?”

“Yeah.”

“Nine nine nine. Now.”

As soon as Petra heard me talking to the operator she reached up and grabbed the mobile. “Got a baby on the way here, prem, mums’s doing okay but we need incubator and oxygen, adrenaline...” She gave our location. Clothilde was gasping and moaning. Petra handed the phone back to me and wiped Clothilde’s forehead with a handkerchief. She spoke soothingly. “*You’re doing fine. Breathe in and out, steady now. Baby’s coming. I can see the head.*”

Holding Jimmy, I recalled his birth, in a nice clean hospital ward. Petra had insisted on everything – private room, which she/we hadn’t had to pay for, seeing as she worked there, gas and air, lumbar jab, birthing pool, Mozart on the sound system, deferential midwife, and ministering husband. None of the old hippy drop ‘em in a teepee and see the pain as her share of the newborn’s trauma at the separation into the rest of the universe, thankyou, skygod, for her. Technobaby Jimmy had made his entrance into the world with mum linked up to more monitors than a council estate CCTV centre.

Back on the wilderness of the M1 services lorry park Clothilde screamed, and suddenly Petra was holding a tiny figure upside down, banging its back with two fingers to get it breathing. The baby cried and Petra ripped off her jacket, wrapped the baby in it and gave it to Clothilde. "*It's a girl. She's fine.*" Petra had taken out a little knife and was cutting the cord. She tied it, tucked the baby back up again as she lay on Clothilde's stomach. "*Everything's okay. Baby's nice and healthy but she's a bit small. She needs to go to hospital. The ambulance is on its way.*"

Jimmy was staring at Clothilde and the little bundle on her chest. "Baba fuuu." He pointed, and then his head turned as he heard the ululating sirens.

The ambulance pulled up and a woman in medical fatigues climbed out of the back, clutching a clipboard. "Who called us?" She looked at me. "You?"

I shook my head, and pointed down to where Petra was kneeling by Clothilde, holding her wrist. "My wife's the doctor."

The woman held out the clipboard to Petra. "Sign here, doc."

Petra signed. "And here, please." The woman produced another form. Petra impatiently scrawled on that. "Is she safe to move?" asked the paramedic.

"Yes," Petra said irritably. "Yes, get on with it. Don't want hypothermia."

The paramedic produced another clipboard. "Transport authorisation. Sign here."

Petra scribbled on it and said a couple of words to Clothilde, who moaned. The paramedic started writing something on the clipboard which Petra had just signed. "Can't you get a move on?" I asked, unable to restrain myself any longer.

The paramedic looked at me coldly. "You're medically trained?"

Petra said, calmly: "You need to move her immediately. We don't want baby getting hypothermia."

A second paramedic had climbed out by now, holding a shortened aluminium stretcher. "Which county are we in?" he asked, looking round at us.

"What the fuck does that matter?" I burst out.

"If we've crossed the boundary we need an FU94 border transit authorisation chit."

I looked in bewilderment at Petra, who looked down at her phone. "You're still in Bedfordshire. Anyway, maternity emergencies are covered by protocol AK47."

The two paramedics looked at each other, shrugged, and lowered the stretcher to the ground, struggling to detelescope it. I tried to help, but the woman pushed me away. "Insurance is void if you touch it." The paramedics manoeuvred Clothilde plus babe onto the stretcher and slid mother and baby into the back of the ambulance. I could see the driver craning out of his window to see what was going on.

The female paramedic climbed back out with another sheaf of papers. "Where you from, doc?"

"Doctor Mary Thornton, Newark General," lied Petra smoothly, signing sheet after sheet of bumf. I peered into the back of the ambulance. Clothilde was lying still, the baby a little bundle under Petra's jacket on her chest. At last the paperfest seemed to be done, and the paramedics climbed into the ambulance, shutting the doors. The sirens and lights came on, but it rolled off at a leisurely pace, disappearing behind the petrol station. We could still hear the sirens for a while.

Jimmy pointed after the ambulance. "Baba fuuu."

"Luton General," said Petra. "They'll be there in ten minutes." She took Jimmy from me, kissing the top of his head.

"Are we going there?" I asked, very much hoping that we didn't have to.

"No," said Petra. "They'll be fine. Baby's early but healthy enough. What on earth happened?"

"I just heard something," I said. "I'd come out from the loo and was just waiting for you by the van, just checked inside that everything was okay, which it was, and I thought I heard someone crying or moaning, and I went over, through the hedge, and there they… She was."

"Must have been in a lorry," said Petra, looking over at where trucks from all over Europe, from Aalborg to Zagreb were lined up.

"I didn't ask," I said. "As soon as I realised what was going on I told her that you were a doc and I'd get you. It all happened so quickly. Think they'll be alright?"

"Yeah. Come on." She started towards the van.

"What about your jacket?" I asked.

She shrugged. "Can't be helped. Wasn't my favourite." She was a lot less affected by the whole thing than I had been, but why wouldn't she be? As far as Petra was concerned the woman was just a chance emergency, something which happened for every medic every so often.

We got back into the van. As I put Jimmy into his seat he held up his tiny hands to me. "Dada baba fuuu"

"That's right, son. Baby. New baby. And you're a big boy." I kissed his lovely stubby nose. I could hardly believe my luck at how easy it had been to get shot of those two. All I had to do was unload the van, without Petra peering into the back too closely, and we were sorted, and that fucker Bogdan could go and screw himself. We pulled out of the services. I was careful to concentrate on the road, especially as we went past a couple of cop cars parked after the petrol pumps. Then we were indicating right and coming out onto the slow lane.

"Good thing you knew about that form, you know, the one about maternity emergencies," I said.

Petra laughed. "You mean the AK47 cross border permit?" I nodded. "Made it up. I do it all the time at work." She was in a good mood. All was well between us and she'd done her good deed for the day. "That woman was okay, bit underfed maybe, and the baby was a bit light, but they'll be fine..." My conscience was easier as well; instead of throwing them out in the middle of nowhere, at some God-forsaken lay-by, maybe in the dark, Clothilde and babe'd got a ride to a hospital in the middle of a town. What happened after that wasn't my concern. But where the hell had Maurice gone?

"You did well," said Petra, breaking into my thoughts.

"Did I? I didn't really do anything."

"You did. You wondered what that noise was. A lot of people would have ignored it, not seen it as their problem, but you're not like that. You're bothered about people, Bill, I've seen it before. It's one one of the things I love about you." She was smiling and her hand reached over our son to caress my leg. I started to get a hard-on, even as the little demon on my left shoulder was whispering in my ear that I was a scoundrel who didn't deserve a wonderful wife like that, and jabbing his pitchfork painfully into my neck, just by the spot where Bogdan's mate had pushed the knife.

"And that's why you need to think about the band," she went on.

"What?"

"Did you enjoy the gigs in Brussels?"

"When you two were there, yeah."

"Okay, you know you're sick of it." She was like the proverbial canine in the ossuary. "People know you, Billy, you've got connections, you could do your own thing. You know, when I met you, the music was still fresh. I loved it. That first gig where we got talking. It was great. But you've been doing the same old thing for years. I am so bloody sick of hearing the same old songs. I hear them in my sleep."

"So do I, but the others won't do anything new. I've tried. Anyway the fans wouldn't stand for it. All they want is what they know."

"Exactly," said Petra, triumphantly. "Why is someone like you squandering your talents to placate a bunch of sad old blokes? Like that loser on the passports, for God's sake? *I* want to hear something new from you. When we get back home, tonight, I want you to tell the others that you're leaving."

"Tonight?"

"Tonight. Ring them tonight."

"I don't know… We've got Zedstock. The biggy, sixty years of the old bastard and all that. Got that Georgian bloke coming."

"Billy," said Petra firmly. "Just do it. For me and Jimmy. You don't need to keep going out with some useless retreads." She smiled down indulgently at the lad, who gurgled and tried to grab her hand. "Daddy's going to get a much better band than with those sad old gits…"

I said nothing more, but focussed on getting us home safely. We had to stop for fuel around Birmingham. Petra went off again with Jimmy as I filled up the van, gazing sourly at the side panelling and wondering how best to get it sorted without her noticing anything amiss. Outside our house in Nottingham I said to Petra: "You take Jimmy in. If I'm quitting the band we don't want all their gear round at our gaff, do we? I'll take it round to the rehearsal rooms."

Petra was happy with that. The only risky bit was getting our own stuff, our clothes *etcetera*, out of the back, but I let Petra busy herself with extricating Jimmy from the cab whilst I opened up, grabbed the cases, and shut the doors again as fast as I could. I unlocked our front door, stepped over the mini-Everest of advertising stuff that had managed to build up in only two mornings of neither of us being there, and switched off the old burglar alarm. As persistent as ever, Petra insisted that I contact the band before I went out again.

"I'll email," I said. "I can't face talking to them."

"Okay. But do it now."

So I sat before the computer, listening to Jimmy splashing away happily in the bathroom upstairs, and Petra's soft but firm voice keeping him under control. My life had changed so much since I had met her. She was right. I didn't need to spend the rest of my natural with those narrow, blokey blokes. Tommo was okay, a bit more like me with his family but we never hung out together. I only ever had contact with him through the band and I'd never thought of inviting him and Suzy round, with or without the kids. Reluctantly I concentrated on what I really needed to do – compose the text that would bring nearly thirty years of my life to an end. "*Dear Otto, Mitch and Tommo...*" No, fuck it, I wasn't saying "*Dear*".

"*Guys, I have some news. As of now I am quitting the band. Sorry for the short notice...*" Don't apologise.

"*...As of now I am quitting the band. It's not working out and I need to do something else. We can settle up the financial side as soon as you want. I will contact the venues and call off our gigs tomorrow, but I will give you time to get this first. Also, you will have to decide what to do about Zedstock. Bill*" I showed it to Petra. She okayed it, so I pressed send. That was it. The end of the Zed Beddington Band. Zed had recruited me in nineteen eighty two to replace Matty, and now it was over. Petra had got Jimmy ready for an early night, in his sleepsuit, tousled hair still wet, ready for a kiss from Daddy.

As I left the house the grumpy old git who lived next to us was just stepping out of his door, on his way to a BNP meeting or suchlike. He pointed with his stick at the van; I'd left the nearside tyres on the pavement. "Hope you're not leaving that there. It's a hazard. I'll get the council onto you."

"It's going in a minute." I thought it politic to be polite – after the last couple of days I'd had I didn't want anyone snooping around. My neighbour shuffled off, muttering about noise and fooking foreigners, though what that had to do with me I wasn't sure. It was only half past five, Blighty time, but the early morning meet in the Gare Midi car-park seemed to belong to another century.

I set off for the rehearsal rooms – to our rehearsal room – the band's rehearsal room, in the old cycle factory. And, ironically, the whole building had become ours a year before; it had come onto the market and Otto, who fancied himself as a bit of a property tycoon, with his string of slum dwellings across the city, had talked the rest of us into buying the place. We had all subbed a share, and indeed we'd spent plenty of spare time working on the building on free days, another source of friction between me and Petra at the time, replastering, rewiring, and laying new floors, so as to bump up the value of our investment, which was now another financial knot to be severed.

I parked up in the little bay by the door, and went round to the back of the van. The ice bucket had got knocked over and the van smelt of stale urine. I pulled out the first few things, revealing the space which Maurice and Clothilde had been in. At the rehearsal rooms, dating back from the time when the place had been a working factory, there was an old kitchen, with cleaning materials and even a kettle. I took some equipment in and came out with a steaming bucket of water in one hand and a big sponge in the other. I pulled out the rest of the gear, pushing it through the doorway, slotting it between the building gear, wheelbarrows and planks and bags of cement which were still hanging around on the ground floor.

I scrubbed the van floor with the sponge, then dumped it and the empty water bottles and Armand's ice-bucket in the big dustbin just outside the rehearsal room door. I also had to throw out the old carpet which had lined the van floor. When I'd done as much as I could I put my own amp and speaker and guitar back into the van – the floor was still wet but I needed to get back or Petra would be wondering what was taking me so long. I had meant to hump Mitch's and Otto's gear up the flight of stairs, rather than leaving it all at the bottom, but I didn't want to spend any more time away from my family, and anyway, fuck them, I thought, the band was over and they could sort themselves out.

I did go upstairs though, to carry down my spare bass amp and the other bits and bobs that were mine. I looked round the dusty room, seeing the piles of empty drinks cans in each corner – Otto's by far the largest and Tommo's the smallest, then turned out the light, locked up and went back down the steps.

Fifth Bar

Chord of D

I drove back through the city, thinking about my new life. I was going to get the violin up to speed, learn some jazz, get a new outfit… I parked up outside my house, and pulled my gear out, taking it into the hallway, leaving the heaviest things, the two bass amps, until last. As I lifted the first one up a voice behind me said: "Want a hand, Wurzel?"

I jumped, letting the amp fall. Otto caught it. "Chill, Billy. Looks like you're worn out." He grinned at me, and then, unbelievably, lifted the amp with one finger. "Like you said to me once before, we need to have a little talk."

"Really?" I said, as calmly as I could. "What about?"

"Aren't you going to invite me in? We're still mates aren't we?" He'd never referred to our being "mates" in all the years I'd known him.

"Okay." I opened the door and Otto carried my amp into the hall. I followed him with the other one.

"That you?" called Petra's voice from the front room.

"Yeah." I led Otto through to the middle room. He sat himself down without invitation. I stood nervously under the light. "Things go okay?"

"Yeah. No problem." Otto folded his arms. "So. So you're leaving us?"

"Yeah." Least said, the better.

Otto said nothing – he just sat there, staring at me in his unblinking manner, unembarrassed, thews swelling out from under his T-shirt, not in the least showing any sign of looking away. Then he smiled. "Okay, Billy. Okay. Don't call off the gigs."

"Why not? We can't do them."

"*You* can't do them." He looked pleased with himself.

"What do you mean?"

"Billy, you've left the band. None of your fucking business. Don't call them off, that's all."

"What about Zedstock?"

Otto pursed his lips mockingly, as if he were a schoolchild considering a sum in an infant class. "Let me think…" His face lit up with *faux* inspiration. "I know, Billy, don't fucking call that off either. Okay?"

"Okay."

"Oh, yeah, and I'll have the wedge from our trip. You can give me Mitch's as well, if you want. I'll be seeing him later."

I pulled out my wallet and counted out a thousand euroes. "I'll have to keep some back for petrol and stuff. We'll sort it exactly later."

Petra opened the door. She looked at Otto for a moment, and then said evenly: "I didn't realise we had company."

"You don't." Otto began to get up. "I was just going."

"How's your Auntie Lil?"

"Who?"

"The sick relative you had to drop everything for to rush back and see."

Otto snorted. "She died. Pity. Van keys, Billy."

"You're banned," said Petra. I'd told her about Otto's final drunken drive into a Wolverhampton department store.

Otto was nodding and grinning. He turned to me. "That was the one good choice you made, Wurzel. I've always liked your wife. She's got balls…." He paused and then went on. "And she's told you to leave the band, and you've done what she's said, so you can give me the bleeding band van keys right now, okay?"

I looked at Petra. She gave the slightest of nods, so I fished the keys out of my pocket, and passed them over to Otto, who enclosed them in his massive hairy fist. "Thankyou, Billy."

"We'll settle all the money stuff next week," I said. "When we've had a chance to think everything through."

"Whatever. I'll bid you goodnight. Remember Billy, leave those gigs." With both hands he snapped an imaginary stick, or neck. "I'll see myself out." After the front door opening and shutting we heard the van engine roaring, and the sound dwindling as Otto drove off.

"You did the right thing again, Billy. I'm proud of you." Petra came up to me, and began to kiss me. She led me off upstairs, where we didn't wake young James Arthur.

***

And afterwards, again, I couldn't sleep. The next gig that we – the band – had scheduled was tomorrow night. Grantham. And I wasn't going to be there. For thirty odd years I had played the bass, in a succession of bands, never leaving one until I had a berth with another, and now I had nothing. I'd had time on my own, out of relationships, and I'd coped with that, but this – this felt ghastly, far worse than when I'd been dumped by a girlfriend. And it wasn't just the end of an affair – this was going to be a divorce, as we were going to have to sort out all the finances, make provision for the kids, *ie* the songs, and make the break final and clean. I'd once read how in mediaeval Japan any samurai who fell out with their overlord would be condemned to wander the country, fending for himself and never being allowed to join any other court. That was going to be me. I'd never find anything like the Zed Beddington Band again. I shouldn't have quit. I rolled over and looked at the sleeping Petra, feeling a sudden rush of recrimination. It was alright for her, bouncing me into leaving – she had her career and the status of being a doctor, but I'd never have the adulation and the sense of being at the centre of things again.

Petra stirred, and I felt ashamed. We had made love half an hour before and now I was filled with anger towards her. She was right. I had been vegetating with the band. No, it was worse than that. Getting out was like getting away from someone who was battering you. You had to do it, no matter how hard it might be. I got out of bed, and padded downstairs. From out of my leads bag I drew Maurice's CD, put it into the stereo and listened to it on headphones. I shut my eyes. It was familiar and yet alien, our songs, Zed's songs – Mitch's songs, really, mostly – translated, not only the vocals, I mean, but the musical idiom as well. The drum rhythms and chucking guitars transported me up into the air, southwards over a sleeping provincial England, over the stormy Channel, over France and the Alps and Italy and the Mediterranean, over the sands of the Sahara to the rain forests of equatorial Africa… Then someone was shaking my shoulder. I pulled off the headphones. It was Petra holding a red-faced Jimmy. "What are you doing?" she asked. "Didn't you hear him? I've got to go to work in a couple of hours." She was anxious. She dumped Jimmy and changing bag onto me and stomped back upstairs. I spread out the mat and laid son and heir on it. He grinned devilishly at me. "Mumu fuuu…"

***

Petra was at King's Medical Centre the next day. At breakfast she said nothing about my not having heard Jimmy in the night. Once I had taken him to nursery, I went back home and got my old fiddle out, the one I'd learnt on as a kid. I tuned up the strings and riffled through the music which I had retrieved from a dusty box in the loft. I recalled the weekly boyhood trudge round to my teacher, a spinster of a certain age who'd lived with half a dozen cats in a dimly lit villa in an overgrown garden. The whole smelly house with its musty furniture and Victorian piano, complete with candelabra, had seemed as wizened and ancient as she had been – I'd started as a compliant seven year-old and had had my last lesson as a mutinous sixteen-year-old who had discovered punk and wasn't going touch anything that wasn't electrified ever again. "He has such talent," Miss Bellchambers had said mournfully to my parents as they had given her a bottle of wine as a parting gift at the end of my last lesson. Still, now I was going to vindicate the old biddy's faith in me. If she were still alive she must be pushing a hundred by now. Here's to you, Miss B. I'd give myself three months to get Monti's *Czardas.* I scraped away for an hour or so, then murdered some Bach and Brahms. I moved onto some blues, my fingers tripping over each other as I tried to bend the notes. With a cup of coffee I sat down before the computer and did a search of bands seeking musicians.

A ceilidh outfit in Ashbourne was looking for a fiddle player, four hundred quid for the whole band bottom price per gig. I downloaded the dots for a couple of Morris session tunes and tried them. They were pretty easy, if uninspiring. By way of relaxation I had a squint at *www.britishbluesgoss.co.uk*.

bluesfiend666, *nakedblueslady*, *beermonster37* and *whitecliffs* are in the room

beermonster37: they got back from brustle's ok

whitecliffs: yeah i spoke 2 bill at dover he asked me 4 1 of my bands cd's he arsked me weather i coud find time 2 cum 2 zeestok this year 2 play

nakedblueslady: bill is so clever he spoke frensh to audien's and he did fantastik improv on bass

Volcanoes on a velocipede, had *nakedblueslady* really been in the crowd at the *Le Mannekin Pis*? It was great to have such devotion but certainly she (he?) couldn't be living up to her (his?) name, as I reckoned someone in the bar would have noticed. And what about *whitecliffs*, who of course had to be that eedjit in the passport booth, assuming that he was going to get a gig, just like that? Now I had got shot of Maurice and Clothilde and cleaned out the van I had nothing to fear from him or his crappy tribute outfit.

whitecliffs: yeah bill also gave me speshul comp tickit's 4 zeestok

Wanker, I thought. We financed all the Zedstock acts from the drink sales. I'd better be careful, otherwise people might start thinking that they had to pay and would stop coming. But did that matter? I'd left the band, I had to remind myself. Nevertheless, I signed in.

wurzelman is in the room

wurzelman: That's bollocks, whitecliffs, you don't need tickets for any of the events at Zedstock

whitecliffs: piss off wurzelman i mean he gave me speshul backstage pass

wurzelman: To get into the Grey Swan? It's a pub. Anyone can get in there

bluesfiend666: fuk off wurzelman i hav backstage pass as well

nakedblueslady: i don't need one i am naked 4 bill

I gave up and logged out. It was time to retrieve the lad. Petra came home, we had tea, Jimmy pulverising the top of his boiled egg with gusto. When he had eaten the contents, I placed, as I always did, the empty shell upside down in the eggcup again and he roared with laughter as he smashed it in with his spoon. I said: "I've got to chase something up this evening." Petra looked up enquiringly over her plate. "I was checking out bands on the net today. There's some people who want to meet me."

"Sounds good."

"They're playing out near Woolsthorpe. Is it okay if I nip out later?"

It was, so at eight o'clock I set out for Grantham. At nine o'clock I was outside the Iron Queen pub. I had to be careful; the venue was not one of our – the band's – regular haunts, although we had played there a couple of years back, but I didn't want anyone to recognise me. I had a beanie hat which I pulled down over my forehead and I wore shades. I probably looked a right poseur.

I could see activity through the windows so I went into the bar from the further door. Otto and Mitch were just about to start. And who the fuck was that on stage, with a bass? After a moment I recognised Matty. Hell's bells, I'd thought he was in Australia or somewhere. Of course, he'd know all the bloody songs. Otto must have moved pretty damn' fast once he'd got my email.

I lurked behind a pillar; it was a big pub and there were plenty of folk between me and the stage. Otto was behind his kit; they'd already retrieved everything from the practice room. Mitch lumbered up to his mike. "Good evening," he said flatly. "We are a Tribute to Zed Beddington." He nodded at Otto and Matty and then they were off, playing the opening song, the same one that I had begun the set with for years. But they were bloody awful. Mitch kept hitting dodgy chords, majors when they should have been minors, and vice versa, and he was on the wrong frets for his solos. Matty kept nervously losing touch with Otto, who simply banged out an uninspired four-square beat. I thought of the eel-like subtlety of Maurice's drumming at the *Mannequin Pis*. Where was he now, I wondered. Sleeping in a barn on a Bedfordshire farm? And Clothilde and the baby? It had all happened only yesterday, but it seemed as distant as the Palaeozoic. The band limped to the end of the song and after some lukewarm applause they launched into the second, "*Green Turtle Blues*". Matty yelled the first line, his mouth flapping open and closed like a beached chelonian himself, and then he seemed to forget the rest of the lyrics. The three of them carried on playing a while and then he started again, bellowing out of tune into the mike. Things were looking up, I reckoned.

At the end of that song somebody in the audience actually had the *cojones* to boo. Otto stared menacingly at them over his kit. "Where's Bill?" a voice called out. "We want Bill," someone else shouted, and in an instant the audience were all chanting the same thing. "We want Bill! We want Bill!" Should I cast off my disguise, rush forward and seize the bass from Matty? Before I could nerve myself to do this Otto had started the drum solo which led into the next song, "*Drop Dead Blues*". The crowd, such as it was – I could see people picking up their coats and slipping out – quietened a bit. There weren't enough folk left to hide me properly so, a bit regretfully, I left by the further door. I'd seen enough anyway. What the fuck were they up to?

Outside I listened a bit longer through the windows. People were making comments as they unlocked their vehicles. "Fucking shit." "They won't last long." "What's happened to Billy? He was magic." I felt like rushing up to the bloke who had said that and shaking him by the hand, but I just got back into the car and drove home.

Petra was watching telly when I got in. "How was it?"

"Not really my thing," I said. "First day of trying though. I need to keep at it." What I really needed to do at that point was get online and see what the maniacs on *www.britishbluesgoss.co.uk* were saying. "Do you want a coffee?" She didn't, but I was able to take the laptop into the kitchen where I filled the kettle and logged on.

bluesfiend666, harpmouth, nakedblueslady, whitecliffs and *beermonster37* are in the room

bluesfiend666: well that woz shit woznt it

harpmouth: wot u mean?

bluesfiend666: just got back from grantam bill not playing got sum useless twat instead

beermonster37: that woz matty he usedter play with zee b4 bill did ☹ zee sacked him mind u mitch woz crap as well and otto is getting past it imho

bluesfiend666: u woz there @ grantam?

beermonster37: yeah they do gold fartwangler on handpump

bluesfiend666: didn't c u

beermonster37: i left b4 brake they woz so yuseless

harpmouth: i am going to herryford next week 2 c trib 2 zb

bluesfiend666: dont bother unless they get bill bak

nakedblueslady: i want bill bak as well i am naked 4 him

beermonster37: u r man but i say sak matty we awl want bill bak

Right on, brothers, and sisters, I thought, feeling more cheerful than I had for a while. I heard Petra's light footsteps going up to bed, so I logged off and followed her. But later, afterwards, lying there, once again, I couldn't sleep. I was thinking about the Grantham gig, and getting angry. How the fuck could they just replace me like that, as if my contribution to the Zed Beddington Band had been nothing over all those years? I had dirt on them – I could ring Mitch and point out that one phone call from me, directing the cops to the basement of the Grey Swan, would pull the plug on the whole shebang. About four o'clock I did manage to drop off and of course then Jimmy woke up at half six and I was too dopey to deal with him properly, which fucked Petra off, as she was trying to sort herself for going to work. Having eventually got Petra, who was now in a foul mood, out of the house, and Jimmy round to the nursery I settled down, with a black coffee, to scouring the net for bands who wanted either a fiddle or a bass player.

The invites to auditions started coming through. The first was from "*Sunset Theory Jazz Collective*" in Lincoln. I drove out one afternoon, having borrowed Petra's satnav thingie. At a pebble-dashed semi on an estate I knocked at the door, and it was opened by a round man with the face and beard of a garden gnome. "Come in, come in," he said effusively, in a sing-song Scandinavian accent, pumping my arm. "You are Bill? I am Lars." He ushered me into the living room, where a chlorotic girl of about twenty was cradling a saxophone, and an Asian guy with a goatee was sat behind a set of bhangra drums. "This is Esmerelda and Bart."

"Hi." I had my little practice amp in one hand and my bass in the other. I set up in a corner.

Lars sat down behind an electric piano. "Okay, Bill?" I nodded. "Okay, this we call *No Fish No Bicycle*. You listen and join in, okay?"

"What key's it in?"

Lars looked a little pained. "It has no key. You listen, you join in?"

With no more ado Esmerelda starting wailing on the sax, and seemingly at random Lars and Bart plonked and bashed away. I listened for a point to hang a bass line onto but it all sounded like complete fucking freestyle chaos to me. In the end I started to play an irregular riff on my D string. Without warning all three of them stopped, with impressive simultaneity.

"No, no, Bill," said Lars, sadly. "Eleven eight, one bar, then seven eight one bar, then eleven eight and seven eight and so on."

I tried to make sense of this as they began again, Esmerelda yowling into her sax with her back turned to the rest of us, and Bart's hands banging away on his drums in a rhythm which was either unbelievably sophisticated or completely bloody random. I counted four three four for eleven, then four three for seven, then repeated it, but again they stopped as one. Lars' tone was melancholy. "Bill, you play this kind of music before?"

"Not really," I said, "I told you online, I played blues for years."

Lars' expression became as grave as if I had told him that I had a conviction for kiddy-fiddling. "I think Bill, you need to free yourself from preconceptions."

"Okay," I said. "Eleven then seven is eighteen. Why don't you just make it nine eight?"

Five minutes later I was on my way back to Nottingham. My next audition was the following day, with the ceilidh band I'd seen on the net when I'd first begun looking, in a room above a pub in the Peak District. The Derbyshire Tup Tuppers were, according to their website, the oldest established dance band in the county and went out earning thrice weekly. Picking my way through the dim bar, I could hear something folky coming from upstairs. After banging my head going up a dark twisty stairwell I found myself in a low-ceilinged room. Three blokes with beards and a lady without a beard, scraping away on a cello, all stopped in mid-play.

"Hi," I said uncertainly, unstrapping my violin from my back. "I'm Bill. Fiddle player?"

The nearest beardy, who was holding one of those irritating accordeon things with buttons – a melodeon – stood up. "Aye. Let's see what tha't made of." Before I'd even got my fiddle out he'd looked round the others, received a collective nod and had asked: "Tha knows *Buxton Sergeant's Brass Monkey*?"

"No."

"*Killamarsh Queer Boy*?"

"Sorry."

"What about *Melbourne Mountaineer*?"

"Give me the dots. I'm a good sight-reader."

Once more, as *chez* Lars, I realised that I had unwittingly transgressed. The man with the melodeon regarded me mistrustfully. "We don't do dots, lad. We keep the spirit of t'music live."

Lad? I'd had my forty-ninth birthday three weeks before. "Okay. Play it and I'll pick it up by ear."

The melodeonist gave a grudging nod, and they all started again. One of the other guys was strumming a guitar and the third had in his hands something like a mediaeval serpent, with a little pick-up lead to a microamp. It was a simple tune, too damned simple, and I could pick out the changes no problem. After a while I started playing the melody, adding little flourishes here and there. The serpent thing was flat the whole bloody time. Mr Melodeon raised a leg, and we all stopped. He looked at me mournfully. "Where tha from, Bill?"

"From? I've come over from Nottingham."

There was a little flurry of muttered conversation between them all. The guitar-player said: "You're not from round here? Where were you born?"

"I told you on the phone, Tiverton, Devon…"

"Devon?" interrupted Mr Melodeon. "I thought tha said Derby?"

"You must have misheard me. Does it matter?"

"Oh aye, lad, it does," said the guy with the serpent, grimly.

They were like one of those collective bloody alien organism borg things you see in sci-fi films, all of the same mind. "You see lad, we're all Derbyshire and proud of it," went on Mr Melodeon. "We only play gigs inside Derbyshire, and we only have folk who're Derbyshire born and bred. Max here…" – the guitarist nodded –"He's from round here, Ashbourne, and Anne…" He nodded at the cellist "…She's from Belper and I'm from Dronfield. And Pete…" – he indicated *Monsieur Serpent* – "He's from Mosborough."

"Mosborough's in Sheffield," I said. "South Yorkshire."

Melodeon Man looked a little embarrassed. "Aye, lad, it is now, but before local government re-organisation in Seventies it were in Derbyshire. We've got to be careful. Keeping old traditions going. We had another chap here last week on violin, great bloke, but he were from Tintwistle so that were no go."

"Tintwistle *is* in Derbyshire," I said

"Nowadays, aye," said MM with relish, "But before 1971 it were part of Cheshire, so we had to say no."

I took the hint. Back home, in front of the computer once more, I thought to myself that I was being too passive. Why didn't I advertise for musoes and set up my own band? So I composed an ad. "Former bass player in well-known band seeking to form..." What kind of band was I looking for? A blues outfit, I decided, in the first place, anyway. If I were going to be trying to run things let it be on familiar ground. "...Seeking to form new R&B..." No, hang on, that'd get me lots of wannabe soul singers. I didn't know who'd appropriated the term R&B for that dreadful bland stuff sung by artistes with stupid names who appeared in the charts for one hit and then who were never heard of again, but when I'd been a lad R&B had stood for proper ballsy Rhythm and Blues... "...Seeking to form new Blues outfit. Gigs waiting." This wasn't true of course, but I had umpteen contacts in the biz and getting a few local appearances in the pubs round Nottingham wouldn't be a problem.

I did get one outing with a band soon enough, though – on the net a message came up through a *Musicians Wanted* site. A band from Nuneaton had had their bass player break two fingers that morning in a bondage ritual related incident (more information than I needed to know, I thought, as I was told this by Sharon Slinky, the lead singer) and they had a big gig that very night. Here were a list of the heavy rock covers they played. Could I stand in? Of course I could – the songs might not be *ma tasse de thé* but it was a challenge that a professional like me would enjoy. Petra okayed it, so I zoomed down to Warwickshire, humming the tunes to myself, and found my way to the dark smelly basement club to meet Satan's Slinkies, four twenty-something maids dressed in schoolgirl outfits, and to play with three of them whilst the injured bassist, her arm in a sling, looked on from the wings. I felt like Old Father Perve. A denim-clad crowd of youngsters shook their heads and writhed on the floor before us. I got temporary tinnitus, one hundred and fifty quid and bad thoughts all the way back up the motorway to Nottingham.

"Good time?" muttered Petra sleepily, as I climbed into bed at last with her.

My ears were still ringing. I'd forgotten my muso earplugs. "Yeah, but a one-off." I hadn't asked Satan's Slinkies whether they needed me to cover for any more gigs and they hadn't asked me whether I might be available.

And one bright Tuesday morning, having dropped Jimmy off, I strolled into town with my fiddle on my back. I'd learnt a dozen Celticky tunes by rote and thought I'd see how much I could make doing a spot of busking. I ambled along the shopping lanes around the Lace Market trying to find a suitable spot – I'd done a few stints of street music years ago, in my punk phase, playing an acoustic bass with a couple of out-of-tune mates, but that had been for a laugh rather than anything else. Now, the town seemed full of buskers, in a way that I hadn't noticed before, although maybe they'd always been there. It was a bit like when Petra had been preggers with Jimmy – we'd remarked on how many fat ladies there seemed to be around, something that I'd never picked up on before I was a father-to-be.

First I passed a couple of Gypsies playing accordians, and fifty yards later a bloke in a beret parping a sax to a track coming out of a portable amp. At least he was playing a recognisable tune, in contrast to Esmerelda back in Lincoln, but I'd always thought that using electronic backing was cheating. Next was a woman playing a zither, then two blokes juggling – not busking *strictu sensu* but still taking up a pitch. All the main drags seemed occupied but in the end I found an alley opening between two shops – it wasn't great but it would do.

Grasping the violin in one hand, I laid the case before me and primed it with random change from my own pocket, three pounds forty three pence (seven cubed, a good omen I thought) to start the ball, or coins, rolling. As quietly as I could I checked that the strings were in tune with each other, rubbed some rosin on the bow, and then, finding nothing else that I could procrastinate with, tentatively scraped my way through *The Leprachaun's Balls*.

Nobody came up and told me I was crap – on the other hand no-one came up and threw any dosh in either. I played *The County Leitrim Potato*, a bit louder (a nice easy tune with no awkward turns or triplets against two beats) and a little old lady who probably couldn't afford it put a two pound coin in my case. She smiled benignly at me before wandering off. Had she realised how much she'd put in? Maybe she wasn't going to be able to afford to eat after that generosity. Should I rush after her and give it her back? Of course I didn't – I carried on, and after a quarter of an hour or so, eyeing my case, I reckoned that I'd taken about four quid.

Gazing around, trying to make my technique look nonchalant and effortless, I became aware of a guy in a hoody, leaning against the wall opposite, watching me. His manner made me uncomfortable. He seemed to be keeping an eye on me, and on my takings. Was he going to rush over and grab the money? Discreetly, with my toe, I pulled the case a tad nearer to me. Having exhausted my repertoire I began again from the beginning. Every so often someone walking past would chuck a coin down, usually a few coppers, but sometimes silver. I'd try to mutter "Thanks" without going out of my stride. The hoody bloke was still hanging around, his shadowed face directed towards me.

A young woman with purple dreadlocks came and stood a few feet away, watching me, or rather my fingers. When I had got to the end of the tune she put a pound coin in my case and asked: "Do you teach?"

"Sorry?"

"Do you do violin lessons? I love that folk style. I'm looking for a teacher."

Hell's bells, I thought. Am I that good? Having learnt from three decades in the music biz that you never say no straight off to any proposition, no matter how unlikely, I hedged. "Er... Yeah.. Sometimes..." The upshot was that Jasmine, as she introduced herself, walked away with my email on a scribbled piece of paper. Hoody was still there. I started again, and after an hour my fingers were too sore to play any more. Time for a break. Without touching the money I laid the fiddle in its case on top of the coins, shut the lid, picked everything up and walked off. Hoody was following me, I saw out of the corner of my eye. What the fuck was this? Surely he wasn't going to try mugging me in broad daylight on a main street? Looking over my shoulder I didn't see where I was going, and struck someone. "Sorry…."

A strong hand grabbed my arm. A shaven headed man was staring into my face.

"Sorry, mate," I went on. "My fault, I wasn't…"

"Shut the fuck," said Shaven-head. Hoody had caught up with us.

They exchanged a glance, and Hoody pointed a finger at me. "Rent."

"What?"

"Rent. You play, you pay."

"What the fuck are you on about?" For a bizarre moment I wondered whether these two were some kind of undercover Council operatives, making sure the local authority got its slice of all business.

"One hour, that's a tenner," Hoody went on. He had a web tattoo on his face and a strong local accent.

"You must be…" My words trailed off. Shoppers bustled past. No-one was going to intervene in our little drama.

Shaven-head was nodding. "You want to play, you pay us."

"I didn't make ten quid." Not true, I was sure, but worth a try.

"Your problem. Now." And Hoody had a knife, held down low where no-one hurrying by would see it. I thought back to the hotel in Brussels. And Otto half-strangling me at *Le Mannequin Pis*. What the fuck was going on in my life? I thought of saying that I needed to get the money out of my case, but the idea of their perhaps damaging the violin and leaving me even worse off made me delve into my back pocket, where I had my wallet with a couple of notes. I produced a fiver and a twenty. Shaven-head took the twenty, and then weird of weirds, groped in his own pocket to bring out a tenner, which he handed me. "Next time, remember."

And that was it – they were walking away down the sunny street. I stood on the pavement, in a disbelieving paralysis, until they had turned a corner. I urgently needed somewhere to sit down with a cup of tea and think. And I needed a pee. I hurried along the street, past a long-haired guy, with a New Age traveller kind of look, who was playing a guitar. He was good, and he had a fair collection of coins, and even a note in his case. I dashed into the café opposite him and hurtled into the Gents. The café was the very one where, years before, I'd first met Petra, although I couldn't sit in "our" seats as they were taken.

Refilling my cup every so often, I watched the busker for half an hour, until, sure enough, Hoody reappeared, there was a quick conflab and I saw hands pass something across. It made a brutal kind of economic sense – don't take so much that it wasn't worth the musicians' while, but keep bleeding them regularly. I paid up and left the café. I wasn't going to be dracula'ed. Nobody was going to stop me playing music. It wasn't just performing – it was the being out, the sense of freedom, even though most of the time I had been wedged into a smelly van with three fuckwits. I needed a band. I needed the attention, the sense of being someone, not just another bloke on the daily grind. As I headed back to the Market Square my phone rang.

"Hello?"

"*Bill? It's Maurice.*"

I took the phone away from my ear and stared at it, as if somehow that would help. I heard a tinny voice saying something, and I put it back up to my head.

"*Maurice? Where are you?*"

"*London. But it's all a disaster.*"

"*Did you find your daughter?*"

"*What?*"

"*Your daughter. What's her name? Laure?*"

"*No. No trace of her. Bill... You've got to help me.*"

Not again, I thought. Then I remembered Clothilde, and the baby.

"*Your sister. What happened there? You just fucked off from the services and left her.*"

There was a pause. Then he said: "*Bill, I'm sorry. That was bad, I know. I was just scared of the police, of the uniforms.*" His voice trailed off. Here we go, I thought. I knew that I was going to get sucked in, as surely as someone doggy-paddling past a hydroelectric plant. Maurice went on: "*I've got no money. I've got nowhere to live. I've only got a couple of cents on my mobile. Where are you?*"

I hesitated. If I told him where I was, I was committed.

"*Hang on, didn't you have a thousand euros in Brussels?*"

"*Matey, that wasn't mine. I borrowed it, and when you didn't want it, I gave it back.*"

"*Fuck me, Maurice, this is out of order. You took the piss bringing Clothilde along and now this...*" An echoing quality on the line made me aware that I was talking into a void. Of course, the fucker's credit had finished.

I walked on, speeding up, wanting to get home. My fiddle bashed against somebody again and I muttered an apology, but this time it was just a normal person, not some parasite seeking to suck me dry. I was halfway back to our gaff, muttering to myself like a homeless nutter, when I stopped, and went into call registry. There was Maurice's number, a bloody Belgian one of course, so ringing him would cost me a fortune. No wonder his money had run out so quickly, calling my UK number. I pressed dial and it rang, and was answered.

"*Bill?*"

"*Yeah. Do you know where you are?*"

"*Yeah.* Veectoria."

"*Do you know King's Cross station?*" I explained to him where it was, told him to look at a tube map. How the fuck he'd get that far I didn't know, but I wasn't bloody miracle worker.

I picked up Jimmy from nursery, and sat out in the garden, with the laptop on the rustic wooden table, watching him in the playpen on the lawn, as he threw his wooden building bricks around. He kept making "naaaargh!" noises like aeroplanes divebombing. I went onto *www.britishbluesgoss.co.uk*.

harpmouth, whitecliffs, bluesfiend666, nakedblueslady and *beermonster37* are in the room

harpmouth: u shoud all check out my new website *www.zbvan.co.uk*

bluesfiend666: wots that about??

harpmouth: dont tell rozzer's but ive hacked into police camra's and ive got pic's of the zeebee band van off of camra's in all different plaice's *whitecliffs*: cool ☺

bluesfiend666: torking of band wots happened to bill?

harpmouth: ive seen him on camra

nakedblueslady: i am naked 4 bill we all miss him

bluesfiend666: fuk off nakedblueslady we talk about music hear not feeling's ☺

beermonster37: we al kno nakedblueslady is bloke anyway

nakedblueslady: i am not i am woman

harpmouth: well y dont u post pic of yorself up then 2 pruve it?

nakedblueslady: fuk off i am naked but not 4 u u r all inaddequat's

whitecliffs: van site is cool ☺

harpmouth: cheers but like i woz saying about bill gess wot

bluesfiend666: wot?

harpmouth: i woz wotching the van cumming back from ferry on camra's they hadnt stopped sinse they left dover i thougt oddson they mite stop @ toddington so i went down there and i saw there van!!

bluesfiend666: the real zb van?

harpmouth: i saw bill and his missus woz weerd bill must have been giving some frend's a lift coz i saw him help sum peeple out of back of van but it looked like she was preggnant

bluesfiend666: wot bill and his missus having anuther baby?

harpmouth: no u twat the woman wot bill helped out of van

I stared at this. Fuck me, didn't these sad fuckers have anything better to do? What the hell had *harpmouth* really seen? I hit the keyboard.

wurzelman is in the room

wurzelman: Are you sure it was Bill? How near were you?

bluesfiend666: fuk off wurzelman u r wanka

harpmouth: it woz there van i took a picture on my sellfone its on the site

wurzelman: Did you actually see Bill?

nakedblueslady: i am looking at yr site harpmouth i am naked i can see bill and his van

whitecliffs: bill told me he woz leaving band but he still running zeestock cos he arskd us 4 cd and woz real pleasd wen we sed we coud play festivle

harpmouth: yeah wotever witecliffs fuk off in my pic he is just letting his frend's out who r thay?

whitecliffs: looks like bills van 2 me

nakedblueslady: the man woz playing with bill in brustle's

whitecliffs: i hope bill isnt going 2 change his mind about us playing @ zeestock

There was nothing for it. I went onto *harpmouth*'s site myself, and there, sad of sads, were loads of shots of our van passing under motorway bridges, overtaking lorries, in the wet, with the sun shining, plagues of bloody frogs tumbling from the sky, locusts munching everything on the central reservation *etcetera etcetera.* But there was one pic which must have been the one which *harpmouth* had taken on his, what he bloody called his cellphone. It showed Petra kneeling down beside a prone Clothilde, and me standing there gormlessly with Jimmy. The only minor mercy was that Clothilde's face was not very clear, and there must be hundreds of light blue trannies on the road. You'd have a job proving that it was me, although of course *harpmouth* probably had the van on time-recorded police cameras the whole fucking way up the M1 with the number-plate clocked. And now of course, *whitecliffs*, Mr Bluesfan in the passport booth, was putting two and two together and realising that he had quite a massive hold over me…

Jimmy was yelling – he had stumbled over and bashed his head on a brick, a house brick that was, not one of his wooden ones. I'd somehow overlooked the bloody thing when setting up the playpen.

It had left a nasty red mark on his forehead. I scooped him up and comforted him, part of my mind hoping that the mark would have gone by the time Petra got home, otherwise there'd be hell to pay, and part of me wondering what the fuck was going on with that website.

***

Once again I didn't sleep too well – Petra, her eye as sharp as a kestrel's hovering over a motorway verge on the look-out for helpless fieldmice, had spotted Jimmy's bruise the moment that she'd stepped into the kitchen, and had had me in a metaphorical cellar with a swinging naked lightbulb for interrogation about it. And of course I was going over and over my coming meeting with Maurice. I'd dropped off in the end as it was getting light.

Breakfast was strained – Petra kept glancing across at Jimmy's head, and it was clear, although she didn't say anything, that she was having doubts about whether she could trust me with him. But once she had zoomed off down the road on her racing bike, work-bags strapped to the panniers, and I had waited a couple of minutes to make sure that she didn't come back for anything forgotten, I wheeled Jimmy, clutching his favourite teddy, out of the door towards the tram stop.

Jimmy didn't go to nursery on Wednesdays – I normally took him to a playgroup in a local church, where, as the only father amongst thirty cliquey mums, and thus not having anyone to talk to I would drink too much coffee and take care not to risk accusations of being a paedo by lifting up anyone else's children should they fall off the climbing frame. I could get down to London and back in five hours, and there was no risk that Petra might ring the nursery to find out how he was.

We got on our train, Jimmy standing on a seat, his padded bum pointing in the direction of travel, whilst he vainly tried to engage the businessman who was studying spreadsheets at the table behind in conversation. I was just about to intervene, and stop Jimmy from pestering the bloke any more when my phone pinged – I had a message. I opened it.

i know wot u were really doing @ toddington What the fuck? There was no name, just a number. Was it *whitecliffs*, piling on the pressure, to make sure that he and his bunch of derivative saddoes didn't miss out on their chance of glory at Zedstock? But thinking of derivatives, integrals, calculus, I looked at the number. 271828… I knew that from somewhere. Who was it? Hang on, I thought, it's not anyone I knew, it's the opening digits of the decimal expansion of *e*, the base of natural logarithms. For Pete's sake, it wasn't *whitecliffs*; it had to be bloody *harpmouth*, who probably had chosen that sequence on purpose, being some kind of personality disorder maths obsessive, and who must have got hold of my own mobile number somehow, and who had been sitting in his lonely flat surrounded by pizza cartons and porn mags working out exactly what it was that he had captured on film, and who now wanted to blackmail me into being bezzies.

Sipping from the coffee I had managed to bring on board the train without scalding Jimmy I looked at the text again. It was probably best to try flattering him into complicity. I tapped in a reply. **Harpmouth you are a clever fellow**

A minute later I had an answer: **don't wurry bill I will keep quite**

Well, that was okay then. After all, what could anyone prove with that photo? An angry voice broke into my thoughts: "Excuse me, I'm trying to get some work done here." It was the guy behind me. I twisted round to see that Jimmy was dangling himself over my neighbouring seat and waving his bear in the bloke's face.

"Sorry," I said, pulling Jimmy back. "Come on, let's ask Teddy what he'd like to eat."

***

Maurice was there, at the King's Cross barrier, looking haggard, his tattered and grubby suit, the one he'd been wearing on the journey over in our van hanging off his large frame. Jimmy, on my back, regarded him curiously. "Dada fuuu…" He pointed. "Dada fuuu…" We didn't have much time if I were to get back to Nottingham without Petra having known anything about all this, so I marched

Maurice straight to the ticket office, bought him an expensive single and we caught the first train back. Maurice wolfed down the sarnies I'd brought along. He had a tatty plastic bag with him, and that was it.

"*Where's your drums ?*"

"*They got stolen. I was sleeping in a park...*"

He told me that he'd managed to catch a bus into London, where he'd spent a couple of weeks living rough, trying to fend off attacks at night.

"*I tried busking with the drums but the cops kept moving me on.*" He'd approached people whom he'd heard speaking French but by that point he looked so dirty and unkempt that no-one would help him. On the train, now, we were getting strange looks. I dandled Jimmy on my knee, and wondered whether anyone would think that I'd abducted him from his real parents. Then Jimmy did a massive dump and I had to take him unsteadily down the rattling gangway to the smelly and cramped train toilet. There was a changing mat which you could let down from the wall, but the foam was missing and Jimmy kept shifting around in discomfort whilst I declagged him.

In a right-on, we're all fathers together kind of way, when I was back in my seat, I dug out one of Jimmy's nappies, and showed it to Maurice. "*What did you use in Congo*?" I asked. "*Cloth*?"

He shook his head, confused, and I suddenly thought that I'd somehow insulted him, showing off how convenient every bloody thing was here compared to Kinshasa, or wherever he was from. To cover my embarrassment I ordered a couple of coffees from the passing buffet wagon.

Anyway, we made it back to Nottingham. We caught a cab to the rehearsal space – there were several rooms which were never used or even opened. He could stay there, at least for the while. And the place was still partly mine. It was summer, there was running water and a toilet, and he could survive. The cooker was working in the kitchen and there were pots and pans in the unit cupboards. And there was the cleaning stuff in the little pantry, or utility room, one could call it, seeing as it even had an old washing machine and an ironing board in it. I left Maurice in his new quarters, went round the shops with Jimmy, bought soap, razors, loose clothing I reckoned was the right size, and food and drink.

When I dumped the bags before him Maurice looked as if he were about to weep. "*Bill. I'm really sorry. I didn't know what else to do.*"

"*Don't worry about it.*" I pointed to the lights. "*Don't use the lights after midnight. People might wonder what's going on.*"

And I left him on his own in the dark, in a strange country. He'd seen his wife shot before him and his child had vanished on a flight, whilst I went home with my son and cooked supper for Petra. She didn't seem to suspect anything when she got in from work. We ate, Jimmy sitting in his highchair and smearing Marmite everywhere. Yet again, that night I lay restlessly beside her whilst she slumbered peacefully, her conscience unburdened. Should I tell her about Maurice? Would she have him at our house? It was too risky. Once I told her what I'd done today, and what had really happened in Brussels there'd be no going back.

***

After I'd offloaded Jimmy the next morning I went back to the rehearsal rooms, with some more food and a couple of French books which I'd found on our bookcase. Maurice had washed and shaved and changed, and looked passable now in a preppy sweatshirt and slacks. I had an idea though – I'd checked the Zed Beddington Band gig list on the net and Otto, Mitch and, presumably, Matty, God rot the lot of them, had a couple of gigs in Inverness that evening and the next night (ones which of course I had gone to all the trouble of booking about six months before), so presumably the fuckers were somewhere on the M7 in our van. Thinking about the van, I needed to get my money from them. I hadn't contacted them and they hadn't contacted me.

I told Maurice that we could make some noise and led him upstairs, where he seated himself behind the drum kit. For the first time he looked happy. He picked up some sticks and tapped out a rhythm. He grinned. "*Hey, Bill, listen to this...*" He started playing some complex cross-rhythmic pattern, even weirder than what he'd played in Armand's bar. It sounded like seven over four or something. Lars from Lincoln, or Oslo, I suppose, would have loved it. I'd brought my bass – I had to plug it into Mitch's spare guitar amp, not a proper bass cab, so it sounded a bit weird and probably fucked the speaker cone, but we jammed intricately away. Petra was right – I could do better than bang out four fours in the Tribute to ZB.

I felt a bit better about Maurice that night. After putting Jimmy to bed, whilst Petra was luxuriating under a layer of foam in the bath, I settled down for the latest online chat:

bluesfiend666, *beermonster37*, *harpmouth* and *nakedblueslady* are in the room

bluesfiend666: wot u reckon 2 matty? any better?

harpmouth: hes still shite herryford woz fukin awful

beermonster37: bring bak bill

nakedblueslady: i am naked 4 bill maybe that will bring him bak

beermonster37: i work as porter at same hospital as bills wife she is posh docter i reckon she made him leave

harpmouth: when i saw her she looked ded fit actully

beermonster37: fit and posh

nakedblueslady: i am naked 4 bill i am all he nede's

beermonster37: i hav spoken to her at wurk she is alrite but a bit stuk up

harpmouth: i bet bill like's havin posh burd 4 wife lol ☺

beermonster37: yeah well wot he woudnt like is that her boss really like's her ☹

harpmouth: wot u mean?

beermonster37: doc cridland he is seneor registrar every1 @ hospital rekon's he want's 2 shag her

Great, I thought. Not that I hadn't suspected. But this was like walking down the High Street naked – they knew about Cridland, they knew about Maurice, they knew about Petra. I was in a fucking goldfish bowl, swimming round and round and round whilst they turned my life over.

> *bluesfiend666:* any more new's on wot bill woz doing at todington?
>
> *harpmouth:* havnt hurd anithing havnt seen the van on any camra's sinse then so dont kno wot bill is up 2
>
> *bluewallace* is in the room
>
> *bluewallace:* bring back bill he woz control freak numptie at least he woz relible
>
> *beermonster37:* wot u mean?
>
> *bluewallace:* last nite drove 100 mile's 2 invaness 2 see band @ birnam club fucker's didna turn up
>
> *beermonster37:* wot they canselled?
>
> *bluewallace:* no the audien's awl there awl ready to go but no band just didnt show

I read this a couple of times before the significance hit me. Hades in a handcart. If Mitch and Otto hadn't gone to Scotland then they could be going round to the rehearsal rooms at any moment, finding Maurice bashing away on the drumkit and demanding explanations. I furtled in the drawer for the car keys, trying by sheer willpower to keep myself calm, not wanting to make Petra suspect anything, then stuck my head round the bathroom door and said, dead cazh: "Got a call, some blues band need a bass stand-in tonight, Burton on Trent, is that okay?"

She shifted under the bubbles. "I reckoned there was room for one more in here."

"It's two hundred quid," I said. I stepped into the bathroom and knelt down beside the bath. "Sorry. I've already said I'll do it…"

"If it's that important."

I was riled now. "Fuck it, you wanted me to leave the band. How the fuck do you expect me to earn a living?"

Petra looked away. “Okay.”

It obviously wasn’t okay. Petra did sound a bit hoity-toity imperious when she was annoyed. Maybe *beermonster* was right. She probably treated the porters and suchlike at the hospital with a bit too much professional disdain. I recalled the way she’d been a bit *de haut en* fucking *bas* with the paramedics when we had got shot of Clothilde. “I’ll be as quick as I can. I couldn’t turn that amount of money down…” I got up and edged out. There wasn’t time to hang about.

I grabbed my bass from the sitting room to add verisimilitude to the story, then realised that I should be taking my amp, and leads bag, both of which were in the front room, if I really were going to a gig, so I lugged the heavy fucker out as quickly as I could and hoyed it into the rear of Petra’s hatchback. I scorched across town to the old bike factory. It was all dark – Maurice at least had obeyed my injunction about the lights, and it looked as if the band weren’t there either. What the fuck were they playing at, not turning up for a gig like that, not even giving any notice? In all the time I’d been sorting things out we’d never let anyone down like that.

I left the car in the little bay, cautiously unlocked the door, and flicked the light on. The corridor leading down to Maurice’s suite was partially blocked by all the building and decorating gear – I’d actually piled a few more things up to discourage any casual investigation of the rooms down there. I picked my way over the barrow and ladders and quietly knocked.

“*It’s me, Bill. Are you there?*”

No answer. I rapped again and then turned the handle, opening the door. It was dark inside. I whispered again. “*Maurice? It’s me.*” No answer. I turned the light on and opened the door fully. Maurice’s things were laid out, and the rough bed of blankets on wooden planks, with a scruffy pillow that I had scrounged from our house was still there. I stepped across and peeked into the little room where the toilet was – no-one. Where the fuck had he got to? He had to be fucking about with the gear upstairs, too keen after our jam yesterday to leave the stuff alone. I went out into the corridor and up the stairs to the rehearsal rooms proper. Again, when I opened the door it was dark inside. “*Maurice, what the fuck are you playing at?*"

No answer. Once more I put the light on, and jumped a foot in the air. Otto was sat at his drum kit. Grinning at me, twice. Two mouths. His normal sardonic one and a bloody gash below, where his throat had been slit.

Sixth Bar

Chord of D

I shut the door, and leant against it, standing on the metal landing at the top of the staircase. I was calm – super calm. Super super calm Bill the problem-solver, that was me. Think of this as an especially difficult mathematical problem, the kind of thing I used to chew over as a student. This was a probability problem really. Think over the paths open to me – I could almost see them as actual physical tracks through a wood of possibilities.

Track one a: I just go, leaving everything as it was, and let either Mitch, or, possibly, Tommo, the only other people who had keys to the building find Otto, and deal with it.

Track one a i): Mitch finds Otto. He'd also find Maurice's stuff and know that something fishy had been going on. And Mitch didn't have the nous to deal with everything quietly, so he'd let the various cats about Zed and Danny out of the bags, and we'd all be in the brown stuff.

Track one a ii): Tommo, coming to the rehearsal room for some perfectly innocent reason, finds Otto. Tommo, being a straight kind of bloke, would go straight to the police, leading us again to the situation outlined in *one a i*) above

Track one b: I take all Maurice's stuff, get rid of it and leave the building as above.

Track one b i): Mitch finds Otto. He'd still fuck up and get us into trouble.

Track one b ii): Tommo finds Otto. He'd still call the police, and there'd be less to connect me. But I'd still be a suspect, and I already had plenty of business to keep *shtumm* about. I didn't fancy trying to finesse my way through a police interview.

Track two a: I clear away Maurice's stuff and call the police. As above I'd be in the frame, newly-resigned band-member, and worse in this scenario, the first person on the scene. I'd read of too many cases of the fuzz being called by someone they then saw as the prime suspect. They'd have a motive – my having left the band. Why was I back in the rehearsal rooms after that? Collecting stuff, okay as a reason perhaps, but sounding too much like a convenient excuse for being there.

Track two b: If I left Maurice's stuff, called the police and told them about him, then, although I'd be landing myself in it anyway, bringing in illegal aliens *etcetera*, it would make my claim to have stumbled upon Otto already dead more plausible. But, see track *one b ii)* above, if the police followed up Otto's career, or mine, for that matter, they might come across too many inconsistencies and oddments and mysteries, like what had happened to Danny McPhee, for example, who had disappeared without trace a few years before, and where Otto had been getting the money to buy all his slum properties from. I might have had nothing to do with Otto's dodgy financial and narcotic dealings but would the cops believe me, especially as I would already have admitted to bringing in illegal immigrants? I couldn't risk it.

Track three: I could get rid of the corpse – I'd done it before and I could do it again. Danny and I'd interred Zed's body in a Nottinghamshire wood, after I'd found him in the back of the van, but we hadn't buried it deeply enough – a fact which Otto had not let me forget – and a woman walking her dog had found a skeletal hand sticking up through the earth, as if Zed were reaching out from Erebus for one last riff on Ida May. And then, of course, later, when Otto had strangled Danny, we'd buried *his* body under the cellar floor at the Grey Swan, and, appropriately, to quote the late Mr Anderson, on the other side of that door, or on the other side of the Styx by now, I expected, we'd "done it properly that time".

Otto would have to disappear, too. I went down the stairs and started rifling through all the building tools and materials. There was some lime, and ropes, but I needed a pick, and somewhere suitable to dig. I searched through the rooms on the ground level – the first one had a solid concrete floor, and even with a pick to get through it would have taken me hours. Then I would have to dig a grave with the cement mixing shovel and relay the floor. I couldn't do it. I tried the kitchen. It was all neat and tidy here – it looked like Maurice had actually cleaned it up, to make it a bit homelier. The packets of food and tins I'd got for him were neatly stacked up along the shelves. The floor here was covered in lino – Maurice had even washed all the accumulated dust and crap off. I peeled back part of the floor-covering, but the surface underneath was as solid as in the first room. It was no good. The whole ground floor was the same, nowhere to get through at all.

Reluctantly I climbed back up, and after taking a deep breath I opened the door. The light was still on. Otto was still there – well of course he was; even Otto, terrifying as he had been in life, wasn't *Monsieur* Cheatdeath. He'd been propped up onto the kit, his head leant against the wall behind him. His flesh, showing on his arms below his trademark T shirt had a bluish marble tone. His throat was a mess of dried gore. His sunken eyes stared at me with an expression I'd never seen on them in life – it was so alien on Otto that it took me a while to realise what it was. But this wasn't the first new emotion I'd seen on Otto recently. Thinking back, in *Le Mannekin Pis*, when he'd been bested by Maurice I'd seen a reaction on his face which I'd never noted there before, but then it had been jealousy. This time it was fear – for once, as he died, Otto Anderson had been frightened of something.

And that something, or rather someone, had been the same something, or someone, who had caused Otto's humiliation in Brussels – Maurice. Fuck me, I thought suddenly, in my super calm, icy calculator state I'd been going about the building without even checking that the murderous fucker wasn't still there. But then I'd been through all the rooms, looking for a pick and spade, so he wasn't around. I'd misread Maurice completely – bloody hell, he could have killed me and Petra and Jimmy…

I was staring at Otto's unmoving form. Other things were

incongruous, now I looked more closely. His throat had been slashed, but where was the blood? There was the odd smudge on the kit, but nothing on the floor. And his flesh – Maurice and I had been in here yesterday, and yet I was pretty sure that Otto had been dead for longer than a few hours. I nerved myself and, using my jacket as a shield I tried moving an arm. It swung freely – no *rigor mortis* – and Otto's body overbalanced. His other arm flailed out and hit a cymbal, which echoed like the crack of Doomsday. He crumpled onto the floor, his head striking it first whilst I waited for the din to subside. Would anyone have heard it? Would anyone come to investigate? Don't be silly, I told myself, it's a rehearsal room, and anyway no-one lives within four hundred yards. That's why we'd taken it on in the first place.

But I'd learnt enough from Petra about pathology to know that if the *rigor* had passed he must have been dead for at least twenty four hours or so already. And he hadn't been killed in this room, given the lack of blood on the floor and walls. So Maurice had killed him elsewhere, waited until after our little jam session and then brought the body here as some kind of sick joke. Or warning, to me?

But why would he have killed Otto? And where had he done it? The body was lying outstretched on the floor before me, the wound in the throat gaping horribly, sinews and veins hanging out. I recalled the knife pressed against my own neck in the *Hotel du Duc*…

The *Hotel du Duc*, where I had moved to get away from Mitch and Otto. The killer wasn't Maurice. No. I'd asked Otto how he'd managed to get three gigs at *Le Mannekin Pis* off the monoglot Armand, and Otto had answered: "…Through my mate, who's a Moroccan, alright?" When the guy had waylaid me outside my room I'd thought that he'd looked familiar, and that I'd seen him before. And indeed I had. He had been at the wheel of the car which the ethnic Russian Kazakh woman had got into when I'd pulled up outside Otto's house before we went off to Belgium all those aeons ago.

He'd also been driving the saloon which Bogdan had got out of in the car park of the *Gare Midi*, and he'd even made a cutthroat gesture at me, then. It had been the same bloke, whatever his name was. And how had he known to find me at the *Hotel du Duc*? He must have followed me, and, from that, I suddenly realised that he'd shared the information about where I was with someone else. And that little fact led on, in a nicely algorithmic way, to letting me know just who was going to help me to get rid of Otto's body.

I got out my mobile and dialled a number from the registry. The phone was answered after a couple of rings.

"Mitch," I said. "It's Bill. I'm coming round, with Otto."

"Otto? Is he with you? I've been trying to get hold of the fucker."

"He's here. You were meant to be in Inverness."

"Aye. Couldn't raise him so we didn't go."

"We being you and Matty?"

There was a pause, then Mitch said, slowly: "Aye."

"No-one in the Swan band room tonight?"

"No. Why?"

"I'll explain when we get there. Oh yeah, and leave the gates round the back open."

I snapped the phone off and fetched a canvas rubble bag from downstairs. Grunting with the effort I manoeuvred Otto's body onto it, then dragged the bag across to the door. Downstairs I got the bucket and sponge out again. I also checked the outer door. When you shut it it couldn't be opened from outside without a key, so if the Moroccan hadn't been in the building when I searched it he couldn't be in now. That didn't mean to say that he couldn't be lurking somewhere outside. And how the fuck had he got in? The answer was, logically, that he'd come in with Otto, and there had then been some kind of altercation. But where the fuck had Maurice got to? The whole thing didn't make any sense.

I cleaned off the smears from the kit, and set up everything to look undisturbed. The cloths I stuck into the bag with the body. I emptied the bucket down the sluice in the kitchen utility room, swilled it out and stowed it away innocently under the sink, and then I pulled out my mobile once more. I had Maurice's number. If he had any power left he could answer. But it just rang and then I was told in French that the number was unavailable.

Otto's head, in the corner of the bag, bumped horribly on every step as I brought the body down. At the bottom I let go of the bag handles and opened the door cautiously. It was still just about light and I couldn't see anyone about. I nipped over to the car, ten yards away, and opened the passenger door. This was the riskiest bit – with my gear for the non-existent gig in the back there was no more room there. I could get the equipment into the building but that would cause more complications, as Petra might ask me where my amp had got to after the gig, and I couldn't think of a legit reason for the stuff not being with me. And the thought of coming back later to pick it all up again was too much. After a last glance I dragged Otto in his bag over to the car, and with much straining and risking popping my back I managed to get him slumped in the front. I shut the building door, reaching round and switching off the lights, and stuffed the rubble bag and cloths into the back of the car between the music gear. Then, leaning in from the pavement I had to take the seatbelt across Otto and clip it in. I couldn't risk an over-zealous cop spotting an unbelted passenger. I could smell putrefaction. Otto had been dead for a while, for sure.

I shut the passenger door and got into the drivers' seat. Otto's head lolled back, exposing the gash in his throat. I had to push the cold lump against the seatbelt bracket to get him into a natural looking position.

"Well, matey," I said, having a quick look round to make sure that I didn't pull out into a passing car. "This is a turn-up, isn't it?"

Otto said nothing as I carefully eased us along the little estate road to the roundabout connecting to the main highway. I headed out of town. I felt like talking, even though Otto didn't.

"You know, I was rather naïve to believe all that nonsense you told me in Brussels. I mean, I suppose strictly speaking you were telling the truth, there wasn't any smack in the van, but you and Mitch set me up nicely. And when we get to the Swan we're all going to have a cosy little chat."

Otto was still silent. I'd said enough for the time being, so I put on some music. I had a CD of Bach, solo cello works. I knew how much Otto hated classical music but he could fucking well listen to some culture for once, as we cruised out to Coatstall, with Yo Yo

Ma coming from the speakers, Otto leaning against the window and me in the driving seat.

The Swan's gates were open. I turned us straight into the yard at the back of the pub and switched the engine off. Mitch must have listening out for me because a moving parallelogram of light appeared as he opened the door from the band room. I got out of the car, picking up the large spanner which was in the door pocket.

"What the fuck's going on?" asked Mitch. "Is that Otto?"

"Yep."

"Where the fuck's he been?" Mitch had started to realise that something wasn't quite right – the living Otto would have been out of the car by now. He came closer and peered at the bloody mess. "Fuck me. What the...?"

I was shutting the gates. "He was at the rehearsal room. I found him like that. It was your mate Bogdan's little helper who did it."

Mitch was crouching down, staring at the gashed trachea of the unmoving form in the passenger seat. "What?"

"The Arab guy. Don't look so fucking surprised, Mitch. I know that you and Otto were working with them. We've got to get the fucker out and into your cellar."

Mitch shook himself. "What? Fuck off."

"Oh no, Mitch," I said. "Very much not fuck off. You set me up, you and that fucker there, and now it's time for you to help me."

"What the fuck do you mean?"

"You set me up, all that bollo in Belgium... Anyway, we get him downstairs, then we talk." I came round to Otto's side of the hatchback, the spanner hidden in my arm, and opened the door abruptly. Otto's body toppled out, and lay on the ground, one of his legs still twisted into the well of the car.

Mitch began to back away. "I'm sorry, Bill, you get rid of him. It's not my problem."

"It so is," I said, lifting the limb out so that Otto was free. "You don't want to help me, fine, I'll be off. First port of call is Coatstall nick, where I tell them there's two stiffs at the Swan, one in the backyard and one buried in the cellar." I went back over to the gates to open them up again.

Mitch was prodding Otto's body with his shoe. "No way."

"Try me." I drew back the top bolt. I couldn't see him physically attempting to stop me; he was too old and too out of condition for that, but I had the spanner in my hand just in case.

"Fuck me," said Mitch. "Alright. Alright." He began to cough, leaning himself against the wall.

I shot the bolt on the gate back and, cautiously, making sure that I kept Mitch in view, opened up the hatchback and got the rubble sack out. After all, Mitch had broken Zed's neck with a blow from a keg pole, and he might try the same stunt on me. But he was too shaken to be dangerous. Together we got Otto's body into the sack, and tugged and humped it up the two steps into the band room, across there and then through the little side door that led down to the cellar. Otto's head bumped once more on each step. We went down to the first floor, where all the barrels were kept, and then, as he had done on that night five years before, the last time I'd been down here, Mitch turned on the light from a switch amidst the spaghetti of cables, and we dragged Otto down to the lower level.

In the corner was where Mitch, Otto and I had buried Danny's body. There was nothing to see – no mysterious staining of the concrete, no unexplained anticlining of the floor. As Otto had said, that time we'd done a good job, and Mitch had piled up some old planks and lumber to stop anyone looking too closely. He and I both dropped our fistfuls of canvas at the same time. Mitch looked at me. "Where are we going to talk? Here or upstairs?"

"Up top. I need a drink."

He went first – I wasn't being clocked from behind, and in the bandroom he put on the bar lights. I could hear conversation and the odd shout through the bolted door that separated us from the main bar.

"What you having?" Ever the landlord.

"Nothing alcoholic. I'm driving."

He got out a bottle of apple juice. "I'll open it myself," I said.

Mitch passed it to me, and poured himself a pint of Guinness. Then he leant on the bar and looked at me again. "Okay Billy, what the fuck's going on?"

With my penknife I levered off the bottle cap and took a sip. "You tried to fuck me over, Mitch, but if you're going to set someone up you need to be a bit fucking smarter than you two." Mitch said nothing, so I went on. "Come on then, tell me. When you got back to London whom did you meet up with? Bogdan?"

Mitch nodded, and drank half his Guinness in one draught.

"Good old Bogdan. Your continental link in the old transport chain. But for some reason you all decided to smuggle some people instead of smack for once. You tell me some bullshit, fuck off back to Londinium and leave me, soft fucking bleeding heart liberal Billy Fuckwit to bring Maurice and his sister back to England, where we were due to get picked up by customs at Dover. Billy gets slung in gaol for a stretch and Maurice and Clothilde get a free one-way ticket back to the equatorial hellhole of the Democratic Republic of Congo. Right so far?"

Mitch nodded once more. I went on. "Only Zed, bless his cotton bloody syringes, got me through Calais, as they're all such *biiiig* fucking fans of his that they didn't bother to switch on the infra-red gear and see who was in the back of the van. First time I've ever felt grateful to Zed actually... Anyway, why don't you ask me where you fucked up? How I know all this?"

Mitch drained his glass, put it under the tap and poured himself another. "Okay, how the fuck did you suss it out?"

"Glad you asked me that. First off, Matty. I saw you at Grantham. You were shite with him." Mitch shrugged. "Right, well, when I pathetically came out there, nothing better to do with my life now, wondering how the hell you and Otto were managing to carry on, you played our usual set, and Matty was fucking lousy, but even so, you must have rehearsed with him beforehand, before we went to Belgium, I mean. You and Otto, you'd had some secret pracs with him, waiting for him to step into my shoes when I was off the scene. Where did you do it? Here?"

"Aye." Mitch was already two thirds through his second pint. Despite himself, I felt, he asked: "How did you know?"

"*Green Turtle Blues*. You played it at Grantham. Zed wrote it, but not until Matty had left the band and I was in. "

"He could have learnt it anyway, on his own, because he wanted to."

"He could have done," I said, "And yeah, that's not conclusive, but the clincher, *le clou,* was you, actually, Mitch. Trying too fucking hard. You asked Petra what the old Duke's Hotel was like. Very polite, trying to show an interest and all that, but the only fucking problem for you was at that point I hadn't told you where we were staying. So how the fuck did you know?"

Mitch was already pouring himself a third pint. I went on: "Bogdan's mate held a knife to my throat there. Threatened to kill me, fuck it, threatened my fucking wife and child. You fucking knew that, didn't you, you bastard?" I was getting too worked up. "And there was me, genuinely trying to help you sort things out with Alison."

Mitch wouldn't look at me. I drank some apple juice and let the anger ebb away. I needed Mitch – I couldn't afford to lose control. I turned my mind to the music, away from Petra and Jimmy. "I reckon you'd been training up Matty for a while. You couldn't have known that all this was going to happen a few months ago, but you were planning on getting rid of me from the band, anyway, weren't you?"

Mitch said nothing but sank half his third pint. I knew what he was thinking though; we had all got sick of each other, I was in the way with their business and they thought I was a stuck-up middle class prick with a posh bird for a wife who despised them. Anyway, I told Mitch what had happened with Maurice and Clothilde and the baby, and told him how I'd installed M at the rehearsal rooms, which is how I had discovered Otto. "And now we've got your mate Bogdan's homicidal Moroccan knifewielder on the loose, and a Congolese drummer somewhere, and Bogdan's love child and ex somewhere else, and this dead fucker..." I pointed downwards, through two floors to the bottom cellar, "…To get rid of. You got the picks still? We need to get a move on. Petra thinks I'm subbing at a gig in Burton, so I need to home by about one at the latest." I looked at my mobile. It was only half past nine. So much had happened that I had thought that it must be already midnight.

"Okay," said Mitch, draining his glass. "We'll be okay until stop tap. Better get on with it."

We went back down, Mitch leading the way, of course, and on the bottom floor we pulled away all the stuff that was covering up where Danny was. All the time, whilst we were hacking at the concrete, I had to keep half an eye on Mitch to make sure that he didn't try to Trotsky me with one of the picks. The concrete wasn't too hard, and we were through in a few minutes. Mitch produced a spade and started to dig down. Wrappings and cords were uncovered, and then he paused as a skeleton was exposed. We were both looking down on the mortal remains of Danny McPhee. A ribcage, and a spine, and a skull, still with some curly auburn hair attached to it, grinning toothily at us.

He had been Mr February in the Zed Bed calendar, aptly the shortest month, posing like an oversexed hobbit with his guitar thrusting out from his minuscule groin. He'd been the only one of us who'd interested himself in male grooming products, or bothered to iron his band clobber, but what use had that been to him? And he'd always tried to crank his amp up to eleven on stage, strutting and fretting, full of sound and fury, signifying fuck-all. Mitch looked away.

"What's the problem?" I asked.

"Dunno. Just don't like the idea of digging him up."

Fuck me, Mitch'd once killed a man from behind, and was selling smack to schoolkids, and yet he had scruples about a few bones? "We don't have to dig them up," I said. "Just make enough room for one more on top."

At that moment a mobile sounded. I groped for mine, then realised it was coming from the rubble sack. Grimly, I poked my hand in after the sound, and by dint of luck managed to fish Otto's phone out of a pocket before the ringing stopped.

Seventh Bar

Chord of A

"Otto?" said a voice. "Where fuck you are?"

I knew who it was. I had to think very quickly. This might be my best chance, but I had a split second to get it right. "Bogdan," I said. "Great to talk to you."

"Who fuck this?"

"It's Bill. You know, I brought your lovely Clothilde and her brother over to England."

"Fuck off. Where Otto?"

"Otto can't talk right now. But I can, and you listen, Bogdan, *tovarishch*. You meet me tomorrow at twelve o'clock, the main entrance to Nottingham Railway Station. And you bring Laure with you."

"What fuck you talk about? Where Otto now? Why you have his phone?"

"I'll say it once more, and that's it." I spoke deliberately and clearly, to make sure that Bogdan knew exactly what I was on about. "I will bring this mobile, Otto's, with me and give it to you in exchange for Laure. Otherwise I'm going to the police. I'll give them the phone so that they can trace everything you've been up to... Everything you have been doing..." I had had a sudden doubt as to whether Bogdan would have understood the idiom I'd used. "And I'll tell them all about you and Otto and your operations. You meet me at Nottingham Railway Station, main entrance, just you, twelve o'clock, midday, tomorrow, and you bring Laure with you."

"Who fuck Laure?" But from his tone I could tell that he sensed that I had something on him. It was truly an inspired riff, but my hunch had been right.

"You know who she is. Maurice's daughter."

"I don't know he has fucking daughter."

"Yes, you do. You got her off the plane in Brussels and bundled her straight onto another one to London, using false documents." Lars would have been proud of me. Who said I couldn't do jazz? I was improvising better than Bird. Mitch was staring at me, mouth agape, but I didn't have time to deal with him. "Twelve o'clock, or it's the police." I snapped the phone off and put it in my pocket.

"Fuck me," said Mitch. "What the fuck are you playing at? He's off the fucking planet. He'll kill all of us."

"Yeah, which is why I'm doing this. You want to wind up like him?" I pointed at Otto's sprawled body. "Or have Alison dead?" Mitch shook his head. "Then fucking well do what I say. I'm going to have to go. You get that fucker buried, good and proper. I'll ring you."

"Where the fuck are you off to?"

"To sort things. Just you sort your bit here, your end. By the way, what's that mad Moroccan fucker's name?"

Mitch scratched his head. "I dunno. I never really spoke to him. He only speaks Frog and Arabic. Dalek?"

"Khaled?"

"That's it. Why the fuck do you want to know?"

"Just curious. Wait a sec, if he doesn't speak English, how come he arranged the gigs with Otto?"

"He didn't. That was Bogdan."

"Does Armand know what's going on?"

Mitch shook his head. "No. He was just a way of sorting things..." I'd grabbed my car keys from the bar. "Wait a sec, Billy, there's something..."

But I couldn't hang about talking any longer. I felt that Mitch was trying to hold me back, that he didn't want to be left alone with the task of burying Otto's body, and that he would say anything just to keep me there. I ran up the stairs; I needed to move fast now. I got out of the band room and into the yard, where I undid the gates. I reversed the car – it smelt horrible inside – out onto the road, got out, shut the gates, drove the mephitic vehicle two hundred yards up the street, stopped and got out my phone. I sat there for a minute or two, at first unable to do anything, but in the end I forced my shaky fingers to dial.

Petra answered. "Hello." Her voice sounded distant. "What do you want?"

"We've got a break. I just wanted to say hello. And say sorry for dashing off."

"Okay." She said nothing more, but she was still on the line. We were back to those horrible silences, the not quite knowing what to say. But this time I was overwhelmed. I'd been running on adrenaline and shock and suddenly the enormity of the situation, the fact a couple of hours ago I found one of my oldest – if not friends, then certainly acquaintances – horribly murdered began to kick in.

Despite the need for haste, I just sat behind the steering-wheel, trembling. "I'm so sorry," I said. "I love you. I can't explain what… I wish I'd not come out…"

Petra still said nothing.

I said: "I'm sorry I dashed out like that. Look, there's a reason I rang you… I mean as well as telling you that I love you."

"Go on." Her tone was cold.

"I heard on the radio that there's a bit of a gang fight going on in Forest Fields. Don't open the door to anyone."

"What do you mean?"

"Just what I said. They've been knocking on doors and threatening folk, steaming into the house and taking stuff. I'm worried about you and Jimmy." It was the best I could do.

"Okay." I needed to know that she and the boy were safe. One day I might have to tell her the truth, but not now. "I've got to go. They're starting up again. Good band, actually. Bluesy, my kind of thing."

"What are they called?" Was she asking because she was interested or because she was suspicious?

"Er… Umm.. Blues Cellar or something." I laughed nervously.

"I'm not actually sure." I hoped to fuck that she wouldn't try checking up Burton gigs on the internet. "I've really got to go. I'll see you later. Keep the door shut, please."

"Okay. If it makes you happier." She was gone, abruptly, but I had no more time for relationship analysis at that moment. As long as she and Jimmy were physically safe, the psychology stuff could wait. I dialled another number. A voice answered.

"Hello?"

"Joe?"

"Yeah. Who's this?"

"It's Billy. Billy Silverthwaite… Listen, I'm sorry to ring at this time of night, but I need to see you now. It's urgent. More than urgent."

"Right." He sounded as sceptical as Petra had, but presumably for different reasons. He probably thought I was having a breakdown.

"I need to meet you now. Where do you live?"

"Hell's bell's Billy, it's ten o'clock. Kids have just gone to bed, I'm relaxing."

"I'm sorry. I wouldn't ask if it weren't…" It sounded so crap to say it, but I did. "If it weren't a matter of life and death."

"Jeez. Rock and roll, eh? Okay, as it's you." He gave me an address in Beeston. I thanked him and managed to put the postcode into Petra's satnav. A mellifluous Welsh voice, which sounded suspiciously like Tom Jones, guided me back over the M1, and in less than fifteen minutes I was pressing the doorbell to a large detached house set back from a suburban road.

Joe opened the door, a glass of whisky in his hand. He looked all normal and relaxed. "I hope this is worth it, Billy." He ushered me into a neat hall with a grandfather clock ticking away comfortingly. A handsome blonde woman appeared, dressed in a pair of paint-spattered dungarees. "This is Billy," said Joe. "Bass-player with the immortal Zed. This is Melanie, artist and light of my life."

"I've heard all about you," Melanie said, smiling. "Joe's always raving about your music. Can I get you a drink?"

"Do you know," I said, "I could murder a cup of tea."

Joe led me through into a room lined with files and legal tomes.

"Take a pew. How's Petra? And the boy. How old is he now?"

"They're fine. Jimmy's nearly one. Walking and talking. A bit, anyway. By the way, if you ever bump into Petra, I didn't come here tonight." I looked round, envious of the solidity and professional steadiness which this chamber intimated. Why didn't I have a life like this?

Above the fireplace, neatly framed behind plexiglass, hung an old poster of the Zed Bed band, me, Otto, Danny and his satanic maj himself, Mr Brian Beddington. Joe grinned. "I'm your biggest fan. Hey, have you seen this?"

On the desk was a plastic skeleton, about a foot high, wearing shades, a porkpie hat and clutching a golden guitar in its bony claws. A gravestone at its feet had *Zee Bedington RIP* carved into it. Joe pressed a button and the bloody thing began to strum, whilst a tinny voice broke into our first chart hit.

"Cool, isn't it?" asked Joe. "It's got your whole repetoire." He pressed the button again and the skeleton began to jive to "*Reptile House*". "I got it on a trip to China, saw it in a shop."

"They're not paying me royalties, I'll bet. I wrote that bloody song."

"That's the world we live in now, Bill. They don't need you and the band any more when they can turn these out for twenty yuan. I see it as a symbol of globalisation and the end of intellectual property rights. Not that you'd exactly have called Zed an intellectual… " Joe leant back in his office chair. "Anyway, to business. How can I help you with this life and death matter, then?"

"I can't tell you," I said. "You don't want to know, but what I want is a pen and paper, or a computer stick. I need to write something, and I want you to keep it."

"What the hell are you mixed up in now?"

"What do you mean, *now*?"

Joe stretched himself and smiled at me. "Billy, I may be a blues fan, but I'm not stupid. There was something odd about Zed's death. I don't know what, I never asked, no names, no pack drill and all that, but you know, lawyers are like sharks, they can sniff trouble a long way off."

"Is this a privileged conversation?"

"Yes."

"Well, I'm still not bloody telling you."

Joe laughed at that, and brought out a posh biro with his firm's name on it and some paper. "Don't use the PC. Even if I delete everything, it's still there on the hard drive and I'm not lying for you."

I wasn't used to writing by hand much, but, with the tea beside me that Melanie brought, and with Joe furtling around on the computer, playing poker or something online I think, I wrote a short but clear account of what had happened since our first night at the club in Belgium, naming names and giving as much identifying info as I could about Bogdan, Dalek, Otto (now he was dead it couldn't hurt him) *etcetera etcetera.* I also stated that Petra and Armand had known nothing about anything.

I folded the paper. "Have you got an envelope?"

Joe passed me one. "So what's this? A new version of your will?" He had mine, in fact, at his office in town.

"No. More like my death warrent. This is in case something happens to me. If you hear that I'm dead, or if I disappear and you can't get in touch with me, for a fortnight, say, you open it, and act on it. Do what you think fit."

Joe was laughing again. "Billy, you're playing in a blues band, not working for MI5."

"I've left the band," I said. "Didn't you know?"

"Haven't been to a gig for ages. But I was going to come to Zedstock. You still doing that?"

"I haven't had a chance to think about it. But as for the rest of them, don't bother. They're pants now..." Hell on horseback, I'd forgotten for a moment that Otto was dead. There weren't going to be any more gigs. "I haven't got time to explain now. Just keep the envelope. And thanks. I'm on my way. Thank your wife for the tea."

And I was out of there, driving back into town. I took the car to the twenty four hour valeting service on Lenton Boulevard and had the whole thing steam-cleaned. It smelt lovely after that. It was eleven o'clock. I headed for home, stopping off at a cashpoint. I popped down the lock on my door, and twisting round in my seat I stared up and down the road. Cars came and went but I didn't think I was being followed. I got out, and still glancing around me withdrew two hundred notes.

I parked fifty yards from our front door. My conscience was giving me a kicking. I should have rung Petra and told her what was really going on, warned her against Bogdan and Khaled, told her under no circs to open the door to anyone she didn't know, maybe get a friend round, but somehow, I couldn't. I just couldn't risk letting her know that anything was up.

There seemed nothing amiss in the street. But it was bit early to have got back from a gig, so I sat in the car for half an hour, listening to music before starting up again and parking right outside our front door. I staggered in with my amp, which I dumped noisily in the back room. I could hear the television from the sitting room. I went back out, got my bass and leads, and was relieved to shut the outside world out. I stuck my head round the sitting room door. "Hiya"

Petra didn't look up from perusing some medical journal through her cute intellectual specs, the television burbling in the background.

"Is everything okay?" I asked, nervously. "No trouble in the street?"

"No."

"You didn't hear anything outside?"

"No."

I shrugged, trying to appear as nonch as I could. "Maybe it was all a rumour. Anyway, they didn't go on late and I just fucked off. Two hundred big ones." I waved the wad I'd just got out. "His nibs okay?"

"Yes."

I sighed and sat down in the armchair. She read on. I sighed again, got up and went out to the kitchen. "You want anything?"

"No." She did sound upper-class and dismissive, I decided. I hoped that she didn't really treat the underlings at the Med Centre like this, or she'd make herself really unpopular. Later I lay in bed beside Petra, a six inch gap between us. When I was sure that she had dropped off I got up, and looked in on Jimmy, who was on his side in his baggy sleep suit, his thumb lodged in his mouth. He was happily away. I crept downstairs and rang Mitch. Everything was okay his end, he assured me, by which I assumed he meant that Danny and Otto were now closer than a couple in the marital bed. I tried Maurice's phone again. Still nothing there, either. He'd probably run out of power. I didn't know whether he had any kind of charger or adaptor with him. Not the kind of thing you'd keep with you on the streets.

So what had happened at the rehearsal rooms? Otto had turned up with Khaled, there'd been some kind of argument and Khaled had slit Otto's throat. Then he'd lugged the body up to the top floor. But how? It had been hard enough for me to get the body down the stairs, and I was a lot bigger than Khaled. And where the hell had Maurice been whilst all this was going on? Had he witnessed the killing and fled because he was scared that he would be next, or had he been afraid that he might be suspected of it? Or had Khaled threatened him, made Maurice help him with the body, then perhaps told him to scarper? Of course, Bogdan must have been there as well – the two of them had been able together to overpower Otto, kill him and carry Otto's body up, and they had told Maurice to get lost. Why hadn't they killed Maurice as well, though, to silence a potential witness against them? One more murder wouldn't have troubled them.

And surely Maurice would now be trying to contact me. I was the only person he could call on. But how could he get hold of me? He didn't know where I lived, his phone was dead and he probably hadn't written down my number. He was likely wandering round Nottingham hoping that we would bump into one another. I heard a yell from upstairs; Jimmy had done his small hours dump.

After I had changed him and got him back to sleep I slipped back once more besides Petra. I still couldn't relax. The gaping slash in Otto's throat smiled at me, and somehow, although I was still awake, the skeleton on Joe's desk and the bones which we had unearthed in the Grey Swan's cellar performed a *totentanz* round my aching skull. I had been at least an accessory to Danny's death, and now I was condemned to eternal wakefulness. *Macbeth doth murder sleep.* I got out of bed and went downstairs. In the kitchen I powered up the laptop. There was one message on the musoes' site. "*Yo, Billy my man, my name's Plastic Andy, and I'm just what you're looking for. I've got a 1966 Ristjob guitar and a Katzenficker amp combo. I'm hanging at my chick's in Sneinton at the mome tho' I'm normally based in Mansfield, but hey, that ain't too far away. Get back to me for meet.. My influences are...*" He went on to spunk a whole load of bluesy namechecks. Wanker, I thought. I switched the laptop off and went back upstairs. I wanted to touch Petra, I wanted to wake her up, make love, not feel so alone, but that miserable six-inch gap was still there. It was beginning to get light.

***

Petra was still curt in the morning. What the fuck that bad had I done, at least that she knew about, I wondered, through a sleep deprived haze, my head thumping as if some bloke were pressing a pneumatic drill against my skull. She busied herself feeding Jimmy his breakfast porridge, cutting me out of the process, then went about getting herself ready for work wordlessly, leaving me to get an unco-operative lad into his coat. Jimmy had picked up on the tension and was being difficult, pulling his arms out of the sleeves every time I got them in, and kicking his boots off gleefully. When Petra had left the house, having made a show of kissing him goodbye and ignoring me, I held Jimmy down and forced the clothing onto him, then strapped him into the pushchair and wheeled him as quickly as I could to nursery. As we rattled along I thought gloomily to myself that Petra and I were back to where we'd been before the Brussels weekend. I didn't know how the hell to keep her happy and deal with everything else. I was doing what I was doing to protect her and J, and she should be grateful, instead of biting my head off or cutting me dead.

I couldn't go on like this – the lack of sleep and the nervous tension were beginning make me doubt my own judgement. Maybe I was doing everything wrong. I needed help – pharmaceutical help. I rang our local surgery, and tried to book an appointment. The receptionist sounded as if she knew that there was nothing really wrong with me and that I should just pull myself together. "We have a slot a week on Thursday at five thirty."

"Nothing earlier? It's important."

"All appointments are important," she said dismissively.

"Be too bloody late by then," I muttered, half to myself.

"Sorry? What did you say?"

"Nothing. Forget it." I put down the phone. Wretched NHS, I paid my taxes, well, some of them, like everyone else, and then when I needed them they weren't bloody interested. It was because I was a middle-aged bloke, and I never went to the doc's. If I had been some woman with fertility problems they'd be seeing me like a shot. I wallowed with melancholy pleasure in various right-wing talk-show complaints and then decided that I really did have to pull myself together and do something. If I were going to get myself and my family out of this bloody awful mess then I needed a clear head, calm nerves and decent sleep.

I opened up Petra's filing cabinet, the one in the spare room. As I'd thought, there were some prescription forms. I did an on-line search, and found details about a suitable tranquilliser. Using an old filled-in form as a model, I made out a chit for twenty eight hypnoproctane tablets, then faked Petra's signature, and a false name for me. Petra used her maiden name for work, fortunately. As I walked to the pharmacist's I realised that I should have kept Jimmy with me; no-one was going to query the *bona-fides* of a harassed father with a toddler, but short of pulling him out nursery for an hour to take him with me, which seemed overly baroque, it was too late now.

Anyway, the pharmacist, or rather the assistant, looked curiously at the prescription, and disappeared into the back of the shop with it. There were several other prescription forms on the desk – all typed, I realised, whereas mine was handwritten. Hell on a unicycle – it was so long since I'd had any kind of medicine that I hadn't realised that they were all typed now. I should have done, because I'd taken the odd thing in for Jimmy and they'd all been printed off. Trying to seem cazh I nervously looked at the rows of tubular bandages and haemorrhoid creams, expecting at any moment a police car to pull up outside and the cops to come rushing in to collar another junkie and get another box ticked. The assistant and the pharmacist, in earnest conversation, glanced over at me, suspiciously. I began to edge towards the door, and then my nerve failed and I just made a bolt for it. I squeezed out through the half-open door as a little old lady with a huge wheely shopping basket tried to get in, and ran down the road, taking first left, then first right, then first left, and wound up a quarter of a mile away, doubled up over a garden wall, five-year-old smoker's tar coughing its way up from the depths of my lungs.

Hades in a hatchback, what a cock-up. Had they got CCTV in the chemist's? I couldn't remember seeing any, but I was pretty sure that they would have – every bloody where had it these days. When I had got my breath back I made my way home by a roundabout route – not passing anywhere near the pharmacy, natch – and let myself in. I sat miserably on a chair in the kitchen. I was even more agitated now than I had been before this latest farrago. With half an ear expecting a knock on the door and the DS outside, I made myself some coffee, whilst thinking to myself that the last thing I needed was more stimulant. I couldn't go on like this.

Five minutes later I was driving out to West Bridgeford, trying to be as attentive to the rest of the traffic as I could. I wasn't sure of the street I wanted, and I had to circle around a bit before I found it. I'd only been to the place once before, years ago, on a mission with Otto, but I had no difficulty in remembering which house number it was – 91, always one of my favourites, as everyone thinks, wrongly, that it's a prime, as it doesn't appear in the times tables. I parked a discreet distance away. The house was surrounded by a high wall and the barred front gate was locked. Through the wrought iron gate I could see a suburban garden with rosebeds and a path leading up to a thirties brick residence. I rang the bell set in the wall and after a moment a voice crackled out of the intercom speaker. "Who is it?"

"It's Billy Silverthwaite. Friend of Otto Anderson's. I'm looking for Baggins."

The speaker went dead, and for a few seconds I stood there, twisting round anxiously to see whether anyone was coming up or down the street. But it was one of those posh quiet areas where no-one's around during the day – hubbie is at the insurance company office and wifie has gone out in the Jag to the country club to play bridge. The bolts scraped suddenly as they were dragged back by a solenoid, so I pushed the gate open. I shut it behind me and the bolts clicked back to. As I came up the path the front door, panelled with art deco glass, was opened, and a little rush of adrenaline made me jump when I recognised Shaven-head, the fucker who had relieved me of my tenner's rent for busking. He recognised me as well, but he said nothing, merely raising a sardonic eyebrow and letting me into a Minton-tiled hall which smelt of polish. He pointed to a door.

I knocked, and a voice said: "Come in."

Baggins was sat at a desk, working at a laptop. The room was light and airy, a big Swiss cheese plant coiling out of a pot in one corner and shelves along the walls, stacked with boxes and padded envelopes. There were bars over the French windows. Shaven-head had followed me in and was standing by the door.

"Billy," she said. "Long time." She made no effort to get up. "How's tricks? How's Otto?"

I hesitated, then said: "Fine. We're all fine."

"How's the band?"

"Fine. Gigging."

Baggins pushed a strand of her long grey hair back behind her ear. "You know, I was always one of Zed's biggest fans." I knew that she'd shagged him at some point. And Otto, for good measure. "Still can't believe that he's gone."

"Neither can we, but we're doing the best we can to keep the music alive." As the words came out of my mouth I though that it was a stupid thing to say, but I felt horribly ill at ease. I'd felt grim enough already and Baggins' manner managed to combine hippy-chick laidbackness with a sly superciliousness.

She was smiling ambiguously. "Nice. Hey, you know, I was thinking of coming out to Zedstock… Anyway, Billy, what can I do for you? Sit down." I did so, in the chair opposite her. "You want a smoke?" She picked up a rolled but unlit spliff from an ashtray.

"No thanks…" I nodded my head at Shaven-head. I didn't want

to talk in front of him.

"Of course," said Baggins. "Keep it confidential, eh? Malc, do you mind?" Shaven-head disappeared.

I told Baggins that I couldn't sleep, and that I needed something to calm me down. She listened consideredly. "Rock and roll lifestyle, eh?" She swivelled round and sorted through a cardboard box on one of the shelves behind her, then brought out a packet. The labelling was all in Hindi, or something. "This should do you. Twenty four pills, take one every eight hours."

"How much?"

The roll of notes which I'd got from the Satan's Slinkies lighter, and, having promised to give my regards to Otto, I was escorted out by the expressionless Malc. Did Baggins know what else he was up to? I drove home, and in the kitchen immediately washed down one of the pills with a glass of water. The rest I stashed away in the back of my bass amp.

Then I caught the tram to the train station. I was far too early and sat in one of the coffee-house franchises in the main concourse. I had too many cups and had to hurry off to the loo, worrying that I might miss Bogdan and Laure. Did I feel calmer? Was the pill working? I wasn't sure, but I didn't feel half as shit-scared as perhaps it would have been rational to have done. Laure. I recalled the photograph which Maurice had shown me. I hadn't really thought this through. What was I going to do? I couldn't take Laure to the practise rooms – I couldn't have left a child – who'd gone through God knows what – on her own in the place *before* I'd found Otto's body there, let alone afterwards. I'd have to take her home, and that meant I was going to have to confide in Petra after all, a task made doubly hard by Petra's bloodymindedness towards me at the moment.

I could sell things to Petra by saying that Laure could be our *au pair* – she could teach Jimmy French and look after him sometimes, cut down on his nursery days and our fees. But the kid wasn't going to be some normal happy girl. Petra wouldn't let some teenager suffering from PTSD or whatever look after our son. She'd probably insist on Laure having psychiatric treatment, and that'd mean the whole fucking story coming out... And how easily were they going to let me have Laure? I'd have to be careful – make them let Laure move a distance away from them so that she could run to me as I slid Otto's phone across the floor. I flipped the phone open and idly scrolled through his contacts. I'd better have a look before I got shot of it. There weren't many names in the directory – security, I suppose. When you had as many phalanges stuffed into as many *pirozhki* as Otto had had you wouldn't want someone getting hold of your mobile. I was there, under Wurzel, and so was Mitch, under Mitch. I got my phone out and compared messages in the registry. Bogdan's number was there, in Otto's mobile under Chicken. From Kiev, I supposed, which showed the limits of both Otto's imagination and his sense of humour. Scrolling down I noticed the sequence 271828... I flipped my own phone open. There was the message *harpmouth* had sent me, from the same number. He must have been in contact with Otto as well, but why? As far as I knew Otto's interaction with the fans was limited to a half-hour's post-gig bonking the best-looking ones, who were usually, but not absolutely exclusively, female.

At quarter to twelve I paid for my drinks, had a last waz and took up my place at one end of the concourse, by the ticket offices. In my haste last night the station had been the first place I had been able to think of which was public enough for me to be able to deal with the Ukrainian and his sidekick with any degree of safety. I scanned the people streaming in and out – was that Bogdan? No, it was another bloke with the same blondish hair. Five to twelve by the big Roman numeral clock on the wall.

Twelve o'clock came and went. Ten past. I was just starting to think that I'd been very foolish, not to say reckless, in thinking that I could tackle someone like Bogdan when I saw him. Against what I'd assumed, he'd come up from the platforms below, rather than in through the arches from the street. I resisted the temptatation to go up to him. Where I was standing was good – a wall behind me and plenty of people getting tickets. Even better, two Transport Police were on duty, watching the ebb and flow of travellers.

Bogdan was scrutinising the crowd, glaring at the world in general. He spotted me. He didn't smile or acknowledge me – instead he padded over to stand a few paces away. He was trying to draw me nearer to him, but I held my ground. “Where’s Laure?” I asked, gauging the volume of my voice as precisely as I could – loud enough for him to be able to hear me, but not loud enoough for the coppers or anyone else to know what I was saying.

Bogdan answered with something but it was lost in the echoing hubbub of the concourse. I beckoned to him, and, reluctantly, he came a few feet nearer.

“Don’t fuck with me,” he said, loudly this time. “What fuck you want?” I could hear him fine now but it was weird talking to someone at a distance amidst so much ambient sound. Over Bogdan’s shoulder I saw that Khaled was now loitering by the steps down to the trains.

“I want two things,” I said, slowly and clearly. I wasn’t sure how much English he really did understand. “First, I want you and your henchmen and your schemes out of my life. I’ve left a letter with my lawyer, with all the details about what you and Otto have been doing, and if you try anything on with me or...” I was about to say “My family”, but I thought, why give the fucker ideas? “...Or try to involve me in anything again that letter goes straight to the police, and even if you’re in Brussels or even fucking Dniepopetrovsk or wherever, Interpol will be on your case.”

“Fuck you,” said Bogdan.

“Yeah, okay, and secondly, I want Laure, so where the fuck is she?”

Bogdan was enjoying himself now. “You like fuck young girls? You like them with no hair? You want her dress as girl from school, maybe?”

“Fuck you, Bogdan. You fucking owe me, and this is quits. Just give her to me, we all fuck off, end of story.”

“You think this game, Bill? You think I give you girl who make me hundreds of euros for phone? What you give me?”

I wasn’t sure what he meant. “I’m not fucking paying you. I’ll give you Otto’s phone, that’s all.”

Bogdan smiled again, wolfishly. “*Nique ta mere*. You fuck knownothing. You give me information, I give you girl. You tell me where fuck Otto now?”

“You should fucking know,” I said. “You, or rather your mate over there, you killed him."

For once I think that I saw a genuine expression on Bogdan's face. "Kill him? What you say?"

"Otto's dead. I found his body, and you killed him."

"What fuck you mean? We didn't kill him."

And at that point I realised how wrong I'd got everything – I'd been so hyped up the night before that I'd overlooked the bleeding obvious; why the fuck would Bogdan have rung Otto on his mobile if he knew that Otto was dead? And even more pertinently, seeing as he clearly wanted Otto's phone for the info on it, had he and Khaled killed Otto he would scarcely have left Otto's body behind the drum kit without taking the mobile. What else had I got wrong? I'd been so preoccupied with my coming *rendez-vous* with Bogdan that I'd dropped Jimmy off at nursery without considering whether I might have been followed there, and Petra had cycled off to King's as per normal. I must be in a state of shock to have behaved so stupidly. Hell on a hobbyhorse, had it been Maurice all along? But why?

Bogdan must have had some inkling of my confused thoughts. "You, Billy, you think you so clever. You want that girl? You have her, you fuck her and you think what her father do when he finds you with her. He already murderer. You think just in England – he telled you what he do in Congo?"

"He was a musician."

"Fuck you, Billy, he plays drum but he kills lots people, that why he must go to Belgium."

I shook my head. It was all wrong, but my brain was spinning, trying to concentrate on not letting my guard down and allowing Bogdan too close, and trying to make sense of his words at the same time. "I want Laure," I said, attempting to keep control.

"I tell you something, Billy. I like you. You stupid but you... *Audacieux*. That's why I come here as person to tell you to get fuck out of my business. Now you give me phone, and you fuck off, and it will be end of story."

I started to back away. I had indeed been stupid to think that I could play in the same league as this psychopath, but something, a little something, perhaps the tranquilliser kicking in, maybe even

Bogdan's own backhanded compliment about my boldness, maybe a sense that Petra would have been proud of me for standing up to Bogdan, and perhaps would have looked down on me a bit less, made me to start to edge away without handing over the phone. Bogdan was watching me, calculating, but he was hesitating – he'd seen the policemen and he wasn't sure that he could get away with jumping me. Behind him I saw Khaled, crossing over the concourse, but I was already sliding my way out through the doors. I sprinted for the taxi rank and pushed an outraged bloke in a pinstriped suit aside. "I'm sorry, mate, sir," I said, "But there's a bloke after me who wants to kill me."

I'd already scrambled into the vehicle and shut the door before he could answer. The taxi driver was watching in his rear view mirror. He shrugged – one fare was as good to him as another, I suppose, and he didn't want a row which might cost him time. "Where to?"

"Trent Bridge." That was the first place that sprang to mind – not home. I wanted to make sure that I wasn't being followed, although, as I afterwards realised, Otto, or Mitch for that matter, could well have already told Bogdan where Petra and Jimmy and I lived.

Off we went, me twisting round like they do in films to make sure that we weren't indeed being followed. I couldn't see anything suspicious – the car behind kept being a different one. As discreetly as I could I melted into the throng outside the cricket ground – England were playing Tierra del Fuego or somewhere, and it would have been hard for anyone following me to have kept on my trail as I dodged around the knots of chaps in Panama hats and blazers exchanging alcohol-fuelled views on the morning's play. I was just making my way back over to get another taxi back to the City centre when my phone rang. I huddled against a shopfront and looked at the number. It wasn't Bogdan.

"Yo, is that Bill?"

"Yes."

"Plastic Andy here. I play guitar. Saw your webvert. Didn't you see my reply?"

Hang on, I thought to myself, I didn't actually answer his

message. “How did you get this number?”

“Right man, well, I kind of deduced who you were...”

“How the fuck did you do that?”

“Well, I went out to Grantham the other night, Zee Bee band had sacked you, I made the leap, you know...” I wasn’t sure what was irritating me more, the guy’s gall, the fact that he thought that I’d been fired, or the way he, like all those other fucking dorks on and off the net called Zed “Zee”.

“Okay, and how did you get my number?”

“Easy, man, easy. I’ve got an old poster of yours, from when Zee was still alive, and it’s got your cellphone on it.”

Hell on a trike, I thought, he could well have. Petra had made me drop the landline from the poster when she’d moved in, and for a while I’d kept my mobile number printed at the bottom, as Plastic Andy had said, before moving over to doing bookings through the website.

“Okay, so what do you want?”

“Let’s meet up. Fuck them, Mitch and the rest, I dunno why they decided that you weren’t up to it any more because they were fucking shite when I saw them. That new bassist, he can’t fucking play.”

“Right.” I sighed. I might as well give it a go. The guy sounded like a pillock but then I’d played with Danny for years and a bigger knobhead you’d have to go a long way to find. Mind you, Danny was dead largely through being a knobhead. “Okay. Can you come to...” I gave him directions to the rehearsal room, and we arranged to meet the next day at two.

“Cheers, man, you won’t regret it. I know we can do great things,” he enthused before I hit the off button. I was carrying on towards the taxis when my phone beeped. It must Mr Dick Guitarist, with some other pearl of wisdom. I opened up the text.

u r the gr8est base player

Fuck I thought, who the fuck is this? Either some obsessed fan, and worse, some needy woman whom I’d exchanged a few words with for two minutes at a gig three months ago somewhere and who had somehow managed to convince herself that I was the one… 271828... *harpmouth.* Why the hell was he texting me with this unctuousness?

I dialled back. It rang, and kept ringing, nothing more. I got into a taxi, and we cruised home, me nervously looking round again to make sure that no-one was after me. In the back of the cab my mobile beeped. I opened it up.

dont try 2 talk 2 me

Fine, I thought. Fuck off then. Our street looked normal and the house was okay. I just had time to pick up Jimmy from nursery. I had barely started to make tea where I heard the scrabbling sound of a key and the front door slamming. "Mumu fuuu…" said Jimmy, tottering out towards the hall.

Petra appeared in the doorway, holding Jimmy who was squirming with delight, and with a very cross expression on her face. "What's up?" I asked, as innocently as I could. It was bound to be something I'd done.

She sat down at the table with Jimmy on her knee. "I need a cup of tea," she said, abruptly.

"Okay, but tell me what the matter is."

Petra sighed. "Some bloody junkie got hold of one of my prescriptions. I don't know how, but we had a phone call from a chemist's, near here actually. Someone came in with a faked bloody form with my name on the bottom."

I poured out boiling water into a mug, trying to keep my hand steady. "Was it really your signature?"

Petra looked up at me for a moment. "Yeah, that's the problem. It looks like I did sign it, but I don't recall ever writing one for the drug the guy was trying to get. It's banned in this country, anyway – it's been linked with testicular cancer." She took the tea without thanking me, holding it away from Jimmy who was glancing curiously from me to her and back again..

"What happened at the chemist's?" I asked. "Do they have a description or the guy on camera?"

"No, no pictures. They just said he was some scruffy weirdo who ran off after a couple of minutes. He must have realised that they were getting suspicious."

Thank fuck that they didn't have my mug on video was all I could think. "This must happen all the time."

"It's not meant to," snapped Petra. "It doesn't look good. Doc Cridland's not happy." We ate in silence, Petra brooding on what this might mean for her career, and then she took Jimmy upstairs. I got my violin out to practise a bit, only to have her call down to be quiet as I was disturbing his nibs.

Having surreptitiously swallowed another pill I sat on the settee in the front room with the local news burbling away, picking quiet pizzicatos on my fiddle. I felt strangely calm. Baggins had picked the right things, anyway. When Petra came down she looked irritably at the instrument and sat at the other end of the settee, reading the paper. Despite my absorption I heard the newsreader say: "A man was found dead in a residential street in Rushcliffe this morning, apparently having fallen from the window of his third floor flat. Neighbours have identified him as Matthew Barker, who played bass in the Seventies with Zed Beddington, the Nottingham blues star, until arguments about money led to him splitting from the band. Beddington and his band went on to achieve their greatest chart breakthroughs after Barker had quit, and it is thought that Barker, who was aged about sixty, had been in a depressed state of mind for a long time."

Petra had come to life. "Isn't that the bloke you replaced?" At least she was now talking to me.

"Yeah. I didn't really know him, though." I was just wondering whether I should let Mitch know the news when my phone beeped. "Sorry." I opened it. **matty woz nowhere neer as good as u billy** What the fuck? How the hell had *harpmouth* known that we'd been watching the telly? I stood up. "Getting cramp," I said, unnecessarily.

"Who was that?"

"What?"

"Text?"

"Oh... Just someone about an audition. I'm meeting a guy tomorrow for a try-out. At the rehearsal rooms." I went to the window and peeked out past the curtain. No-one outside as far as I could see.

"What you doing?" asked Petra.

"Just thought I heard a noise. Probably a cat. Back in a mo."

I went into the kitchen and checked that the back door and windows were locked. Pressing my nose up against the glass I couldn't see anything unusual in the back garden. Upstairs Jimmy was microsnoring away happily in his cot. Something struck me. *harpmouth* lived down somewhere near Bedford, yet the news about Matty had been on our local TV station. I sat on the toilet and texted back.

You are not harpmouth, are you?

u r v smart bill

What do you want? How did you know I knew about Matty?

just lucky gess i woz wotching tv and saw news

How did you get this number?

ive had it 4 yrs

I thought of what Plastic Andy had said this afternoon. Of course, any bloody loony could have my mobile, and I couldn't change it because all the promoters and landlords knew to get me on it. I′d also taken care never to tell the fans where I lived, although that had been much more to do with not wanting some drunken fuckwit turning up at three o'clock in the morning and demanding a jam session with me than because I′d ever been scared of stalking psychoes.

Whoever you are, just leave me alone

zee is with me

What do you mean?

i mean i hav zee with me here i am naked

So that was who it was. I didn't understand what was meant by Zed being there, but there was something else more important I needed to know. **Why was your number on Otto's phone?** I sent the message, and I sat on the loo, awaiting an answer, but none came.

After ten minutes or so, I checked on Jimmy again and went downstairs. Petra was asleep. I sat on the arm of the settee and looked down at her. I could wake her up and tell her everything, about Mitch killing Zed, and Otto killing Danny and Maurice and Clothilde and Laure and Matty and and and… It was too much. I'd juggled everything out of her sight, and that was how it had to stay. I fired up the laptop.

bluesfiend666, *andreplastique*, *harpmouth* and *beermonster37* are in the room

beermonster37: u awl herd about matty?

andreplastique: i saw him @ grantam 2 he woz crap but bill has joined my band now

bluesfiend666: who the fuk r u? andreplastique wot kind of name is that u wanka?

andreplastique: easy man im just saying that bill dont need 2 wurry coz him and me got new thing going

I scratched my head and stared at the screen. Should I log on and tell them all that Plastic A was being rather bloody previous, a bit like wretched *whitecliffs* saying that his lot were gigging at Zedstock this year? They all wanted a bit of my stardust, not that I'd ever noticed that I was trailing any.

beermonster37: wot about matty eniway?

bluesfiend666: i saw him b4 bill joined band he woz crap then good riddan's he desurved 2 die

wurzelman is in the room

wurzelman: Isn't that's a bit harsh? He may not have been the greatest but the poor sod's dead

bluesfiend666: fuk off wurzelman why do u cum on2 site? evryone h8's u

harpmouth: they got rid of bill to get matty bak thats why we dispized him i am glad he dead

beermonster37: do u think theyll get bill bak in now?

andreplastique: no like i say hes wurking with me now

bluesfiend666: fuk off plasticwanka u r not bluesman

harpmouth: yeh rite fuk off plastic i hope they get bill bak 2

bluesfiend666: i don't kno about that awl there gig's hav been called off it says on there website

What? What the hell did he mean? I quickly opened up another window and got onto *www.zedbeddington.co.uk*. And *bluesfiend* had been quite right. Across the scroll-down gig list was a big banner saying "*Canselled!*" in red letters which flashed on and off. How the fuck could that have happened? Otto and I had been the only people with the codes to access and alter the site. My phone beeped with a text. I opened it up. **they don't kno u r wurzelman**

Do they know that you killed Matty?

haha bill u r smart trying 2 catch me out

How did you get into our website?

That was it – no more texts came. I went into the kitchen and made myself a drink, and when I went back into the front room Petra had disappeared, presumably up to bed, although if she had inaudibly slipped out of the front door and were wandering the streets of Forest Fields at that instant I didn't think that there was much I could do about it. But she was upstairs when I checked, asleep at a diagonal across the bed, leaving no room for me. Rather than risk waking her by trying to shift her I went into Jimmy's room and pulled out the futon which was stored under his cot, and lay on it,. I could hear him breathing gently and I could see the street lamp light round the edge of the curtains. Did *bluesfiend666* really think that Matty deserved to die for being a crap bassist? And Plastic Andy was a wanker, like *bluesfiend666* had said. And had *nakedblueslady* really pushed Matty out of that window? Not only that, but *nakedblueslady* had talked in the chatroom about my speaking French at the gig… She (or he, whatever) had been there. Or knew someone who had been there. Or knew someone who knew someone who had been there. Or knew someone who knew someone who knew someone…

Eighth Bar

Chord of A

Even though I still felt better and quite bloody tranquil actually, which must have been Baggins' little helpers, another one of which I palmed down with the first cuppa the next morning, we had a rerun of the day before's silent breakfast. Silent between Petra and me, that was – she was demonstratively over-attentive to Jimmy's every need, cutting me out of being a parent again to make her point. Once more she went off to work without saying goodbye to me. I rolled Jimmy to the nursery, where I left both him and pushchair. Thence I walked into the city centre and headed for Otto's flat on the Meadows estate. The band van was parked up across the road, seemingly unmolested, but I needed to move it pronto before the riffraff sussed out that Otto was no longer at home and decided to put the Tranny up on bricks, or worse. It was registered in my name and I didn't need the police seeing it vandalised and asking questions. I hesitated outside the drawn-down slat blinds of Otto's flat, then pulled out the keys and let myself in through the triple-locked door. I had been in the place once or twice a few years ago, and I had been right in my uncertain memory that Otto hadn't had any kind of alarm system, preferring to rely on his fearsome reputation to deter the junkie burglars. I relocked the door once through.

In the dark hallway I flicked on the light. Otto's bedroom held a neatly made double bed, an anglepoise lamp on the floor, and a chest of drawers opposite, upon which was a CD player, with a stack of discs by it. I pulled the drawers open. Black T-shirts, underwear, black trousers, socks. There was a suit hanging on the back of the door. I went through the pockets but found nothing except a packet of Zed Bed condoms.

The kitchen was equally bleak, with aseptic surfaces empty but for three storage jars labelled coffee, tea and sugar. I checked inside each one; the contents were respectively what each said on the tin. In the cupboards were a few plain mugs, some plates and bowls. I opened the fridge, to see rows of neatly stacked beer cans, and a pint of milk, which I took out and sniffed. It had gone off.

In the living room was an ironing board and iron, a flat screen TV, a set of weights, and an electronic drum kit with headphones. Otto's public existence might have been debauched but he had lived a home-life of monkish austerity. No pictures on the walls, no carpets, no books, nothing to cook a meal with, no computer… Now, that was odd. I knew he had a computer, and moreover, he'd had it recently, because he'd reacted pretty sharpish to my email about leaving the band. And by the TV was a modem, its green lights winking on and off. I went back through the spartan rooms. Under the bed, resting on the wooden floor there were spare pairs of shoes and some kind of metal apparatus, which I pulled out cautiously, and identified as a fold-up rowing machine, but nothing else. In the bathroom I checked the cupboards and examined the panelling round the bath for signs that it had been moved. Nothing unusual in any way.

I'd searched everywhere. No PC, no laptop, no nothing. It couldn't have been stolen – there was no sign of a break-in, and anyway, a burglar would have made off with the other electronic goodies as well.

In the end I went out, locked up, opened up the van and drove it back to a couple of streets away from *chez nous*. I couldn't leave it any nearer lest Petra see it and get suspicious. I parked the van up in a little cul-de-sac that was off any route which Petra might take, either to work, or anywhere with Jimmy, as far as I knew. The tax disc had several months to run, so it could just sit there for the time being.

I didn't know how long it would take before anyone official noticed Otto's disappearance. Possibly they never would. He had illegally sublet the flat from its real tenant, I knew, a guy who was now in retirement in Costa Rica or somewhere, and presumably if Otto's bank account kept paying out the rent and council tax *etcetera* the bods at City Hall had much more pressing things to do than come round wondering why no-one ever saw their neighbour any more. On the other hand, his slum tenants might wonder why he hadn't come round to collect their rent. Short of finding the documentation, which probably didn't even exist, and going round to each property in turn, announcing myself as the new rent-collector and getting the moolah to feed into Otto's account to keep the ball rolling indefinitely there wasn't much I could do. If the law or anyone else came looking for him I'd just have to say that I'd quit the band and not seen him since. At least I could point out that the band had carried on for a couple of gigs after I'd quit, namely at Grantham and Hereford, where dozens of witnesses could testify that Otto had been there and I hadn't been on stage, so no-one was going to be able to say that my resignation and his disappearance had exactly coincided, which would have been suspicious.

In Petra's car, I got to the old bike factory at a quarter to two. I could have found somewhere else, a pub upstairs or somewhere, but as I kept telling myself, there was nothing in the practice rooms now, and it had a secure door. Once inside, we were safe enough. I humped my bass and amp up to the top room, and hesitantly turned the catch. There was nothing there, except the drum kit as I had left it that night, only sixty hours earlier, and various cabs and pedals lying around, as well as the piles of beer cans.

At two o'clock my phone beeped. **at door** I went downstairs and opened up. "Hi..." My words went into the empty air. There was no-one standing there. Wedging a brick in the jamb I stepped out onto the street and looked up and down. The road was always quiet, as it led only to a couple of blocks of industrial units, most of which were unoccupied. Petra's car was parked in the little layby. I walked round it. Nothing wrong there as far as I could see. It was a sunny day, but, despite the happy pills I felt cold and sweaty at the same time. The text's number was the same one on which I'd spoken to Plastic Andy yesterday. I dialled it. It rang, and then the answering service kicked in. I didn't leave a message.

I stared up and down the road again. No-one about on foot, although a builders' merchants' van backed out of one of the gates further up. There were two guys in plaster-stained clothes in it, who drove past without looking at me.

Sitting on the step of the rehearsal room door, I texted *nakedblueslady*: **What the fuck are you playing at?**

After a few seconds I had an answer: **he woznt good enuff 4 u**

Who wasn't?

plastic andy

I knew that I shouldn't be getting drawn in to whatever game she (he, it, they, what the fuck) was playing, but I couldn't help it.

Decisions about my band are up to me. If you do anything else to interfere I will go to the police

i am naked 4 zee he is here with me now

How can Zed be with you? He is dead

i will b naked 4 u as well bill

I sat for several minutes after this message came through, and then I tried Plastic Andy's number once more. Nothing but the answering machine. I left a message this time. "Hi. This is Bill. Please get back to me as soon as possible."

I shut the outer door carefully, making sure it was locked, putting down the latch, and went into the kitchen. I needed a cup of tea. I recalled that there was some dried milk powder lying around – I'd forgotten to bring a bottle of fresh with me. I opened the cupboard to find the powder, and clumsily knocked an old salt cellar out. It clattered onto the floor and rolled under a unit. I cursed, got down onto my knees to get it out, and grasped it, but when I withdrew my hand it was smudged and stained with something, brownish red, jelly-like, and smelling.

What was this? I lay down full length and peered underneath the unit. There was some kind of long arc, a splash of congealed liquid underneath, where something was spilt. Blood, viscous, but still fluid enough, after separating into clumped corpuscles and plasma, to have stuck to my fingers.

I scrambled to my feet and rushed over to the sink, where I

washed off my hands and wrist. Luckily, it being summer, I only had a T-shirt on and there was nothing on that. Breathing heavily, I leant against the sink. The kitchen was unnaturally clean, I saw now. I'd assumed that Maurice had tidied up a bit, but, when I studied it closely, I saw that someone had seriously gone to town on all the surfaces and crevices. There was no dust, no odd crumbs, nothing. It was as clean as one of those mock-up kitchens you see in furniture stores.

I got my phone out again, went into messages, found the last one and tapped a reply. **What do you want?**

zee and i want the best zeebee band there can b

I thought for a moment, then wrote: **Who is in that band?**

u r i am naked

Who else?

they kicked u out but u r star

That was just what Plastic Andy had said. I started to tap in that I hadn't been kicked out, *au contraire* that I had left of my own accord, but then it struck me that *nbl* could turn her/his fire on me for that, for having disrupted the band, so I plumped for going with the idea that I was the victim of an injustice. And anyway, Mitch and Otto had been going to dump me.

You didn't have to kill Otto

i did hav 2 he woz evil drugdeeler and not good enuff 4 u

How did you get into building to get to him?

he let me in i was naked 4 him ☹

Now that was convincing. Probably the only time Otto might be off his guard would be when he thought he might get a shag. **Where did you meet him?**

No immediate answer. *nbl* had the knack of staying off certain topics. I needed to keep this conversation going, in order to find out enough info to either identify or locate her/him. I tried again.

Is it easier to wash blood off if you're naked?

u r smart bill i am naked 4 u atm

And how did you bring a knife if you were naked?

u r v smart bill u r rite 4 my band

So who would be in your ideal zed bed band?

There was another pause, but this time I had a strong feeling that *nbl* was genuinely considering the question, rather than merely playing with me. I was wandering round the kitchen, examining the surfaces minutely, looking in all the cupboards and under the units, pulling out the drawers and examining their undersides, looking for anything which might give me a clue. In one drawer I found some cutlery – a few blotchy silver forks, a couple of bent teaspoon, and a long knife. There was also a whetstone, and peering in I could see minute filaments of metal on the wood of the drawer. I found a cloth and picked the knife up – I didn't want to leave fingerprints on what could be the murder weapon. It looked clean, again, like the kitchen itself, maybe a bit too clean. I tested the blade's sharpness with my thumb. It cut through the outer dermis.

My phone, which I'd left on the drainer by the sink, beeped again. **u & tommo & ur african frend**

My African friend?

u brort him and his wife hear in yr van u let them out @ todington

Well, well, well, *nbl* wasn't all-knowing. Should I say that Clothilde was Maurice's sister? Probably best not to appear over-keen to help.

You saw that?

he was playing with u when i killed otto u didnt heer us

Good grief, Otto had turned up here with *nbl*, bringing her/him here for some kind of rumble, whilst Maurice and I were jamming in the band room. *nbl* had somehow taken Otto by surprise and slit his throat in the kitchen, then cleaned up, and all the time Maurice and I were making a racket above their heads? Surely Otto would have wanted to know why he could hear the drums and bass?

Didn't Otto want to find out who was playing upstairs?

he new it was u and yr frend he was mor interested in me i was naked

That made sense. Otto had of course known that Maurice had been in the van, and he had known that Maurice was a drummer, and he had also known that Maurice was somewhere on the loose in England. Neither would it have been a total surprise for him to find that I had come back to use the rooms, and more to the point maybe, if Otto were about to indulge in some kind of unusual shag experience he would have left any curiosity about who was playing up top until later. Something else struck me – *nbl* didn't seem to know Maurice's name, either. This lack of knowledge on *nbl*'s part was scarier in a way than if s/he had known everything – it suggested that I was actually dealing with a real person, a real psycho, rather than some prankster or even, I don't know, some diabolic supernatural force.

Thinking about our website, I decided to risk a direct question. **Do you have Otto's laptop?**

☺ u r v sharp bill

This comment made me glance at the knife I'd found, which was lying on the drainer. My thumb had a little pricking sensation from where I'd tested it. But it was hard to get a straight answer from *nbl*. I'd try another question. **What is my African friend's name?**

i dont know u tell me

Damn. Now I had to say, otherwise s/he might take the old hump and end matters.

His name is Sylvain

dont lie 2 me bill or i will not b naked 4 u

Ok, his name is Maurice. How did you hide Otto's body from him? He must have seen it

lol he did he came in2 kitchen and then he ran away ☹

Did he see you?

no i woz in yutillity room

Fuck me, I wasn't bloody surprised that Maurice had cleared off and left everything. It all made sense, now – he comes into the kitchen after I've gone, sees the corpse, panics, both out of horror and because he can see himself immediately in the frame for the murder, and scoots *asap*. Then, of course, *nbl* takes the body upstairs and puts it behind the drum kit.

Must have been hard getting the body upstairs on your own

not if u r naked *nbl* had a knack of finessing difficult questions.

Did you kill Matty?

he woz rubish @ grantam

You were there?

u were there bill in audiens i was naked 4 u *nbl* hadn't actually said that s/he had been there, but was trying to make me read things that weren't in the texts.

You were in the audience in Brussels, weren't you?

u r so clever bill u can speak frentsh

I chuckled to myself. Bogdan might think me stupid but I had at least one admirer for my intellect. **How did you stop Plastic Andy from coming here?**

I was watching my phone, waiting for the answer, but a couple of minutes went by and it didn't beep. Maybe I needed to try another angle. **I don't see how we can get your ideal line-up together seeing as Maurice has gone missing**

I waited for five, ten, fifteen minutes, pacing round the kitchen, holding my phone like a talisman but no further text came. In the "yutility" room I found a mop and bucket and cleaned up the blood under the cupboard which *nbl* had overlooked. I locked up, and went out to the car. I left my amp and bass upstairs – I rationalised to myself that they were my spare kit, and that I might well need it up there for another audition, but the real reason was that I had had enough of this gruesome place and I couldn't even face going upstairs once more. I needed out, now.

I looked up and down the street. Nothing out of the ordinary. I closed the door behind me and checked the car, even peering underneath for a bomb or something.. There was nothing unusual there either. The builder's van with the two guys in it headed back past me, having presumably ripped off enough grannies for the afternoon. It was time to fetch Jimmy. I nipped in at home *en route*, to drop off the car and looked at my website advert once more – nothing but Plastic Andy again, who had left a second message, clearly before managing to trap me on the phone.

At the nursery Jimmy was in the "Aquatic Room", a large brightly painted hall. He was standing, his nose pressed against one of three big transparent pillars filled with water, up which streamed columns of bubbles jostling and moving shoals of plastic fish.

"Has he been alright?" I asked the nursery nurse.

"Lovely," she cooed. "Haven't you, James?"

Jimmy was pointing at the fish. "Fuu…fuu…fuu…"

"That's right," I said. "Fish."

He ran over to me and jumped into my arms. I nuzzled him and then carried him out to the pushchair storeroom, where, after disentangling our wheels from all the others I propelled the lad along the quiet streets, calling in at the shop. Inside, as I bought Jimmy one of his his favourite ice lollies, my eye was caught by the pile of local papers on the counter. "*Crash horror on Mansfield Road*" ran the headline. I read down. "*A car hit a tree at high speed this lunchtime on Mansfield Road. The driver, Andrew Darlowski, aged 31, who had to be cut out of his vehicle by the Fire Services, has been taken to the King's Medical Centre with serious neck and shoulder injuries...*"

"You buying that, or what?" asked the shopkeeper.

"Yeah, sure." I picked up a copy, handed over the money and carried on reading outside whilst Jimmy sucked enthusiastically on his lolly. "*...A witness said that the driver seemed to lose control of the car coming up to the lights on Elmore Street, and swerved into the tree at full speed. A spokesman for Nottinghamshire police said that it seemed that Mr Darlowski's seatbelt had been frayed and had snapped.*"

It had to be, I thought. Coming down from Mansfield, about the right time. Thirty one was probably about the right age, given his bumptious and upfront manner. I wheeled Jimmy home, hurriedly, and settled him in front of the telly, something that I always assured Petra that I didn't do during the day.

I made a cup of tea, swallowed another tranquilliser and sat at the kitchen table. Think. Somehow *nbl* had hacked into my advert – possible, I supposed, for someone with a knowledge of IT, although well beyond me. It meant that nothing I did over the net was secure. *nbl* presumably also knew where Andy Darlowski lived as well, as s/he had then managed to tamper with the brakes and seatbelt on his motor. I wondered whether I should visit Plastic Andy in hospital, both out of humanitarian concern and to make sure that it was the right guy beneath the plaster. Anyone I tried to play with was in danger. Apart from Tommo, presumably, thank God, when you think that he had three kids, and Maurice, wherever the fuck he had got to, the two guys whom *nbl* wanted in the Platonic ZB tribute band together.

I glanced at the laptop, which was sitting, turned off, on the kitchen table. I couldn't use that. But I had take control of the situation. I sent a text. **Just heard about Plastic Andy**

After a minute there was a beep **he wont be playing gitar 4 a while lol**

There was something else bothering me. **What did you mean by saying that Zed was with you? You know that he's dead**

u will c

Would I indeed? Now I had to write something risky, drawing *nbl*'s attention to an issue which it was conceivable s/he hadn't already thought of. Anyone else whom I played with, or who was in the current line-up would, it would seem, be a hindrance to forming the ultimate outfit. So I wrote: **If you want your ideal ZB band you have 2 leave Mitch alone** Though as soon as I had sent it I asked myself, seeing as Mitch had tried his damnedest to stitch me up, why the fuck should I be bothered about him?

wy he is not yr frend any mor and he is yuseless gitarrist

Correct but he runs Zedstock and if the band is going to carry on we have to play there

I waited for an answer. I could hear Jimmy giggling at something, and high-pitched voices from the telly. I went out into the hall and glanced round the door to make sure that he wasn't gnawing through a cable or anything. Jimmy was sitting, cross-legged, on the carpet, gazing up in wonderment at the screen where a purple humanoid was prancing about waving a handbag. My phone rang. I retreated to the kitchen and put it to my ear.

"Hullo?"

"Good afternoon, is that William Silverthwaite?"

I was so unused to being called William that it took me a minute to realise that it was me they were after. "Er… Yeah. Who's this?"

"William, this is Arthur McMurray of the Arthur McMurray Six..." He paused, clearly expecting me to give an excited yelp of recognition or, I dunno, become doubly incontinent on the spot.

"Right."

Arthur McMurray carried on, in an evangelical tone. "Well, William, the Arthur McMurray Six is Nottingham's leading showband, specialising in weddings, bar-mitzfahs and funerals..."

He chuckled at the old joke. "And, William, you were recommended to me by Annie Higginbotham."

"Who?"

"Annie Higginbotham, chair of Nottingham Square Table?"

I'd never heard of the woman, but I said: "Oh, yeah, sorry bad line, Annie, yeah."

"Indeed, William," went on Arthur McMurray, "You might be the very man to help us. The Arthur McMurray Six has a performance tomorrow night, at the Empire Ballroom, and we have a little problem..."

"That being?"

Arthur McMurray coughed. "Well, William, our bass player, Louie Harbourne, has gone down with food poisoning, and our usual stand-in, Reggie Dwindling, is on a tour of the States."

"So you'd like me to step in?"

"Indeed. It's all standards, soul, Sinatra, that kind of thing."

I'd never played any of the old mafiosi's songs in my life, but I scented spondulicks. "What would the fee be? For playing?"

"Well, er, considering the lateness of the request, shall we say five hundred pounds?"

There was a mirror on the kitchen wall. I pursed my lips up, as if considering, and gazed at myself. I looked like a complete pillock. "Seems reasonable enough. What kind of function is it?"

"It's the finals night of Miss Nottinghamshire, swimwear and ballgown rounds. Do you have a tuxedo?

"No."

"I'm sure we can sort something out for you. Can you be at the Empire Rooms for six o'clock tomorrow, for a run-through? Curtain's up at half eight."

A quick flip through the diary showed that Petra was not doing anything the next evening. The way things were at the moment I might as well make sure that I was out earning. "I can."

We finalised arrangements, gear and so on, and Arthur McMurray of the Arthur McMurray Six rang off.

I'd neglected Jimmy for long enough, so I went through. He was standing, swaying and dancing to music from the TV. "Dipsy fuuu." I wondered whether it was worth cooking for Petra and me, or whether she'd just find fault with whatever I made, but reckoned that it was better to show willing, so I dumped Jimmy in his playpen whilst I had hot stuff on the stove. Then I sat him in his highchair and spooned his portion of our vegetarian moussaka supper into him.

Hey, I could text *nbl*, tell her/him about the gig and get the whole Arthur McMurray Six slaughtered before tomorrow evening. But perhaps one-off bookings didn't count. I hadn't heard that any of Satan's Slinkies had come to harm. I lifted Jimmy out of his seat and set him on the rug with his giant Lego bricks, then logged onto Satan's Slinkies' website, hastily scrolling down past the photos to check their gig list. It didn't say anything like "*Canselled*" in big flashing letters, so presumably all was well. I went onto *www.britishbluesgoss.co.uk*

beermonster37, harpmouth and *whitecliffs* are in the room

beermonster37: hay harpmuth, i think i kno who that guy in yor photo is

harpmouth: wot guy?

beermonster37: the guy in the foto u took of the bloke getting out of bills van

harpmouth: wot u mean?

beermonster37: last nite they brouhgt in african guy to hospital he had been on street's quite ill and mad they think hes illegal i reckon hes bloke in yor foto thay hav sum kind of gard on him in case he scarpa's

harpmouth: u mean bill brort the guy in2 the uk in his van?

whitecliffs: i hope bill isnt going to 4get about my gig at zeestok

harpmouth: wot the fuks that got 2 do with it witecliffs u wanka?

whitecliffs: just saying in case bill is reading this

I logged in.

wurzelman is in the room

wurzelman: Why do you think that it's the same guy?

beermonster37: fuk off wurzelwanka it just look's like him and he duznt speak english just frentsh they coudnt find any1 2 transl8 4 him

whitecliffs: bill could get year's 4 doing that

beermonster37: doing wot?

whitecliffs: peeple smugling

wurzelman: What ward is he in then?

beermonster37: y u want 2 kno that, u wanka?

bluesfiend666: wurzelman is queer he like's big black men lol

beermonster37: o rite hah ha take yer vasseline wurzel its ward six

nakedblueslady is in the room

nakedblueslady: i am naked 4 bill

bluesfiend666: hay wurzel u can shag nakedblueslady he is bloke

nakedblueslady: fuk off i am lady

bluesfiend666: yeah and i am muddy water's

I heard the front door opening and quickly logged off – I had been dreading Petra's coming home, and I braced myself for more trouble, but she came straight in and kissed me on the lips. "Mama fuu…" said Jimmy, scrambling to his feet. Petra held her arms around me and pressed herself tightly up against me. This was a turn-up, and I surprised myself even more by becoming rapidly tumescent, but she either didn't notice or didn't mind.

"I'm sorry," she said. "Sorry about this morning. And yesterday." She held me, speaking up to me.

"That's alright." What the fuck was this?

"I know it's hard for you…" She hesitated, then went on. "I realised how lucky I am to have you. They brought in some young bloke, thirty odd, mashed up in a car accident. He was in a terrible state, and it was awful because they had to amputate an arm, and someone told me that he'd said he was a musician and…" She tailed off. She'd noticed my glazed expression. Plastic Andy. Hell on a hovercraft.

"Yeah," I said, shaking myself. "Musician's worst nightmare. You know, if you lost a leg or something you could still carry on, but an arm, fingers… Doesn't bear thinking about." I hoicked little Jimmy up into my arms for a three-way hug. "The only thing worse would be something happening to him…" I tailed off, not wishing to articulate the thought lest it became reality.

"I know," said Petra. She kissed me again. "Anyway, enough of that. I'm starving," she said. "What is it?"

"Moussaka, with real moose…" I might as well tell her now. "Oh, yeah, I've got another gig. It's a Rotarian do, you know, local worthies and their wives, but they pay well. Two hundred quid plus drinks. Tomorrow night. Is that alright?" I reckoned that if I told her how much I was really on for she'd get too interested and try to find out where and at what kind of event I was actually playing, and then she'd get all Germaine Greer on me.

"Of course." She smiled at me across the table. Neither she nor I mentioned the rogue prescription. We had a nice quiet domestic evening lying happily cuddled up before the box with an existential French thriller, the dialogue of which was far too racy and *verlan* for me to understand without the subtitles, although I could never be sure about Petra. We had opened a bottle of wine, and I raised a private toast to Plastic Andy, firstly to wish him as speedy a recovery as was possible in the circs, and secondly to thank him for bringing my wife and me back together.

Ninth Bar

Turnaround Chord of E

The next morning Petra was rooting through her stuff. "You haven't seen my badge, have you? I can't find it. Blast. I'll have to get a sign-in from Doc Cridders. That'll piss him off again." Here we go, I thought, things are going to turn bad again. But fortunately Petra still seemed grateful that I was whole, and she bustled off, blaming herself for being absent-minded, maybe having seen the affair of the dodgy prescription as evidence that she needed to get more of a grip.

Once I had taken Jimmy to nursery I hurried back home, and busied myself anew with Petra's spare medical kit. Her silky deception of the ambulance crew at the motorway services had given me an idea – no-one ever had the nerve to question a medic's *bona-fides*. I got my pills out of the amp, looked at them, and then decided that if Petra and I were getting on okay I didn't need them. I had slept pretty well last night and I felt a sense of confidence which hadn't been there for a while. I neatened myself up, took out the ear rings and put on a decent shirt and tie, then drove out to King's. There was a small risk that either Petra or one of her colleagues might recognise me, so I had a cover story. For Petra it was: how about a surprise romantic lunch date, and for the colleagues, or even Cridland, should I have the supreme bad luck of crossing his path, presumably in the shadows as he would turn to dust exposed to sunlight, it was: don't say anything to Petra about my being here, as I'm planning a birthday surprise and I needed to carry out a recce. Fortunately her birthday really was in a couple of weeks.

Walking along the main corridor of the hospital I slipped into the toilets. In my bag I had a white coat of Petra's and a stethoscope. The coat was far too small, making my arms stick out stiffly like penguin wings, and in the end I decided to fold it up and put it over my arm. I pinned Petra's ID badge to my shirt. I hadn't actually had to lie to her and say that I hadn't seen it, as she'd been too agitated to notice that I hadn't answered her question. Obviously the photo was of her, but I was gambling that no-one would look too closely. Most of the hospital medics whom I'd passed in the corridors were wearing green jackets and gowns, but I reckoned that I could look like a visiting GP, as long as I had a confident manner and the stethoscope around my neck.

I stuck my head out of the gents'. The corridor was not too busy. I found the stairs up to ward six, passing a couple of nurses who didn't give me a second glance. There was another nurse on the door, but she just looked at me and smiled as I walked in. I strode down between the beds. I could see what had to be Maurice's head resting on pillows, but there was some woman in a smart suit standing by the bed, looking down at him. *beermonster* had been right in suggesting that Maurice was being guarded.

"Dr Robert Johnson," I said. "I've been asked to translate some advice for the patient."

"Fine," said the woman. "Susan Thurley, from the Home Office. Just making sure that he doesn't try to abscond." She was rather handsome, green eyes and red hair cut in a bob, and she had that same self-possessed air which had first attracted me to Petra. I looked away, needing to concentrate. Maurice's eyes were shut, and his face was thin, his body covered by a sheet, but it was him for sure.

"Are you here all the time? I mean, guarding him?" I asked, as innocently as I could.

Susan Home Office shook her head. "No. Just popped in to check on him. He doesn't look like he'll be going anywhere." She looked at me curiously. "Do I know you from somewhere?"

"I don't know," I said. "You mean at the hospital?"

Ms Thurley shook her head doubtfully. "No. No, not as a doc. You don't play in the Nottingham Symphony, do you? You know, the amateur orchestra?"

"Not my thing," I said with a laugh.

She was getting a bit too close for my liking, but she wouldn't back off. "Were you at the Hardwicks' dinner do last year? The one where they had the music *soiree*? Jackie Lovell played that marvellous Schoenberg?"

I had no idea who either the Hardwicks or Jackie Lovell were, and anyway, even before Jimmy had been born and our social life had shrivelled as much as our sex life we had hardly been dinner-party animals, the compulsory jaunts out to Doc Cridland's excepted, of course.

"I don't think I know them. I've got one of those faces, people are always telling me that they recognise me. I've got a lot of twin brothers out there."

She seemed happy with that, and even laughed, motioning me to go ahead and sit down by the bed. "Be my guest."

Underworld on a unicycle. I hoped Maurice wouldn't say anything stupid. "*Monsieur? Can you hear me?*" I whispered in his ear. Maurice didn't stir. Susan Friend of the Hardwicks' watched me approvingly.

"What's going to happen to him?" I asked.

"As soon as he's fit enough, he'll be moved to a detention centre pending removal."

"Where to? I mean, which country?"

"We're not sure at the moment. We haven't been able to interview him properly. Police picked him up yesterday evening, delirious, suffering from exposure. One of your colleagues said that he might have pneumonia. What do you think?"

"Oh… Er… Yeah, it's possible." I touched Maurice's head, and made as if I were listening to his chest through my stethoscope. "He certainly seems feverish. I'm not really here to do a diagnosis. I'm meant to find out any medical history I can." I tried addressing Maurice again. "*Monsieur*?"

This time his eyes opened in a flicker and he looked at me, and shuddered. His pupils dilated. He muttered something. *Madame* Susan and I both bent closer to him. "*I saw him... I saw his throat....*"

I looked at Ms Thurley, who shrugged again. "He just keeps saying things like that. Probably something which happened in... Wherever he's from. I deal with all the francophone asylum cases in the East Midlands."

I took hold of Maurice's wrist and felt his pulse. I'd seen Petra do it often enough. Maurice closed his hand round my arm. "*I saw his throat...*" he repeated.

Susan Thurley stood up. "I don't think you'll get anything sensible out of him. The nurses are keeping an eye on things. They're to notify us if he tries to leave. Good luck. See you again, maybe." She shook hands with me in a business-like fashion, gathered up her files and shoulder bag and strode out. I watched her go, and then turned my attention back to the bed.

"*Maurice,*" I whispered. "*It's me, it's Bill.*" Slowly his eyes opened again, looking up at the ceiling and then across at me. He blinked, and tried to push himself up, using my arm which he was still holding as a support.. "*Easy. You need to be careful.*"

He gestured at the cup of water that stood on the cabinet. With my free hand I brought it across and held it to his lips. He sipped it. I said: "*Maurice, they want to deport you, send you back. I'm going to get you out of here – I'll come back tomorrow evening, okay?*"

Maurice nodded. He squeezed my wrist with a surprisingly strong grip, and steadied himself. "*I saw... In Congo I saw lots of bodies, but...*"

"*Don't worry. I know what you saw. And I know where Laure is. Bogdan's got her.*"

Maurice groaned. "*Bogdan? It was him who...*"

"*Don't worry. We'll get her.*"

At that moment I saw a party of genuine quacks gathering in the corridor, about to come in. "*I'll be back.*" I extricated my arm from his hand, jumped up and went over to a corner of the room, by the doors, where I pretended to make some notes amongst the folders which were stacked up there, and then managed to slip out undetected. In the Gents I took off stethoscope and badge, and stuffed them and the coat back into my bag. As I strolled along the corridor I passed a sign for the hospital chapel. I stuck my head in – it was an empty room with a couple of ecclesiastical stained-glass windows at the far end below a plain wooden table, which I assumed could serve as an altar. But the chapel gave me the solution to the problem of how to get Maurice out.

***

I pretended to be a doc again later that day – I rang the hospital in Luton on my mobile, claiming to be a Nottingham GP checking up on a new patient of mine, Clothilde Habarayama – I gambled on the surname being the same, and Clothilde not having given a false first name – and her infant daughter, who was about six weeks old now. I must have picked up enough from Petra to sound plausible, because they told me that Clothilde had been there for four nights, with baby, who had been perfectly healthy and had been taken out of the incubator after the first twenty four hours. On the fifth day Clothilde and daughter had left – with, the nurse I was speaking to thought, a male visitor.

"Ah," I said, "That must be Wojtiech Kosminski, her husband?"

Yes, said the nurse, she herself had been there when Clothilde had gone, and she thought that the man had been some kind of Eastern European. The nurse and the other staff had tried, with difficulty, as none of them spoke French, to persuade Clothilde not to check out, but her husband had been insistent and as Clothilde seemed willing, there had been nothing they could do to hinder her. They didn't know where she had gone. I rather liked the deferential tone I was getting from people in the role of Dr Robert. I could see why Petra slipped into putting on airs. Thanks, I said, and hung up quickly. Bogdan had them, all three, Clothilde, baby, and Laure.

The landline phone was ringing. There were a few clicks and burrs, and then a echoey voice said: "Is Beel?"

"Yes. Who's this?"

"Borjo Janibegashvardze, from Rustaveli Agency in Tbilisi. Listen Beel, is problem…"

Borjo told me that although Zurab Tkupishvili, the famous

Georgian Zed tribute artist, had been given a visa by the British Embassy, for some reason which remained unclear the rest of the band had been knocked back. I had to think quickly – during the course of the phone conversation I had had an idea. Not just about Zedstock, but the faintest glimmer of how I was going to get myself out of this whole shebang with Bogdan and Maurice *etcetera etcetera*, but for it to work I definitely needed the Kartveli Caruso there. "Okay, Borjo…" I said. "We'll sort it. Tell Zurab to come anyway." At the end of the call I hunted through the folders in the computer, found the canonical set-list and emailed it to Tbilisi. I hoped that Zurab could sing them all in the right key.

I rang Mitch. "You okay?" I said warily.

"Aye." *nbl* hadn't got to him yet, anyway.

"Zedstock." I said. "You and me, we're going to play it as the Zed Bed Tribute."

"What the fuck are you on about? You've left, Otto's…"

"We'll have a band," I cut in. "First off, I'm bringing over our new drummer tonight."

"What? Who the fuck's that?"

"You'll see. Get one of the rooms upstairs at your gaff ready. And we're going to have some special guests. We've got that Georgian bloke playing, you know, Zurab What-the-fuck-ishvili. I had a call, he's still coming, but no backing band. He'll need a room at the Swan as well, come to think of it."

"They're already booked out."

"Tell whoever's in them to fuck off. We need them more, we're to make this the best Zedstock ever. And, hey, Bogdan's going to be there, guest of fucking honour."

"What? Have you completely left the fucking planet?"

"No. You want that psycho fucker off our backs for good? You owe me, Mitch. One word from me and you're doing twenty fucking years, minimum. I'm going to ring him, and I'm going to invite him. I'm going to give him a spiel. All you have to do, if he rings you, is to tell him that I haven't lost my marbles and it's all on the level. He'll listen to you, Mitch."

There was a silence and then he muttered "Okay."

I rang off, then carefully composed and sent a text. At six o'clock that evening, I was hanging around in the Art Nouveau splendour of the Empire Ballroom's foyer, having been told that "Mr McMurray" would come and find me. A tubby little man with a grogblossom nose, bloodhound jowls and a halo of white hair scurried across the parquet. "William?"

"Hi."

"Arthur McMurray of the Arthur McMurray Six." He was panting, short of breath. We shook hands. AM of the AM6 led me slowly up red plush stairs and into a dressing room where another four elderly gents were sitting around, reading papers and drinking bubbling G&T's. AM of the AM6 waved a hand. "Allow me to introduce William…" The oldies looked up and nodded cursorily before going back to their crosswords and sudoku. From a wardrobe AM produced a tuxedo which I squeezed myself into before being handed a sheaf of music. "You can read dots?" AM of the AM6 asked me anxiously, having only just realised that he had forgotten to pop the question over the phone the night before.

I had played in the Empire Ballroom years ago, some gig with the Mayor and various puffed-up bigwigs who'd then invested Zed Beddington (and not the rest of us, me, Otto or Danny) with the freedom of the City for having made such a contribution to the local culture, but I'd forgotten how cavernous it looked from the stage. The punters had not yet been allowed in, and a gang of ushers and hands watched us idly from the wings as we ran through the tunes. We were set up on one side of the stage, with Arthur McMurray in profile to the auditorium as he led us from his white Bechstein. I managed to get through without too many fuck-ups, keeping it conservative and only hitting the root chords until I was sure of the notes.

AM of the AM6 smiled approvingly. "Super, chaps. Well played, William." The five seniors went back down to the dressing room whilst I hit the bar, having been told that there was a free tab for the band. An hour later we strolled back onto the stage. The auditorium was buzzing with conversation and I could see tiers of heads gazing down at us. In the centre of the stage an oleaginous MC was warming the crowd up with off-colour jokes, and then we struck up the first tune, "*Isn't She Lovely?*", whilst a line of nineteen-year-olds in swimsuits paraded onto the stage to wolf-whistles and cheers.

The MC went to the first girl. “And what’s your name, darlin’?”

“Chantelle,” she said shyly.

The MC glanced at his notes. “And you’re from Strelley and a nursery nurse?”

Fuck me, I thought. I recognised her as being the girl in the Aquatic Room at Jimmy’s nursery. I was hoping that she wouldn’t spot me, as that way it was poss that Petra might find out where I had been that night, but Chantelle was too busy gazing at the floor for me to have to worry. My fellow band members pulled from discreet hip flasks. Of course, I hadn’t thought to bring a drink onto the stage with me. When the MC had molested all the two dozen girls we played “*When Will I See You Again?*” whilst the beauties sashayed off. After that we were treated to the individual ballgown round, followed by another round in swimsuits, and then it was the break. I went back to the bar, and guiltily glanced at my phone, which I’d switched to silent. I had a message.

dont look at girls i am naked 4 u

I knocked back my buckshee pint and hastily got another. When I went out again with the Arthur McMurray Six I had a good scrutinise of the audience. Mostly sixty-something businessman, a few wives, but I couldn’t see anyone who could be *nbl*. That was the point, though, presumably.

And we played some more drearily safe *mor* standards (I was tempted to stick in some little extra riffs and wiggles but I didn’t want to endanger my five hundred sovs), between rounds, until halfway through “*Fly Me to the Moon*”, as I was watching AM of the AM6’s hand for the beat, I saw him stagger forward, clutch at his chest, and then fall impressively headlong onto his keys. An avant-garde chord – I thought of the handsome Susan Thurley and her Schoenberg evening – the first interesting notes of the evening, and the band stopped. We looked at each other. There was gasping from the audience. One of the contestants screamed. I was the nearest to AM – with my bass still round me I stepped forward, and took hold of his shoulders, pulling his head back. His eyes stared at me, and I knew that I was looking at the late Arthur McMurray of the former Arthur McMurray Six. As gently as I could I lowered the head back down onto the keyboard. The MC was gabbling: “Ladeez ‘n gennelmen, stay calm, no need to panic… Is there a doctor in the house?”

Some bloke climbed up out of the audience – fuck me, it was Doc Cridland. What the fuck was he doing at this event? He grinned sharkily at me, as he passed, meaning, as clearly as if he’d said it out loud, keep *shtumm* about this pal, if you don’t want Petra to suffer. I nodded, meaning I’d understood, but then we both had an interest in keeping this *entre nous*. Doc Cridland lifted AM of the AM6 off the piano once more, checked for a pulse, looked into the eyes, closed them and lay the body back down. The stage curtains swept together, cutting us off from the audience, who were shouting and climbing to their feet to see better.

“Stagehands,” shouted Doc Cridland. A couple of guys appeared and lifted the corpse under the doc’s directions. The rest of the band and I retreated to the dressing room. Someone had sent down some brandy, and we sat drinking it with shaking hands.

My phone beeped. **i am naked and zee is here and arthur is ded**

I had been wrong. Anyone who played with me was in peril. I didn’t know how the fuck *nbl* had killed Arthur Mac – slipped something into a drink, maybe? – but no-one was out of reach. Nevertheless, there was a more pertinent question for me. I wondered which of my fellow musicians would be the best to tackle. The Grim Reaper was soon to knock at a few more doors, judging by their appearances. AM hadn’t even seemed to be the oldest – the trombonist was a slender tottering man who looked to be about ninety.

I went over and sat myself down by the drummer, whose name I had managed to recall. He was staring into his glass. “Sorry, er… Monty… Can I ask you something?”

He nodded absently.

“Bit awkward, but… Well, Arthur did mention some money for tonight, and I was wondering…”

Monty said nothing. After a minute I got up and went out to the box office, where I explained the issue. The girl behind the counter said breezily: "You'll have to see Mr Edgar. He's the house manager. He'll deal with it." Of course she didn't know where the fuck he might be at that moment. I knew that if I left without the wedge in my hand I'd never get it. I found Mr Edgar talking to Doc Cridders – we both carried on pretending that we didn't know each other. Why the hell had Cridland advertised his presence at such a tacky event by coming onstage? Some vestigial sense of professional duty, I supposed, which was to his credit. At a suitable moment in their conversation, when the good physician had just explained that AM had, as far as he could tell without a proper post-mortem, suffered a massive stroke, I said "Excuse me, but…" and made it clear that I'd been promised my monkey.

Mr Edgar regarded me with distaste. "I know nothing about any arrangements you may have made with Mr McMurray." Doc Cridland was grinning his shark grin. It was obvious that I was onto a loser, so I fucked off out of the theatre by a side door, bass guitar in hand. The contestants were being shepherded out the same way, wearing coats and boots at any rate, not just swimwear, but even so there were already a couple of guys from the local press trying to take piccies and asking questions. I slipped down the jitty and made my way to the nearest cashpoint. I got two hundred quid out. It wasn't likely that Petra would go through my bank statements but she might ask me whether I'd got the wonga.

I needn't have bothered. Downstairs at home was empty – Petra must be in bed. I didn't feel like turning in – in my mind's eye I kept seeing Arthur McMurray collapsing at his piano. I made myself a cup of tea, took a pill, and sat stirring the bag round and round. I texted *nbl*.

Why did you have to kill Arthur Macmurray? He didn't do you any harm

After a moment my phone pinged.

did u want 2 play in a showband 4 rest ov yr life?

nbl was right, I supposed, although for five hundred quid a night I'd sell my soul to anyone. Despite how late it was I dialled a number in my registry.

"Hello," said a young female voice.

"Is that Sharon Slinky?"

"Yes."

"It's Bill Silverthwaite here, you know, I stood in with you a couple of weeks ago…"

"Oh yeah." Her voice had an edge of suspicion. She probably thought I was going to try to ask her out or something. "What do you want?"

"Look, something's happened. You need to…" Hell's clangers, I thought, I can't say, watch for some fucking murdering psycho who'll bump you all off one by one for having played with me. "I've just… I've just had some odd messages. One just came through, which is why I'm ringing now. Someone knows that I played with you, and they seem like they want to find out about you. A stalker, you know, some saddo…"

Sharon Slinky laughed. "We get that kind of thing all the time." She actually had quite a posh middle-class sort of voice, and her tone was a bit warmer now. "We're quite used to dealing with that. But, thanks, sweet of you to be bothered." She hung up.

It had been sweet of me to be bothered. I was glad that Sharon Slinky was used to dealing with that, whatever "that" was. Perhaps I should ring her back and get some lessons in stress management. Let's have a squint at the Net.

bluesfiend666, beermonster3, whitecliffs and harpmouth are in the room

bluesfiend666: i just seen bill playing at notingham empire with new band

beermonster 37: any good?

bluesfiend666: they woz rubbish lode of old bloak's didnt play any of zees hit's

whitecliffs: wot bill playing with them 4?

bluesfiend666: money I gess eniway turned out good cos bandleeder just droppd ded on stage

harpmouth: that sounds like good laff wish id bin there ☺

whitecliffs: i hope bill hasnt desided not 2 do zeestok

bluesfiend666: well he wont be playing with old bloaks band again ☺

whitecliffs: well getting arested 4 peple smugling wouldnt help his carear eether

I pulled *whitecliffs'* CD of the shelf, and studied the lookalikes on the cover with distaste. How on earth did anyone reckon that that gurning idiot looked like me? I listened to the first couple of tracks through the headphones. I t was exactly what I'd expected – halfway competent but bland renderings of our greatest hits. You could tell it wasn't us because it was all too well put together. There was no spark. But then there'd hardly been a spark with me and Mitch and Otto for the last couple of years.

I had to make a decision. *whitecliffs* was getting dangerously close. It was late, but I texted the number on the back of the CD envelope. **Hi Bill Silverthwaite here Just listened to your CD and thought it was great I can give you a slot at Zedstock on the Friday night £200**

Tenth Bar

Turnaround Chord of E

I told Petra that I had had another call to sub. Daventry, another two hundred. It was the first place that came into my head. I bathed Jimmy, watching him shoving his soap bubbles around and making sure that he didn't slip on the smooth enamel and wind up under the water, then scooped the lad dripping out of the tub, and wrapped him in a towel, whereupon he started to squirm around on the bathmat like an oversized grub. Petra came in, and kissed me. "I want you to make a go of it," she said. "And the money'll come in handy. Enjoy yourself."

Pilled-up, I loaded my gear into the hatchback and set off back to King's Med Centre. Still in the car, I awkwardly changed out of my gig uniform of black bomber jacket, drainpipes (which were beginning to get uncomfortably tight round the stomach and crotch), and black DMs into a respectable corduroy jacket, jeans, and plain shirt. I attached the dog collar which I had found at the back of the wardrobe at home, a dimly remembered souvenir of a Tarts and Vicars party I had reluctantly attended during the costive interval between Clara leaving my life and Petra coming into it.

As I had hoped, there was no-one sat at Maurice's bed. It was quiet in the wards – visiting times were coming to an end, and the patients were being tucked up, or sedated, or whatever, for the night. I strode into the ward, nodding at the nurse, a buxom West Indian, who was at the desk in the corner. Her not being the sister on the shift during my last visit was a bit of extra luck – otherwise a resemblance between my persona tonight and the French-speaking doctor who'd come in yesterday might have struck someone. I plonked myself once more down by Maurice's bedside. He opened an eye. I patted his hand and leant right over him, to speak quietly.

"*Maurice? You need to get up. We're splitting.*"

The nurse was coming across. "Excuse me, sir, what's going on?"

I smiled in as *simpatico* a manner as I could. "I'm a friend of..." I wasn't sure whether they had Maurice's name, and if not, whether it was a good idea to give it to them. "...Of the patient's." Maurice was fumblingly trying to sit up.

"You do know that we are meant to be keeping an eye on Mr Luwumu?" So Maurice had given them a false name. "Who are you?"

"I... I ... We met at my local church. I run the Questioners' Group, and Mr... Mr Luwumu started to come along. Very interested in theology. I'm meant to be taking him down to the hospital chapel."

The nurse's face had brightened. "Which church are you from?"

I delved desperately into distant memories of primary school RE lessons, sat cross-legged in shorts on the mat before Mrs Petherbridge, four decades earlier. "Er... The Shadrach, Meshach and Abidjan Pentecostal Church. It's only a little place." Maurice was sitting up now. Where the fuck were his shoes?

"I don't know that," said the nurse. "Where is it?"

"Oh, tucked away behind the industrial estates on Derby Road." Maurice, more on the ball than I had expected, had opened a locker and was pulling his footwear out.

"Pentecostal, is it?" The nurse had a puzzled expression. "I thought I knew all the Pentecostalists in Nottingham."

"It's not exactly Pentecostalist. We're a bit different... Quadracostalists." Maurice had lowered himself off the bed now. "I was asked to come specially because Mr Lumumba doesn't speak much English." To Maurice I muttered: "*We're going to fuck off now, okay?*" Maurice nodded. I went on: "So, is it alright if I take

Mr Lamella down for a quick pray? Just a few minutes. His soul needs refreshment." I needed a drink.

The nurse had suppressed any doubts she might have. "Of course. It's so lovely to see that you're concerned with the patient's spiritual welfare, Mr… Reverend… Er..."

"Wolf.... Reverend Harlan Wolf. I don't often like to wear the old dog collar, bit formal. We'd be delighted to see you at The Shadrach, Meshach and Abbott's Church..."

"Abednego," said the nurse.

"Yes, sorry, all these Babylonian names, so tricky, you know." I smiled and started to usher Maurice out, his arm over my shoulder. "*Get a fucking move on.*"

We were a few paces from the door when the nurse called out. "Wait!"

I froze, and turned around, my benign clergyman smile fixed. The nurse was pointing into the corner. "Take the wheelchair. The lift's at the end of the corridor."

"Why, thankyou… *We'll take that chair,*" I whispered in Maurice's ear, and steered him over to it. He plumped down heavily and I wheeled him out. It was harder to steer the bloody thing than I had imagined. "Back in ten," I said to the nurse, who had resumed her vigil in the corner. "Minutes, I mean, not Commandments, ha ha…"

Once we were moving in a straight line our momentum zoomed us down the corridor to the lift. "*I can walk,*" said Maurice.

"*Fuck that. Stay put,*" I said. "*No-one will notice us like this.*" I tugged the wheelchair to a halt by the doors. Again, we were lucky – we were the only people in the lift. With trembling fingers I hit the ground floor button, and we rolled along to the Gents, which had an extra wide-door for wheelchair users. Inside, I scrabbled around in my bag. Maurice was about my height – he had been broader and heavier built, but his ordeals had thinned him out – and I had brought the loosest clothing I could find. An old track suit, which I never wore – the last athletic activity I had done was an unwise game of five-a-side footy a few years back, also before Petra, where my tar-clogged lungs had left me spluttering and gasping after ten minutes – and an extra large T-shirt. He changed in a cubicle and came out looking a bit odd, with the combination of leather shoes and sports gear, but it would have to do. I had ditched the dog-collar, as well.

We left the wheelchair in the loos and strolled as cazh along the corridor as we could, past the main reception desk and out in to the coolness, picking our way between parked up ambulances. The air in the hospital had been stiflingly hot. I'd left the car in the hospital pay and display – five bloody quid it had cost. Talk about ripping off the sick and needy. I unlocked the car doors and Maurice sank into the passenger seat. He groaned again.

"*Okay?*"

"*I'm alright. I'll live.*"

I turned the ignition and we got the hell out. I drove us north-west out of the city. Maurice was slumped in his seat, shaking his head and muttering things under his breath. I headed for the orbital superstore, and dragged Maurice into the concourse. The photo booth seemed to be working.

"*Take a seat there.*" He looked suspiciously into the space, as if it were some kind of sci-fi humane death chamber. Of course, Maurice had never seen one of these things before. Presumably in Congo you actually got a real live human being to take your passport mugshot. "*We need some photos of you.*" I had to spin the seat round to get it down low enough, and managed to get him to sit still whilst the light flashed. We then hung around uneasily whilst citizen consumers wheeled their laden wagons triumphantly past us. A buzzer sounded and a strip of portraits appeared. I snatched them up. In the pics Maurice's eyes were staring out of his sockets and he looked like the kind of bloke you'd cross the road, if not the city, to avoid, but I wanted out of there so it would have to do. I could see a uniformed security guard casting a wary eye our way.

We went back to the car, and when we were out beyond the suburbs I pulled us over into a layby. Maurice stirred and looked at me. "*Are we there?*"

I hadn't told him where we were going. "*No. But you need to tell me a few things.*" Maurice had closed his eyes. "*I want the truth, this time,*" I went on.

"*The truth.*" I would have thought that he was asleep, had he not answered. "*What the fuck's that?*"

"*Ha ha, Pontius Pilate. Tell me what the fuck happened in Congo. Why you had to leave. Whom did you kill?*"

For a long drawn out moment Maurice said nothing. I could see his face, his skin luminescent in the light from the street lamps at either end of the layby, the stubble on his chin, the tired dark rings around his eyes. Then: "*You've met up with Bogdan, haven't you? Since we got to England, I mean. That's why we needed the photos. He's getting you the documents. He said something?*"

"*Yeah.*"

Maurice let out a slow sigh. "*Do you know what tantalum is?*"

A vague picture of the Periodic Table in the school chemistry labs floated up in my mind. "*It's a metal, isn't it? An element?*"

"*Yes. You use it in mobiles. It's rare, but there are deposits in Congo. The Chinese came to Kivu to open up a big mine, for tantalum and niobium and cobalt. Whatever, I'd trained as a mining engineer in Kinshasa but I was back in Kivu. I'd been playing a lot of music, but I couldn't earn a living doing it and this Chinese firm took me on to oversee the mine galleries... My job was to put in struts, stanchions, to hold up the roof...*" Maurice stopped talking. A car flashed by us in the dark, white then red lights..

"*Go on,*" I said.

"*Well, they gave me money for the struts, one every three metres. But the bloke I was getting them through, he said, put one in every four meters and we'll split the difference... He was a mate of Bogdan's, another Ukrainain.* " Maurice laughed. "*Guess what I did with my share?*"

"*Drink? Women? Drugs?*"

"*No. Wrong each time. You'll never believe it, but we bought music gear with it, me and my mates. The ones on the CD.. You know, in Belgium, or here in England you can just stroll into a recording studio, they're everywhere. But in Congo we had to travel to Kinshasa and pay bribes to use the government broadcasting studios. Way beyond our pay-packets, that was.*"

"*And a gallery collapsed?*"

"*That's right. Three miners were killed. They didn't matter, but there was this bigshot Chinese guy, Communist Party cadre below with them. He shouldn't have been there but for some reason they'd taken him down. He was killed too, of course, and the company was in deep shit, and they came after me.*"

"*How did they know that you were to blame?*"

"*They dug the fucking gallery out, didn't they, to recover this Chinese guy's body, and of course they didn't find the right number of struts. Then they measured the other galleries. Those guys are not fucking stupid – they knew exactly what I'd done.*"

"*Maybe it hadn't been the struts.*"

"*Maybe, but they needed a scapegoat, anyway.*"

"*So you scarpered, with Laure?*"

"*I got the hell out as quickly as possible. I pinched a truck and drove straight to Kinshasa.*"

"*And your wife?*"

Maurice shook his head. "*She was already dead, killed by the Tutsis. That bit was true, Bill... I got to Brussels. Clothilde paid for my ticket with money from Bogdan. His mate, the Ukrainian bloke in Congo, he was panicking that the Chinese would come after him if I stayed.*"

Maurice and I sat for a long time. Cars zoomed past on the road, people going out, people coming home, people with their partners, people with their children. I though of green steamy jungle I'd never seen where death could lurk behind any tree, and dark choking dusty mineworkings. Zed and Mitch had been miners, before Zed had got famous and Mitch had begun running the Grey Swan, and I recalled how Mitch had once told me how they had worked in the constant knowledge that the roof could come down at any time. Witout any more being said, I turned the ignition key.

As we drew up outside the Grey Swan, the yard gates opened – Mitch was there – and I carefully took the car in. I helped Maurice in though the back door into the band room. We sat with drinks, me with a fruit juice, Maurice looking around with interest at his first sight of the inside of an English pub. Without asking Mitch I poured out a pint of Olde Stoatfucker from the handpump, and passed it to Maurice. "*That's typical English beer. Try it.*"

Maurice sipped cautiously at it. "*It's warm.*"

"*It's always like that. What do you reckon*?"

"*Not bad*." He drained the rest of the glass quickly enough. I explained *en français* to Maurice that he was going to stay here, and that we were going to gig in a few days, then I finished my juice and got up to go. "Hang on, nearly forgot." From my bag I drew out a French-English dictionary, which I laid on the bar. One of the two of them was going to have to blink first and make an effort.

Once again, on the way back, I withdrew two hundred smackers from a cashpoint at a garage. Problem was that I kept spending these alleged gig payments instead of being Mr Sensible and putting them back into my account. Still parked up on the forecourt I made a call.

"Who this?"

"Bogdan, it's Bill."

"What fuck you want this time?"

"I've got a deal for you. A big one. I'm going to let you in on something."

"What fuck you mean?"

"I'm not telling you over the phone. Are you in England?"

"What fuck that to you?"

"I want you to meet me. Again. Broadmarsh cinema café, in Nottingham, tomorrow."

"Why fuck I come?"

"Because what I've got is big, Bogdan. It's come along, it's too big for me, but you can do it, and I want a share. You meet me, twelve o'clock, do you know the cinema in Nottingham?"

"I find it." From that I knew I had him hooked.

"Good. You meet me there, just you, not that fucker Khaled, no tricks."

"Fuck you, Bill, you waste my time, I kill you and your family."

"I'm not wasting your time, Bogdan. I know better than that. Twelve o'clock." I clicked off the phone. I was shaking. I was in deep now, much much deeper than when I'd agreed to take Maurice back to England.

When I got home I went straight to the cupboard where my amp was stashed and fumbled for the pills. I pushed two out of their foil packet and went into the kitchen, where I swallowed them whilst drinking directly from the tap. Petra was watching TV in the front room. I waved the wad at her. "It's coming in."

She gestured me to silence. "You've got to see this. It's unbelievable." I sat down on the chair-arm. On the screen were a group of dark-skinned chaps with shock-hair, running around naked but for penis gourds and, fuck me, guitars in their hands and woven grass pork-pie hats on their heads. The voiceover was saying: "…This is Zed Tok Pisin from New Guinea, a tribute band to the British blues star." The camera cut to a group of the same tribesmen standing in a half circle, wielding guitars and chanting a song which, despite the odd phrasings, after a moment I recognised. "That's your song, Reptile House," said Petra, "Isn't it?"

We watched and listened, until the documentary moved on. "Just came on as you walked in," said Petra. "I didn't realise how far Zed had travelled. You could have had them at one of the festivals." She switched the sound down. "You pleased with the money? I know you're trying."

I snuggled myself up on the settee next to her. "Jimmy alright?"

"He's fine. I'm sorry about the band, as well."

"What do you mean?"

"Making you leave. I didn't realise you'd find it so hard to get something sorted."

"It's early days. Anyway…" This was my moment, I realised. I'd been watching for the right juncture as carefully as a zoologist waits to get that perfect snapshot of mating wildebeest. I sat down beside her and took her hand. "I've got a problem."

"I'm a doctor," she said. "I've seen it all before."

"Ha, ha. Not that kind. Music… Well, you know you mentioned the Zedstock festival just now… Look, okay, I've got to do a gig with Mitch and…" Of course I recalled that she didn't know that Otto was dead. "...And the others." I explained as quickly as I could about Zurab, who he was, the visa problem, not giving her a chance to object. "And so," I finished, somewhat lamely, "I just need to do this one last gig."

Petra said nothing.

"Do you mind terribly?" I added.

Petra shifted herself, her body language expressing the beginning of disengagement. "Just the one?"

"Yes. Then it's all finished. I don't want to play with them ever again."

"Hmmm..." She didn't sound convinced.

I realised that I needed to change the mood. I would make it into a bit of a joke. "Okay, listen, Petra Silverthwaite, *née* van Rensberg, I, William Richard Silverthwaite, your awful wedded husband, am going to do one last gig with the Tribute to Zed Beddington Band. Because I want to, and because Zedstock needs me."

And, much to my surprise, and relief, Petra settled herself back against me. "That's better," she said. "Actually, I quite want to see that Georgian bloke. Sounds interesting. As long as it is positively, definitely the last one. And I quite like it when you're all masterful."

For the life of me I could not tell whether she was being sarcastic or not. I'd never heard her say anything like that before, but maybe I should have been more attuned. Anyway, the idea of being lord in my house rather appealed, and we didn't switch the TV back up. Later, after we had crawled up to bed, clothes bundled in our arms, I lay running through what I had to do, turning the plan round and round in my head as if I were viewing a 3D model from all sides, looking for weak points and flaws. Petra had dropped off, issuing lady-like snorettes. Then I heard Jimmy. He was back to performing his regular midnight poo. I changed him, fed him with a bottle from the fridge downstairs and, after having pulled out another two pills from my amp and having swallowed them, I decided to try putting him down again. I knelt down on the futon, which was still out, looking in between the bars of the cot. There he lay, the little mite, thumb stuck in his gob, dark curls on the pillow. I reached my hand into the cot and took hold of Jimmy's little mitt, warm and so beautifully soft in the coarseness of my own. The next thing I knew, it was morning, the light streaming through the gaps around the curtains, and Petra was shaking me. "Tea," she said, placing a steaming cup by me.

***

I went round the block to pick up the van. I'd knocked back another pair of pills – at this rate I was going to be needing a repeat prescription pretty damn' soon. Petra was long gone to work, and Jimmy was at nursery. My first port of call was the Grey Swan at Coatstall, where I found that that Maurice had staged a Lazarus-like recovery. Mitch had set up some spare music gear in the band room, amps, a guitar, a bass and an old drum kit, and when I got there Maurice was tapping away, literally nineteen to the dozen or some equally coprime and fiendish proportion, between sips of Olde Stoatfucker, which he had clearly developed a taste for. Mitch was sat at the bar listening, drinking a Guinness and perusing a Teach Yerself Frog. "*Bon djooer*," said Mitch, lifting his glass. "*Common va?*"

"*Pas mal,*" I answered. "*Et toi?*"

Mitch looked confused. "'Ello," said Maurice, suspending his percussion. "'Ow are you?"

"Great," I said, impressed and surprised. "How are you?"

"I'm good," he said.

Oh no, I thought. What the fuck had Mitch been teaching him? "No, you're *well*. Good is virtuous, morally praiseworthy."

Of course Maurice looked at me blankly. He was hurt that I hadn't been more enthusiastic about his learning some English. He started tapping the drums again, until I interrupted him to tell him about his new identity. "*You'll be from Niger, or Gabon or somewhere.*"

"*I won't have the right accent,*" he objected.

"*No-one in England will know that.*"

He looked fucked-off again. "*You whiteys think that Africa's just one big fuck-off country, just one culture...*"

"*And you told me it was all down to the Europeans' frontiers that you all didn't live in harmony.*"

"*Fuck that.*" He bashed a cymbal.

"*Anyway, talking of harmony, we need to practice the tracks.*" I managed to coax Maurice round into running through the traditional Zed set with me and Mitch. When I left. things had thawed a bit and Mitch and Maurice were convivially sitting at a table, each with a beer, trying to converse, books flattened in front of them.

At the airport I parked the van for an extortionate fee and made my way up to arrivals, where the screen told me that flight 1001 from Tbilisi, 7 x 11 x 13, product of three distinct primes, via Chisinau, was two hours late. I sat in a cafe with the paper and an overpriced coffee. When, at last, the flight was called I went to the gate and stood amidst the taxi drivers, hoping that I'd recognise Zurab from the blurry image on the net. I also had a piece of paper with his name written in English, Cyrillic and in curly martianesque Georgian letters, which the agency had emailed me. Next to me was a paunchy bloke in a tight suit. He smiled at me. "Who are you meeting?" he asked, *apropos* of zilch

"Just a friend," I answered neutrally. I felt obliged to answer. "You?"

"My wife," he said proudly. He pulled out a picture. "Valentina. Got her off the Internet. What you reckon?" I was looking at an imperious woman of indeterminate age. She had serious cheekbones and a cross expression.

"Charming," I said. "I'm sure you'll be very happy."

"Yeah. Went over to Moldova to meet her. She's Russian, her husband was a Soviet colonel, stationed there, and he ran off with some Romanian flooze and she's been desperate to get out ever since." I bet she was, I thought, thinking back to that woman who had come out of Otto's flat that morning, to be picked up by Khaled. The chappy went on: "Got wed there after two days. Visas and shit cost me a fortune. I've bought her ticket, and a house in Urmston."

The frosted glass gates slid open, and the passengers began to trickle through. My new friend scanned the crowd anxiously. As the throng tailed off he made for the doors, to be held back by a security guard. "You can't go in there, sir."

"Fuck me," said Mr Paunch. "Where the fuck is she? Three thousand quid I sent her…"

At that moment I saw, not the delectable Valyochka, but a squat looking bloke with a luxuriant moustache who put his head shyly round the glass door. In one hand he was clutching a canvas hold-all and in the other a gold-coloured balalaika, a round, long-necked lute, a Caucasian version of Ida May, Zed's guitar. I hurried over and he looked up at me enquiringly. "Zurab?" He nodded and we shook hands. I took his hold-all. My mail-order bride mate was now shouting and being restrained by two guards. I had to raise my voice.

"Hi. I'm Bill. Good trip?" Zurab looked at me blankly. "Good trip?" I repeated. Zurab shook his head. "Was the flight okay? You were held up a couple of hours."

Zurab smiled. "Yes. Very khappy. *Ty govorish' po russki*?"

"No, *nyet*." I don't bloody speak Russian, I thought, steering him away from the scrum. Valentina's swain was still shouting and remonstrating as we got into the lift to go down to the car-park. At the van we had a pantomime where Zurab tried to climb in on the wrong side, and didn't seem to believe me that the wheel was actually on the right. I also had to demonstrate putting the seatbelt on as Zurab didn't seem to know what one was. As we passed the front of the airport building he looked out of the window, his lips picking out the letters. "Mahnchister," he said slowly and happily. "Mahnchister Yoonited. Bobby Chahrlton. Yes?"

"Yeah. George Best. Bert Trautmann. Bobby Stiles. Gordon Ramsey." I had no fucking interest in the international language of football, though I supposed I should make an effort. Right fucking tower of Babel it was going to be at the Swan.

We cruised back down the M6. Zurab was seemingly fascinated by all the different cars and lorries, and every time we passed a big blue destination sign I could see him trying to read the names of the places. "Kknutsforrrd," he said, pronouncing the K. "Villemslov. Nortivich." He was dressed in a kind of sparkly suit, too small for him, with crepe brothel-creepers just like the ones which Zed had used to wear, and during the journey he produced a porkpie hat from his holdall and stuck it on his head, truly the love child of Brian "Zed" Beddington and Uncle Joe Stalin.

We established Zurab in one of the frowsy upstairs rooms at the Swan, next door to Maurice's one room suite, and by dumbshow and gesture I managed to explain that we, *ie* Mitch, Maurice and I, were going to be his backing band. We set up and had a prac in the bandroom. Amazingly, Zurab's balalaika had a jack-plug socket in it – he stuck a lead in and strummed his way through the first song on the set-list which I'd emailed to him in Gori the week before. The tuning of the individual strings sounded odd, and minorish, but it worked. He knew the whole set. In a heavy accent he growled his way through "*Green Tordle Bloos*", "*Beeg Ant Stomp*" and even my song, "*Repitile Khouse*" though it was clear that he didn't understand what any of the lyrics meant.

At the end, Mitch, Maurice and I gave him a round of applause and he bowed sheepishly. Mitch handed him an open bottle of lager. "*Gaumarjos,*" said Zurab, toasting us.

Maurice raised his Stoatfucker in response. "*A votre santé*."

***

Zedstock. The very word is enough to send joy leaping across the true blues fan's heart, like the word "*Christmas*" thrills a small child, with its images of tinsel and trees and presents. And like the Christmas decorations going up earlier each year, with September becoming the start of Advent, so each year the preparations in Coatstall, Mecca, or Bethlehem, of British blues, crept forward in time. A week before the big concert the large banners with Zed's portrait had been hung, Pyongyang style, from all the buildings. From beneath his porkpie hat he frowned down grumpily on the passers-by and the fans. Bunting in the form of golden guitar cut-outs was strung from lamp-post to lamp-post, and the dusty charity shops on the main street sported multicoloured posters announcing all the acts. The market square, usually occupied only by a handful of forlorn stalls on Saturday and Tuesday mornings was barred off so that the aluminium pole stage could be built, and Coatstall's few bed and breakfast establishments and the single musty hotel had their yearly late spring-clean, ready to receive their guests. Even the Grey Swan, which had a couple of rooms upstairs which were never let out except for this one week in June had had its carpets shampooed and hoovered, its windows polished and the tops of all the mirrors and pictures feather-dusted.

Of course, there wasn't just the main blues fest now, but also a whole raft of fringe events. Following the success of the British group the Last Letters, seven Zed lookalikes in a row, ranging from six foot six at one end to five foot at the other, thrashing away on spray-painted golden cardboard axes, who had debuted at Zed's wake and who had since gone on to club circuit success in their own right, we now had entrants into *The Omega* air-guitar competition from all over the world: *Las Letras Ultimas*, from Paraguay, *Poslyedniyi Bukvi* from Belarus and the hot favourites, the Austrian *Die Letzten Buchstaben*, who had taken the competition a step further by stomping around on stage to Zed's hits, rerecorded for yodeller and alpenhorn, whilst miming on golden cardboard accordeons. There was also the Zedtipple marathon, held at one of Coatstall's other pubs, the Black Horse, where musicians had to sing a Zed song, drink a pint of lager, sing another song, drink another pint, and so on, until either the audience booed them off or they passed out. The canonical Zed set being two dozen songs long, no contestant had ever managed to get right to the end. Nevertheless, as the lager was provided gratis by the pub, there were a large number of entrants, but the amount drunk by the spectators easily paid for the free stuff.

I wandered up and down, visiting the venues, popping in and out of the Swan bar, which served as a meeting point and festival office, making sure that everything was running smoothly. It had soon become clear, once I'd picked up the reins again a couple of weeks earlier, that neither Mitch nor Otto had done a hand's turn in organising anything – once I'd quit they'd just let everything slide, and now I was having to cram months of organisation into a few days. Nevertheless, the bands and the fans were turning up. There were always problems – *Zeddau Bach Cymru*, who sang all Zed's songs in Welsh, had had their gear stolen at a services on the M45 on their way from Betws Y Coed – I had to do a quick mobile ring round and extract favours from folk to set up a backline for them, and the lead singer of *Zee Zee Zee OMG*, a blues rap crew who chanted Zed's lyrics to a drum'n bass backbeat had had a tantrum when he'd seen the smallness of his room at the Coatstall Boutique Hotel. I'd placated him by negotiating a twenty per cent off. And of course, bloody *whitecliffs'* outfit turned up. *whitecliffs*, whose real name (although I may have misheard, as there was a lot of ambient noise whilst he told me) was Don Wankstaff, decided to impress upon the rest of his band and the world in general what great bezzies he and I were.

"Of course," Don held forth, in the Black Horse, before they went on, "Bill knew who I was straight off. He'd seen our act on the Net. Isn't that right, Bill?"

I just nodded. "Yes, Don."

The fucker kept dropping unsubtle hints, jokes about Zed's body being in the back of the van, and "Who else, fuck knows, eh?"

Anyway, A Tribute to A Tribute to Zed Beddington did their gig on a quiet Thursday afternoon. They shuffled on, a disturbing visitation from a parallel universe. Modger (Otto) tripped over a lead and stumbled headlong into his drums, whereupon Potter, who was meant to be me, began to cackle into his microphone in a mad scarecrow kind of way. "Get out of the van, Zed!" he yelled, over and over again, for no apparent reason. Then Don Wankstaff, who had back-combed his hair and stuffed a rolled up towel under his T-shirt to portray Mitch as accurately as possible picked up his guitar and began to strum a riff, whilst the rhythm section clapped their hands above their heads in a ludicrous attempt to whip up the audience. After thirty seconds, when no-one had joined in, Wally strode on in the standard Zed mohair suit and porkpie hat outfit, clutching the regulation Ida May copy, and they launched into a ragged version of "Reptile House Blues". The sparse audience started throwing beermats at them.

I had to get on stage and actually fucking humilate myself by pleading with the gaggle of onlookers. "Give the lads a chance. They've come all the way from Dover…" at which some wag shouted: "Well, why don't they fuck off back there, and keep going through the fucking Tunnel?" I managed to restore some kind of order and ATtaTtZB finished their second set to a grand total of six people, one of them your humble narrator. Afterwards, having swallowed another happy pill I told Don and his mates "Yeah, we'll deffo have you back next year," which I hoped would keep the fucker quiet for twelve months.

The star turn this year, however, headlining on the Saturday night on the Grey Swan stage, confusingly located in the market place, as the pub itself was no longer big enough to host the audience, was of course to be Mr Tkupishvili. He'd settled nicely into Coatstall – once he'd discovered that he only had to set foot in a bar to be given a free pint, he had taken to sitting and drinking all day, nodding and smiling, without understanding a bloody word, to all the fans who came up to pay homage. I noticed after a couple of days that some enterprising person must be marketing Zurab T-shirts, with his fiz and his mispelt name screenprinted onto them, as every second punter who came into the Grey Swan had the Sakartveli songster's face stretched across his beergut. That someone, or maybe a second entrepreneur, was even selling Zurab moustaches on an elastic headstring, which had become the "must-have" accessory at any of the Zedstock gigs. And he hadn't even played yet.

And it was a Zedstock poster, with Zurab's grinning face in the top corner that I had rolled up in my hand as I had sat drinking coffee, washing down another pill, in the Broadmarsh cinema bar, the day before the festival started. The place was full of serious males in roll-necks and horn-rimmed glasses and earnest females with modish crusty-style dreadlocks. As I gazed around me, feeling middle-aged, someone said: "Hello."

I looked up. Not Bogdan, but it hadn't been his voice. A young woman with purple hair was standing before me. "Hi," I said carefully.

"You don't remember me?"

I shook my head. "Sorry." Not being male, or balding, or overweight, she didn't look like one of our obsessive fans.

"Jasmine," she said. "I emailed you. Violin lessons."

Of course. I essayed a smile. "I'm sorry. Did you? I don't think I had anything…" This was true. I couldn't recall any message from her.

"Can I sit down?" I motioned to go ahead. "I sent you a couple of messages. Look, I'm really keen to do something…"

"Hey, Bill," interrupted a voice. "You dog, you have nice girlfriend, no?" It was Bogdan, dressed in his regulation stonewashed denim, as out of place in this fountainhead of trendiness as the proverbial bacon sarnie. He smiled wolfishly down at Jasmine. "You know darling, he has also very nice wife, doctor."

Jasmine was confused. "Take no notice of him," I said hastily. "Listen, I'll ring you. Email me again, it didn't get through..."

"That's right, darling, he rings you when wife's not home."

I was tempted to tell Bogdan to fuck off, but instead I stood up. "Jasmine, I'm sorry, I have to talk to my... friend. Do you mind?"

She shot a look of dislike at Bogdan, then sloped off without another word. Bogdan took her seat. He grinned unpleasantly. "She has good arse."

I reckoned that it would be an idea to let Bogdan think that I was a deceitful philanderer, so I said: "I know. She's crazy about musicians."

"You get plenty women with music. I know that. I play bass guitar in band in Kharkov."

"Really? What kind of stuff?"

"Like you, blues. You know, I have all Zed's albums. Not I pay for them – Otto he give them to me. I am big fan. Maybe biggest. That's how I get to know Otto, I see you play, you too, Bill, Otto talks with me after gig when I am on business in England. I see poster for Zed Beddington Band, I think that in all years in Kharkov I play his music but I never see him, my chance now."

"Where was that you saw us, then?"

"I don't know town name." At that moment Bogdan's hand closed powerfully around my wrist. His grip was as strong as Otto's had been, his nails digging painfully into my flesh. His pale eyes stared at me across the table. "You fuck with me, I kill your wife, then I kill your child, then I don't kill you like I say on phone, instead I cut your fingers off. You understand?" I nodded, and he let go of my arm. He went on: "So what fuck you want talk about?"

I reached down into my bag and brought out a Zedstock poster. "This," I said. "Him." I pointed to Zurab's face.

Bogdan read the name, his lips moving. "Who fuck he? Name is Georgian?"

"Yep."

"I don't like Georgians. Thieves and murderers. Cut your throat when you sleeping."

"You don't have to like him," I said. "Thing is, he's come to England. Otto set it up, using the festival as cover. This guy controls the all the smack coming into the South Caucasus. Comes in via Azerbaijan from Iran, weighed up in Baku, shipped northwards to Vladikavkaz and on." I'd done my homework on Wikipedia.

Bogdan leant back, eyeing me with perhaps a little more respect. "And?"

"And Otto was going to do a deal with him. Setting up a supply route across Europe."

Again, Bogdan seemed to consider seriously what I was saying. "Why you tell me this? What to do with you?"

I sipped at the coffee I had ordered a million years earlier. It was cold, but my mouth had gone dry. It hadn't occurred to me to get Bogdan one. "I picked this fucker Zurab up from the airport yesterday. He doesn't know that Otto is… that Otto's dead. And I thought, I could do with a cut of this, but I don't have the contacts. You can take over the deal."

Bogdan was nodding. "What about Mitch?"

"He knows about it but it was Otto's deal. Mitch's nothing to do with it. He's a drunken fuckwit – you can't trust him not to fuck up."

"How you know so much?"

"When I picked up Zurab from the airport he asked me when he was going to meet Otto, said that he had all the chain worked out and so on. He just assumed that I was in on it all."

"Fucking idiot." Bogdan had leant back a bit. He was less sure.

I shrugged. "Maybe. But you said it. Georgians. They just think everyone is a crook."

At this Bogdan laughed. "You know Bill, I said you stupid."

"I remember."

"Maybe you not as stupid as I thought. So what we do?"

"I want ten per cent of profits. And you bring Clothilde, and the baby, and Laure. We sort everything out."

He was still laughing. "You, Bill, you have wife and already one girl, you want another?"

"Nothing like that. I've talked to Maurice. You know that he knows too much about... Your business. If he gets his sister and daughter, and the baby, he'll be happy. He'll keep his mouth shut."

"You know where that... *Sumashchedshchii...* Crazy man?"

"I do. I can sort everything, if you give me his family. First off, I need false passports and ID, for a man and a woman, and a teenage girl from a French-speaking African country. Not from Congo, though." I dug out the photos which Maurice had had taken in the booth and passed them over. "You'll have to get Clothilde and Laure to have their photos taken as well. And the baby. We'll need a passport for her. All the passports need to be stamped with leave to remain in the UK. You understand?"

Bogdan was studying the strip of Maurice's pics. "Why we do this?"

"Because we have to make sure there's no trouble for them. The authorities find out they're illegal, it'll get back to us maybe."

"I can get you Ivory Coast documents. It cost maybe ten thousand euros, four passports. You have that?"

"You can take it out of my share from the deal."

"Fuck you." He leant back in his chair. "You try get passports for nothing? No deal."

"Okay." I had anticipated this. That morning I had been to the Building Society and cleaned out Petra's and my joint ISA, six thousand eight hundred and eighty nine pounds, eighty three squared. I'd raided the cashpoint yet again, and I had a fat roll of notes stashed away in my jacket pocket. I got it out, discreetly, and passed it over to Bogdan. I recalled Maurice offering the thousand euroes in Brussels and I wished to fuck I'd taken it now. "Seven thousand pounds. That's about eight grand in euros. The rest you'll have to wait for."

Bogdan took the money, without examining it and slipped it away. I took that as a sign that the deal was back on. "Why you spend your money for them?"

I decided that getting outraged was the best way of bluffing through. "Fuck me, Bogdan, okay, I like Maurice, he's my friend, I want to help him, keep him quiet. If I pay for it, it's none of your fucking business."

Bogdan stared at me, his eyes boring through mine, trying to determine whether I was taking the piss, or whether this was really my attitude. He smiled. "Okay Bill, you right. Your money…" But as he smiled, the flickers of suspicion broke through again. "Your wife doctor. They get fuck lot money here, not like in Ukraine. My cousin, he doctor there, he get three hundred dollar one month. Why you need money from deal with me anyway?"

I flicked a finger in the direction in which Jasmine had disappeared. Bogdan chuckled. "Bill, you are true dog. You leave wife?"

"No," I said. "Why should I? But paying for that girl's expensive, and I can't keep using money from my bank account. My wife would see it."

He thought that this was fucking hilarious. "You English, you are so good…" He groped for the right word. "*Litsemyeri…* You do one thing, say another…"

"Hypocrites?"

"Hypocrite. Yes. Anyway, how you know I give you right amount from deal?"

"You're not a hypocrite. You're honest."

He liked that. "Yes. I am honest man. Not like thieving Georgians…" I seemed to have touched on some Soviet-era issue there, but all to the good, maybe. "So," he repeated, "Okay, I like this deal. What we do?"

***

In Petra's runabout, one vehicle in the heavy flow of fans coming into Coatstall the next morning, I crawled up to the Grey Swan, parked in the back yard, and went into the band room. Maurice was sat at the bar, eating his breakfast, a pint of his usual beside him and Mitch was fucking about with the beer pumps, doing unneeded polishing, a bottle of Guinness in hand. He looked up at me. "They coming?"

"Haven't heard otherwise. Anyway, this is the plan." I said. "*Maurice, you fuck off once they get here, okay*?" Maurice nodded.

"Mitch, fuck off as well. Go now, before they get here. I don't want Bogdan seeing you. I need keys to the door."

Mitch nodded reluctantly, laid his keys on the bar and cleared off. I was to meet him in the Black Horse. He didn't like leaving his pub in someone else's hands, but this was going to be delicate. Maurice was finishing his repast in a leisurely fashion, sipping at his ale. Even after nearly thirty years in the music biz I couldn't have stomached beer for breakfast, although of course I'd seen him have exactly that before, aeons ago in the Café Kinshasa. Bloody hell, that seemed like it had happened in the Cretaceous period, though when was it? Six, seven weeks ago.

I went out and waited by the yard gates, watching as the traffic grumbled past and the throngs of fans heading on foot for the first gigs hurried by. A car came up, half on the pavement. Leaning out of the window was Khaled. As he saw me he accelerated to try to make me jump and step back, but I'd been expecting something like this and I stood my ground. The car skimmed by an inch from my thigh and halted. "*Bonjour*," I said, cheerily.

Gearbox in neutral, but treading on the pedal to make the revs roar, Khaled leant back and said something to the shadowed figures inside. The nearer one was Bogdan, and beside him, hazardously cradling a baby in her lap – why the fuck hadn't they thought of getting a proper bloody child seat? – was Clothilde. I indicated the Swan's gates, which I'd opened. "*Park through there.*"

Khaled zoomed backwards a few feet then swung the car across the pavement into the yard, without bothering to see whether anyone was crossing on foot. I sighed and followed them in, shutting the gates behind me. Maurice was pulling open the further passenger seat, whilst Bogdan was already climbing out of the car. He had a surly expression and had clearly had time to get suspicious again. "You not fuck with us, Bill. You know what I say."

"I know what you said." I was peering into the dark interior of the car. How many people were in there?

Khaled was still sat behind the steering wheel. He had his knife out and was cleaning his fingernails with it. Clothilde was embracing her brother. They kissed, but chastely, sibling to sibling.

Over Maurice's big arms Clothilde smiled shyly at me. In a cloth sling she had her daughter. "*Salut,*" I said. "*How's it going? What's the little one called?*"

"*Florence.*" Maurice was clucking at the little girl, lifting the shawl off Clothilde so that he could carry Florence around proudly. Bogdan was scowling. I'd forgotten that he was the father. Was he jealous?

I looked at him. "Where's Laure?"

He snorted. "You fuck, you don't know fuck."

"What?" All I did understand was that *he* wasn't keeping to the deal. I looked at Clothilde. "*Laure? Where the fuck is she*?"

Clothilde's expression clouded. "*Bill, you know... You've got to...*"

Maurice interrupted. "*It's alright. I'll explain later. Sort everything with Bogdan first. Don't worry about Laure at the moment.*"

I hesitated, and then indicated the gates to Maurice, with a nod of my head. Still clucking and fussing, he ushered Clothilde and the babe out and round the corner. "Where fuck Mitch?" demanded Bogdan.

"He's gone to get Zurab. They'll be back in a minute."

"I don't like Georgians," muttered Bogdan, yet again. He wasn't going to let it go. "*Vory... Voleurs...* Bandits. Put you knife in back."

By now Khaled was out of the car and grinning malevolently at me across the roof. "*Nique ta mère.*"

"*And yours.*" I shouldn't stoop to his level. "This way." I led him and Khaled into the band room, where the lights on the bar had been switched on. Bogdan looked around suspiciously. I pointed to the door leading to the main part of the pub. We could hear snatches of conversation and laughter. "That door's locked and bolted. You can talk to Zurab – hey, you can rap in Russian – and you won't be disturbed. If you want a drink, help yourself."

"English beer warm piss."

"Whatever. Mitch's got lager, if you can bear it. Right, have you got the passports?"

Bogdan had a padded envelope in his hands. "You give me two

thousand euros still."

Sighing inaudibly, I reached into my jacket once more and brought out a bundle of notes. After our *rendez-vous* yesterday I had gone to the bank. I was already up to my overdraft limit, what with taking the money out for the non-existent gigs, and I didn't dare withdraw the cash from the joint account. Petra might not notice my clearing out the building society for a while but she'd sure as fuck spot something when her card wouldn't go through at Harvey Nick's. I'd asked to see the bank manager and they had ushered me into one of those little glass-sided booths like the rooms in films in which they interview psychopathic murderers strapped to boards. I had managed to negotiate a loan for some new music equipment.

As he had done in the Broadmarsh cinema bar Bogdan pocketed the money, once again without counting it. He trusted me now, it seemed. He passed over the envelope and I slid three green hardback passports out. Three? I opened up the first. There was Clothilde's picture, but she was now called Corinne Gbana. On the first page of the passport was a stamp allowing her indefinite leave to remain in the U of K. The second had one of Maurice's scary pop-eyed mugshots, in the name of Richard Gbana, same stamp, and the third passport pic was of a scrunched up munchkin – Florence Gbana, aged two months, and again the same stamp. "Where's the other one?" I asked. "There should be four. Laure as well."

Bogdan was grinning malevolently at me. "Three passport. Three people. That what you get." Khaled was prowling around like a caged beast. He poked the little skeins of wired-up lights on the bar with his knife.

I didn't want to arouse his suspicions, and risk his, and Khaled's leaving, upsetting my plans, but it would have been implausible for me not to get riled. "Fuck you, Bogdan," I said, with controlled anger, "You haven't kept your side of the deal. No Laure, now no fucking passport. You owe me two and a half thousand euros."

Bogdan snarled: "Fuck you, Billy, I said you stupid, then I say not, now I know you stupid."

I half heard, half saw Khaled come over from the bar and stand behind me. "Okay. Okay." I slipped the three passports back into the bag. "I'll get Zurab. I'll be back in a minute." I stood up and managed to get to the door, keeping my eyes on both of them. Khaled made a lunge as I went past him and I flinched. They both laughed, but I got to the door, already pulling Mitch's key from my pocket, and out into the yard. I shut the door as casually as I could, as if I were merely closing it to keep them private and then, my hands shaking like flags in a gale, despite Baggins' pharma, I stuck the key in the lock and turned it. I secreted the key behind a couple of bricks next to the doorway.

I got out my phone and texted, then hurried down Coatstall High Street to the White Snake pub. Mitch was stood at the bar, Guinness in hand, gawping at an Israeli act called *Oy Ve Zed*, four guys dressed in Hassidic hats and coats who had translated Zed's lyrics into Yiddish and played his tracks with wailing klezmer clarinet. Maurice and Clothilde, with the baby asleep in her sling, were sat at a table by the window. I smiled across to them. What the fuck they made of these four *nebbishes* I had no idea. There couldn't be much *shtetl* culture in Congo. Maurice kept patting Florence on the stomach, almost as if to reassure himself that she was there, and okay. It was weird – he had not even been bothered about Laure, only mentioning her to me to tell me not to be bothered either. I got myself a fruit juice and, back turned, downed another two pills. Now I only had two left, but maybe I just needed to get through the next couple of days and I wouldn't need them any more. When the Lubavitchers had got off stage for a break I handed Maurice and Clothilde their new identities.

Maurice scowled at his passport details. "*What kind of fuck name is this?*"

"*Yours from now on.*" A bit of gratitude would have been nice.

Clothilde seemed happy enough though. She was looking at her and Florence's docs, and nodding and smiling. She took my hand and squeezed it. "*Thanks, Bill. You're an angel.*"

I was just wondering about how I was going to explain that I didn't have the passport for Laure when my phone beeped. **i hav my ideal zed bed band i am naked zee is w8ing 4 u** I nudged Mitch. "When you're ready." Whatever the fuck was going on about Laure, it would have to wait. He slowly finished his pint, and he and I walked back up to the Swan, swimming against the current of the crowds. Part of me was desperate to get there, get the business over and done with, and part of me never wanted to arrive. We let ourselves in through the back gates. In the yard I could hear music coming from within the band room. The keys were back behind the brick. I opened the door and the blast of sound made me recoil, as if I had been punched. It was "*Drop Dead Blues*", being played at full volume. Mitch grabbed my arm in the din.

There, on stage, was the Zed Beddington band, or rather, some ghastly parody of the classic threesome. The music was thudding out of the PA system. Behind the drumkit, propped up as Otto had been at the rehearsal rooms, against the wall, was Khaled. But his head was cocked at us at an impossible angle. In his already darkening hands were sticks. In front of him stood the dummy that I had last seen outside Armand's, still dressed in its pork pie hat and mohair suit, the shades and the golden cardboard guitar in its hands. Now I understood *nbl*'s comments about being with Zed. And Bogdan…

Bogdan… I had seen mediaeval woodcuts of mass executions, and photos, from the war, in books, documentary films of people hanging by their necks from gallows, but never had I thought that I would see such a thing before me. Bogdan was hanging, his toes pointed down, the noose around his neck tied to a large hook in the ceiling. His body turned slowly, the rope creaking, and the tongue sticking out of his livid face mocked our revulsion. His hands were tied together with a guitar string and wedged into his arms was the old bass guitar which Mitch had dug out. There was a large dark patch on the front of Bogdan's trousers – urine was still dripping off his shoes and soaking away in another patch on the wooden floor. Lying a few feet away was a kicked over beer keg. As his face spun slowly round away from us I ran over to the bar and switched the music off. The silence stunned me.

I stood in front of Bogdan's twisting body. There was something particularly horrible about the way that it turned before me, showing every facet of its deadness to the world. Khaled's corpse at least had the dignity of the wall's support, but Bogdan's was fully exposed in the incontinence of death. Bogdan had been a conscienceless psychopath, worse than Otto, worse than Zed, even, but I could not help feeling a twinge of pity for him.

Mitch was standing in the doorway, leaning against the frame. “My God,” he muttered, “My God.”

“Get inside,” I said, impatiently. “We can’t have anyone seeing.” He shivered, and shook his head. But he had been fucking me about ever since we’d first gone to Brussels, and everything that had happened since had been because of his scheming with Otto. He could damn well show some backbone now. I stepped back and grabbed a fold of his shirt. “Fucking get in.” I could hear now the hubbub of voices from the bar on the other side of the inner door. Had they not wondered why there had been all that noise from the band-room? No – it was a bit like my having worried about anyone hearing Maurice playing the drums at the practice rooms – the folk next door would have just assumed it was soundchecking or something.

I pulled Mitch into the band room and locked the outer door. Bogdan and Khaled had left their coats on the stools by the bar – there were two half drunk bottles of lager standing on the counter. Mitch sat on one of the barstools, rubbing his face and pulling straightaway at the abandoned bottles, filling himself with Dutch courage. He was so desperate for a drink that he didn’t mind taking a bottle whose last owner was hanging before our eyes. Meanwhile I went into the Gents’, with the bag of old clothes and boots which I had brought with me. I changed and came out. Mitch was still huddled at the bar, but when I appeared he slowly got off the stool, picked up his own bag of old clothes and went to change himself.

With my gardening gloves on I dragged Khaled’s body off the kit and tugged it over to the cellar door. His flesh was still warm, and his staring eyes were red, where the blood vessels had burst in his death agony, and nearly starting out of their sockets. His lips were blue, and his face was beginning to blacken.

“Who the fuck did this?” asked Mitch, in a hoarse voice.

“The same person who killed Otto. Our greatest fan.”

Mitch was shaking his head, looking up at Bogdan’s dangling body. “What the fuck are you on about?”

I got out my penknife to cut the bonds round Khaled's wrists. "We have a very committed fanbase, Mitch." As I sawed away at the rope I explained briefly about my messages from *nbl*.

"Fuck me, Billy, you set this up?"

Otto had once told me that I was not a killer – well, he had been right. I hadn't had the balls to do it myself – instead I was ever the manager, delegating the dirty work to others. "I told you I'd sort it. Come on. Help me get that Ukrainian fucker down."

Reluctantly, Mitch steadied Bogdan's body whilst I dragged the keg up, stood on it and cut through the knot around the hook. As the last strands broke under its weight, Bogdan's body tumbled with a dull thud onto the concrete, the noose trailing the rope with the cut-open knot at the end.

Mitch stared down at the two bodies, lying crumpled side by side. "I never thought I'd say this, Billy, but you scare me."

"Survival," I said. "It was either them, or us. Me and Petra and Jimmy. And you. And Alison. Your kids maybe. And God knows who else. They wouldn't have stopped."

"And what about…You know?" He meant *nbl*.

"We had a deal," I said. "They sort Bogdan and co for us, I get the best Zed Bed band there is back together. That's me, you, Maurice and Tommo. And it means, Mitch, we have to keep playing together. Any of us quit, we wind up like this. Or worse." I thought of Plastic Andy, still alive but unable to ever play again.

"And who the fuck is it?"

"I don't know. I don't want to know." And that was true. I could have waited, lurking somewhere near the Grey Swan, waiting to see who it was who had come, who it was who had let themselves into the back yard, who it was who had taken the keys out from behind the brick, who it was who had unlocked the door and gone into the bandroom, but the whole point was not to have known, not to have seen. We had had a deal, *nbl* and I.

Mitch had sat himself down on the keg. He kept wringing his hands in a nervous gesture. He looked old, his jowls sagging. "Get up," I said. "We haven't got all day." I took hold of Khaled's hands and started to drag the body to the cellar door. The head caught against the raised lip of the step and I had to prod it up with my foot. Mitch hadn't stood up. "For fuck's sake," I muttered. "Bring the other one. You brought your gloves, didn't you?"

But Mitch couldn't do anything. He sat wheezing and gasping on the keg. I switched on the lights and dragged Khaled's body down the steps to the upper cellar, where the pipes snaked into the barrels. I found the light switch for the lower level and heaved my load down the second steps, leaving it on the concrete floor.

When I got back up I realised that Mitch had been on his feet, because, although he was still sitting on the keg, he now had a pint of Guinness in his hand. He avoided my eyes when I reappeared. We didn't have time to argue, so I seized Bogdan's stiff hands and pulled him down below. Then, taking my gloves off, I got out my phone and dialled Mitch.

"What?" he answered.

"You come down, now. I'm not doing all this myself."

There was a pause, and then he muttered: "Okay."

A minute later, he appeared unsteadily at the foot of the stairs, another full pint in his hand. I put my gloves back on, grabbed a pick and, rather than opening up the grave where Otto and Danny lay, I attacked the concrete in the neighbouring alcove. After a minute Mitch came over and joined me, bringing his pick down heavily, and then pausing to catch his breath after each stroke. Once through, we dug the soil out with spades, piling it up to one side. Then we dragged over the first body, Bogdan. I pulled some rubber gloves out of my bag and went through Bogdan's pockets. I found his mobile phone, keys, some pounds and euros, a document, which looked like a driving licence, written in Cyrillic. "Your turn," I said to Mitch, peeling off the gloves, and proffering them to him.

"What?"

"I did him," I nodded at Bogdan's body. "You can do Dalek."

"Fuck off," said Mitch. "I can't do it. Sorry, Billy. I can't." He backed away towards the steps. Sighing, I rolled the gloves back on, and searched through the garments on Khaled's thin body. I found car keys, some more money, pounds and euros, a phone and his flick-knife. This last I tossed into the hole we'd dug. Then we strapped up the bodies with gaffer tape from the bag, and laid them to rest. Bogdan below and Khaled on top. We shovelled the broken concrete from the floor back first, to get rid of it, and then backfilled with as much of the earth as we could fit it, stamping it down to get rid of the extra volume, but even so we weren't going to fit it all in. "I'll get rid of it," said Mitch. "In the pub garden."

I rather hoped that he would, as I didn't want some bright spark coming down here, spotting a little pile of soil and putting two and two together. We went up to the upper cellar and filled buckets with water, then brought them down to mix up the concrete. The bags were already piled up to one side, with a shovel leant against them. I scooped bladefuls of the wet mixture onto the rubble in the hole, then Mitch screeded it off, nice and level. We moved some old barrels and junk to block the alcove whilst the concrete was drying off. I kept looking at the other new concrete floor, under which Danny and Otto lay. Did it look discoloured? There wasn't much I could do about it, anyway.

We went back up, switching off the lights. And when we got up to the bandroom there was the dummy, dressed in Zed's clothes, still standing on the stage. We had been so intent upon getting shot of the two corpses that we had forgotten about it. Without saying anything to Mitch I went up to it and took off the hat and sunglasses, removed the cardboard guitar, and stripped off the mohair suit. Mitch had headed straight for the bar shelf and got down a bottle of Jack Daniels, from which he had poured a huge slug, hands trembling.

I carried the dummy upstairs and stowed it in the big cupboard on the musty landing. I made a second trip for the clothes and guitar, and shut them all away. Then I went into the toilets, and awkwardly got down my last two pills by jamming my head into the basin and letting the stream of water into my mouth. I didn't want Mitch to have seen what I was doing. I washed my hands and face and changed back into my normal clothes, then texted *nbl.*

sorted

When I came out I seated myself on the other side of the bar. "Right Mitch. Give me an apple juice, and then we'll have our last little chat."

He lifted his bleary head. "What?"

"Let's just wrap things up, eh?"

“What do you mean?” He reached onto a shelf, and passed a bottle over to me.

I levered the top off with my penknife. “Laure. It was all bollocks, wasn’t it?”

Mitch lifted his glass of whiskey and poured what was left down his throat. “Aye. I tried to tell you before…” I recalled that the last time we had talked he had wanted to say that there was something else.

“Who sent that postcard? Was it you? Whose fucking idea was that?”

“Otto sent it. He got Dalek… What’s-his-fucking name to write it and then he put it in the post.”

“To make me feel sorry for Maurice? Poor sod lost his kid? That was the hook, get Billy Family Man to swallow that sob story?”

“Aye.”

“And the money, Maurice’s wonga, the wedge he tried to offer me in the café. Whose idea was that?”

“Otto’s as well,” said Mitch. “Bogdan lent it to Maurice. Otto bet Bogdan a hundred euros that that you wouldn’t take it. He was fucking killing himself when Maurice gave it back.”

“I bet he was. And Otto and you arranged with Maurice to turn up at the bar, all spontaneously like, and get on stage and play. I remember wondering at the time how he’d known where to plug the drum mike in and all that. What was that about?”

“We reckoned that you wouldn’t do it if he just came up to you on the street or summat. You had to feel that you already knew him. That’s what Otto said, anyway.”

I recalled how at the break on the first night in the *Mannekin Pis* Otto had even tried to get me to tell Maurice to get lost. That had been cunning. He’d used my vanity as well, that I’d been puffed-up by being the only one in the band who could speak French – what I’d picked up on summer grape-picking sessions, at any rate. I’d never seen Otto as psychologist before, and maybe I’d underestimated him. It had been a pretty plausible set-up. On the other hand, Otto hadn’t foreseen what would happen onstage. “It bounced back on Otto, though, didn’t it? Maurice blew him off.

Showed him up for the limited four four rock muso that he was."

"He wasn't made-up about that."

"I realised. But why, Mitch? What the fuck was all this elaborate scam for?"

"I didn't understand the ins and outs. Otto and Bogdan hatched it. All I know is, Maurice got himself mixed up in some corruption deal in Congo, some Chinese bigwig mine-owner got killed, and the firm wanted to pin it on Maurice."

"I knew that," I said. "But why all the fiction with Laure? Why did he want to come to England?"

Mitch shrugged. "The Chinkies knew he was in Brussels and were putting pressure on the Belgian authorities to send him back home to face trial. Or maybe even ship him straight off to Beijing for a bullet in the back of the neck. And Bogdan wanted shot of Clothilde, so why not kill two birds with one stone?"

I sat there nodding slowly, sipping at the juice. My mobile beeped. Petra. **Finished work coming out to coatstall with J remember I'm your biggest fan xx**

"We've got to go," I said. "We've got a gig to do."

***

"*A Tribute to Zed Beddington*" announced the banner over the stage. It was a warm night, and I could see heads, many of them wearing the now famous Zurab elasticated moustache, stretching back across Coatstall market place, caught by the spots on the lighting gantry. A row of security guards stood behind the crash barriers which kept the crowd fifteen feet from the stage, and at the back of the auditorium were ambulances, waiting to deal with the consequences of the inevitable fights and overconsumption. I stepped up to the mike. At the side of the stage Petra was holding Jimmy. It was not too noisy there, and he was grinning his toothy grin at me. Alison was there, as well, Mitch's estranged wife. She gave me a cool look. And Don Wankstaff was there too. He'd come up to me when I was ushering Zurab backstage, insisted on shaking hands with him, and then inveigled me into giving him a backstage pass. He gave me a thumbs up. I ignored him and flashed a quick smile at my wife and child before turning my attention back to the audience.

"Welcome to Zedstock!!!" I yelled, and my amplified voice went booming round the town. The crowd yelled and cheered. "Welcome to the fifth Zedstock Festival, the biggest and best ever, welcome to the main event, tonight, all the way from Gori, Georgia, Zuuurrrraaaab Tkupishvili!!!" I'd practised his name.

On the drums Maurice played a massive roll, I beat out a riff over and over again to build up the tension, Mitch strummed his guitar – I thought it was a bit out of tune – and, out from the side, where he had been waiting by Petra and Jimmy, stepped Zurab, holding his golden balalaika above his head as a trophy. The crowd roared. Zurab stepped over to his amp, one of the roadies dashed across, plugged the lead in and Zurab looked at me, nodded, and away we went, the strong timbre of the balalaika cutting over Mitch's guitar and my rhythm. The crowd started clapping along, Zurab sang his accented words into the mike, and we rolled through the first number. The fans bounced and leapt, yelling their approval. I hit the chords for "*Green Turtle Blues*" and we were off again. The audience was roiling like the sea in a storm, moustachioed fans perched on their mates' shoulders, waving T-shirts and banners with Zed's and Zurab's faces on it. We played the third song, the fourth, the fifth, each number greeted by a new ecstatic roar which outdid the one before. As we came to the end of the set the audience all started chanting "Zurab, Zed, Zurab, Zed…."

I gestured to Zurab and we retreated in a line off stage, where we listened as the chanting got louder and louder. Don clapped me on the shoulder, yelling into my ear: "Billy, I don't care how you got him in, that drummer is awesome!"

Petra had brought Jimmy up to me, and he held out his arms. I took him, and then, on an impulse, I carried him out onto the stage. The crowd boomed. I stepped up to the mike. Jimmy was grinning and squirming with excitement. "Thankyou, friends," I yelled into the mike. "Let me introduce the future of the blues…" I didn't know what the fuck I was doing, too high on adrenalin and happy pills and exhaustion and alcohol to wonder whether this was a good thing, but I held Jimmy aloft and said: "In twenty years' time little

Jimmy here will still be keeping Zed's music alive!!!" It was a message to *nbl* – who, I knew, but don't ask me how, was out there somewhere, watching the stage – leave us alone and the music will keep going. The crowd roared and roared, yelling "Jiiimmy! Jiiimmy!", and Jimmy kicked and wriggled in delight, punching a little fist into the air. I turned my head and indicated to the others to come back on. Petra came onstage as well – I thought for a moment that she was angry with me for taking the son and heir out there but again I couldn't foretell her reactions. She was beaming, taking Jimmy from me, and patting me on the shoulders.

Zurab strapped his balalaika back on, I picked up my bass, Mitch plugged himself in again, Maurice eased himself once more behind his drumkit, and we did six encores. They still didn't want us to leave but I and saw Petra, in the wings, pointing at Jimmy's arse. He needed changing – we needed to come off. "Goodnight!!" I yelled into my mike. "Let's hear it for Zurab!! Goodnight!! See you next year!!"

"Yeeeeeah!" echoed the crowd. "We want Bill! We want Zurab!! We want Zed!!! Zed!!! Zed!!! Zed...!!!"

As the chanting bounced around our ears we picked our way between vans and ambulances towards the back way to the Swan. I was holding Jimmy. "Dada fuuu… Nusi fuuu."

"Music. That's right. Daddy's music." I pressed him against me as we walked along, despite his squishy rear. Petra was escorting Zurab a couple of paces ahead, both talking in German. When we got to the Swan, Petra told me that Zurab had spent two years in East Berlin in the Red Army before Gorby had pulled the house down.

In the pub I took Jimmy off to the gents'. I couldn't lay him on the cold hard urine soaked floor tiles so I cleaned him up precariously in the sink whilst rummaging in the changing bag one-handed. I just left the soiled nappy in a plastic bag on the window-sill. If Mitch couldn't be bothered to provide proper baby-change facilities in this right-on day and age he'd just have to deal with the consequences.

I sat in the bar with Jimmy asleep on my lap whilst Petra and Zurab got on great guns. Under the floor, thirty feet down, under our feet were four bodies, I kept thinking. No-one but Mitch and me knew that they're there. What would Petra think if she knew? What would she do if she ever found out the truth? What if I told her, or blurted it out, or said something in my sleep which gave me away? I stroked Jimmy's curls with my fingers, the same fingers which had ferreted through Bogdan and Khaled's clothing a few hours before. I stopped touching Jimmy, suddenly feeling that I would contaminate him. A message buzzed my phone against my thigh.

i saw u with zurab u r the gr8est i am naked 4 u ☺ u r rite wot u sed on stage u can keep the music alive 4ever

I slipped the phone away. Petra hadn't noticed anything. She was too busy translating some enquiry for Zurab from a bloke in a Zed T-shirt and golden porkpie hat. Mitch had recovered enough to be capitalising on the crush in his pub and selling more beer in an evening than he normally shifted in a month. The fans were squeezing into the bar, queuing impatiently to get served, trying to catch Zurab's eye and giving him a salute of a raised pint when they did. Zurab was in blues heaven, knocking back bottle after bottle of lager from a store which successive fans felt themselves honoured to contribute to.

A hand clapped my shoulder. It was Joe Robotham, clutching a pint in one hand and his lady wife's waist in the other. "Geat gig" he yelled in my ear. "Still alive then? Not been on any parachute drops into Macedonia?"

"Ha ha. You can get rid of that paper if you want."

He nodded and grinned, although I wasn't sure whether he had actually heard me. The two of them got squeezed away from me in the melee. Then I saw Baggins and Malc – the latter, adorned with elasticated moustache, sidled up to me whilst I was getting another pint. He pressed something into my hand, muttering into my ear: "Present from Baggins. She's one of your biggest fans." When I had a chance to snatch a glance at it I saw that it was another packet of pills. Baggins winked at me across the room.

At last, at one o'clock, tearing ourselves away from the congratulations, and the entreaties to have Zurab back next year, and the prolonged leave-takings, we rolled home, Jimmy securely asleep in the child seat in the back, Petra, who had nobly restricted herself to fruit juice, at the wheel, me slumped in the passenger seat.

Petra reached down to change gear as we came out of the thirty zone of Coatstall onto the A-road. "You remember that woman?"

"Sorry?" I stirred myself out of my thoughts. I kept seeing Bogdan hanging before me. "Which woman?"

"The one we found at the motorway. Who had the baby?"

"Oh yeah. Her. Yeah." I tried to keep my voice level, but I knew what was coming. "Why did you think of her?"

"Your new drummer. I didn't speak to him, but you were talking French to him, weren't you? Just reminded me of her. Where did you find him? And what's happened to Otto?"

"Dickie? He's a friend of Mitch's, well, some friend of a friend. Mitch brought him in. He's good, isn't he?"

"Yes." I had warned Maurice beforehand that on no fucking account whatsoever were Clothilde or babe to be anywhere in sight in Coatstall, and they had been accordingly confined in purdah upstairs at the Swan for the duration. As little as Petra had suspected that whereas Bogdan *et al* were thirty feet underneath her, the woman whom she had helped, and her child – whose father's death, I suddenly realised with a shudder, as I hadn't seen it in those terms before, I had plotted to bring about – had been twelve feet over her head when she'd been rapping with Zurab. Nevertheless, Petra was not to be diverted "And Otto? Where's he?"

"No idea," I said. "All I know is that he and Mitch had some big row, and that he's stormed off. Mitch hasn't seen him. Nobody has."

"Oh. That's funny," she went on, "Because I thought I saw the van, you know, your van, the band one parked up the other day. Couple of streets away. And I thought that was odd, because Otto had taken the keys."

"Really? What were you doing round there?" My tone was too sharp.

"Round where? You mean by the van?" She sounded put out at my reaction to her casual question.

"Sorry," I said hastily. "I just meant, where did you see it?"

Petra turned a corner and the concentration seemed to take the asperity out of her voice. "I was just going round to see Val. From the NCT group. Just thought I walked past it."

"I dunno. There's hundreds of Trannies like that." Jumping Jehosephat, I was skimming the bloody waves here, having to make up one lie after another. "Like I say, he had a barney with Mitch and fucked off. Least ways, that's what Mitch said."

Petra smiled. "Well, that new guy's good. There's your new direction. You could do something jazzy with him and Zurab. Having that balalaika's fresh, it's interesting. Keep what's his name, Dickie, and get rid of Otto, when he turns up again. I always thought he was creepy. Do you remember how he came round that night after we got back from Brussels?"

How the fuck could I forget that, darling? I thought. "Yep. No, you're right. Dickie's ace."

"And dump Mitch, too," Petra went on, as tenacious as ever. "No more Zed Beddington greatest hits. The Bill Silverthwaite Experience." She giggled, coquettishly, yet another trait I'd never seen in her before. "I like the idea of that. Your band. You can be the man, Bill, and I can be one of your rock chicks."

I didn't like to disappoint her, but I could imagine a text from *nbl* reacting to *that* little idea. A text at best, and a direct and deadly intervention at worst. "Jazz bands don't have rock chicks. And anyway, I don't think that Zurab could stay, even if he wanted to. He'd need residence docs and all that. Georgia's not in the EU."

"He doesn't have family, he told me. No kids. No wife. He doesn't need to go back. All those guys I was translating for were all saying the same thing – that he should stay and play with you. If he could get a work permit or whatever it is you need, you three could do something really special."

"Maybe." We had parked outside our house. I carried the snoozing Jimmy upstairs to bed, and got my axe out of the car (all the rest of the gear was being roadied back to the Swan for me). Petra had already gone up but I was too *agitato* to relax straight off. "I'll be up in a minute," I called. I heard her say something indistinct, and then the shower running. I put the kettle on and fired up the laptop.

<u>*whitecliffs, bluesfiend666, beermonster37 and harpmouth* are in the room</u>
whitecliffs: just come from bakstage with bill and the rest wot a fantastic gig
harpmouth: gr8 2 c bill bak
bluesfiend666: i thouhgt mitch woz a bit crap
harpmouth: a bit crap? his gitar woz way out of tune
bluesfiend666: btw ware woz otto? they hav new drummer
beermonster 37: yeah drummer is bloke from hospital
harpmouth: wot the 1 u woz talkin about?
beermonster37: yeah he dissapeared a few day's ago and they woz lookin 4 him
harpmouth: who woz?
beermonster37: police cos thay think hes ilegal imigrunt i reckon bill smugled him in

Perdition on a penny-farthing, I thought. What am I going to have to do next? I logged in

<u>*wurzelman* is in the room</u>
wurzelman: I thought Bill said on stage tonight that the drummer was from Ivory Coast. He said that he'd been in England for years
bluesfiend666: fuk off wurzelwanka u r not tru blu'sfan u werent in the audien's @ coatstall i bet
whitecliffs: i don't rememmber bill sayin anything like that
bluesfiend666: neether do i
beermonster37: im shore its same bloke
whitecliffs: wen me and bill were chatting in calais it woz just his wife and kid in the van

nakedblueslady is in the room

nakedblueslady: i was naked @ zeestok 4 bill i dont think u shoud say enithing as long as bill is bak in band

harpmouth: i dont think u shood say enithing eether he is fantastik drummer way better than otto

wurzelman: I think he is far better, too, actually. Far, far better.

bluesfiend666: fuk off wurzelman u hav serious problem's

beermonster37: nakedblueslady is bloke but 4 ounce i agree with him

nakedblueslady: u mean agree with her ☺

bluesfiend666: fuk off u r man i didnt c no naked lady @ zeestok 2nite

nakedblueslady: i woz not naked 4 u but 4 bill

beermonster37: no i wont say anything dont want 2 fuk up gr8 lineup but i tell u sumthing bill woz in the hospital day b4 drummer guy went awol

harpmouth: wot u think he got drummer out?

beermonster37: i dont kno he woz walking along coridor looking v smart i didnt recoknise him til afterwurd's but maybe he did

harpmouth: if he did it woz 4 the blue's we shoud thank him

wurzelman: He might just have been there to see his wife. You said that she works there

harpmouth: fuk off wurzelman bill did it 4 the blue's he is our hero

bluesfiend666: cheer's bill

beermonster37: wurd in kings is that doc cridland her boss is kene on bills wife

whitecliffs: he is our hero we shoud all keep shtumm

Thank fuck for that, I thought. My whole life was hanging on what these losers decided to do.

nakedblueslady: i am naked 4 bill

harpmouth: eniway that russhan gitarrist bloke is hot as well

wurzelman: He is Georgian, not Russian, and that was a balaika, not a guitar but you are right he was excellent. And the new drummer is far better than Otto ever was.

bluesfiend666: fuk off wurzel u think u r way clevrer than rest of us u r sutch a prit... pretendingshus...

wurzelman: Do you mean pretentious?

bluesfiend66: wurzelman u r a tossa ☹ they shoud hav zurrub in band instead of mitch he is rubish drunkan fuker

Damn and blast. The last thing I needed was for the fans to be turning on Mitch just as I'd got it all sorted.

wurzelman: I thought Mitch was quite good, actually. I thought his playing had improved somewhat.

bluesfiend666: oh lah de fukin dah, hes improved, ectually ☺ u r such a wanka wurzel mitch need's to go

harpmouth: rite on get rid of mitch and bring in zurrub

whitecliffs: i woz torking 2 bill after gig thats wot bill sed 2 me thay were going 2 do

I couldn't face any more from these arses. I would show them – I'd sort the band and I'd show my wife who was her man. I switched off and, my hormones up after that fabbo gig, went upstairs in time to catch Petra just coming out of the shower.

Eleventh Bar

Home Chord of A

I was woken by my mobile. I reached out for it sleepily, trying not to disturb Petra. “Hello?”

“Bill?” It was Mitch.

“Yeah. What do you want?” I looked at the bedside clock. “It’s twenty past seven. Had a fucking late night last night.”

“Zurab’s dead.”

“What?” I realised my voice was too loud. Petra stirred but didn’t wake. I cupped my hand around my mouth. “What the fuck do you mean?”

“He’s dead. I just found him… I… I heard a noise, and I came out of my room, and there he was, at the foot of the stairs. He’s dead.”

“An accident?”

“I don’t fucking know, Billy.” Mitch was silent for a moment. Then he added: “I didn’t hear anyone else. I don’t know how anyone could have got in.”

“Haven’t you rung the police, or an ambulance or something?”

“No. I thought… I dunno.”

“You thought, whoever…?” I didn’t want to be more explicit on the phone.

“Summat like that.” Mitch knew what I was getting at.

I got out of bed and padded out onto the landing, shutting the bedroom door behind me. “I have no idea what’s happened, Mitch, but you, or we, we can't just bury the fucker out of sight. The authorities would think he was trying to stay here illegally. They know he's in the country, and they'd come looking for him, not to mention that folk back in Georgia might start asking questions."

"So what do we do?"

"For fuck's sake Mitch, you ring for an ambulance. Tell them the truth, that you heard a noise, came out, and there he was. They'll just see it as the accident it was. Presumably they'll contact the embassy or something. If it's all innocent, why would you wait?"

"Okay."

"Ring me when they're there."

I flipped my phone off and had a quick look in on Jimmy. He was fine, lying splayed out on his back, his little chest going up and down. I went downstairs and put the kettle on, and switched on the portable telly on top of the microwave. There was nothing on the news bulletins, but Mitch would only just have called 999. I took one of the pills Malc had given me last night with the tea, then texted. **How many more innocent people have to die?**

A minute later I had a reply. **who is innosent?**

nbl was as morally evasive as Maurice had been. **Zurab was. He was just a musician like Arthur McMurray. You killed them both. What did they do wrong?**

i didnt kill arther

I recalled AM of the AM6 collapsing at the keyboard before my eyes. **What do you mean? I saw him die**

i didn't kill arther he had hart attack ☺ nuthing 2 do with me

I nodded slowly to myself. It made sense. How could *nbl* have made sure that someone was going to pop off in such spectacular and public fashion at just the right moment, short of shooting them with a silenced rifle from the gods? Old Arthur Mc hadn't exactly been the picture of health that night. Of course, I was looking to see musoes being bumped off, after Matty and Plastic Andy, and I'd thought I'd seen something that wasn't there.

I texted again. **What about Zurab?**

he woz big drug deeler What the fuck was *nbl* on about?

No he wasn't he was just a musician

bogdan told me b4 he died all about wot zurab woz up 2 ☺ zurab desserved 2 die 2 i am naked

Fucking hell. The shakes were back in my hands as I picked up my tea. That was on my conscience, the story I had concocted. Lord help me. The rest of them had all had it coming, maybe even Plastic Andy for being such a wanker, but not Zurab.

My phone pinged again. **anyway u wanted 2 hav zurab in the band insted of mitch 4 good i didn't want him**

I had been thinking that, but I hadn't told anyone. Of course *bluesfiend* and all the rest of the crew had been rooting for Zurab, and in fact I'd encouraged that line in the chatroom with my comments about how good Zurab had been, and presumably *nbl* thought we might go along with it.

This has got to stop

i want the best zb band there can b

Why did you stop Jasmine's messages to me?

i am naked 4 u she isnt

Fuck me, *nbl* was jealous and possessive. I sipped at my tea. My phone rang. I was so unnerved that I knocked it onto the floor with my hand and had to get down and scrabble about for it between the chair legs. "Hello? Who's this?"

It was Mitch again. "The police are here," he said, curtly. "You need to get over."

"Okay. Don't say more than you need to. Wait." Something occurred to me. "They might ask about Otto. Where he is. If they do, just say that you, we, you had an argument with him and that he quit. We don't know where he is. We need to get our story straight. You got that? Just say yes or no." The police might be listening to him talking.

Mitch had understood. "Yes. You need to get over. I don't know how to deal with it." Mitch as needy fucker was a new one as well. Maybe that's why Alison had left, not because of the drinking.

"I'll be over as soon as I can. Just keep your trap shut as much as possible." I rang off, tiptoed hastily upstairs and threw on the smelly clothes from last night's gig. Petra muttered something and turned over. I looked in on Jimmy. All well still. He was snoring away minaturely

Downstairs I left a quick scribbled note: "*Problem with clearing up from last night, got to pop to festival site, will ring, love B x*" I had to take Petra's car, otherwise she would have wondered how I had got out to Coatstall, and not the van, which of course was parked up where Petra had spotted it the other day. I needed to move that *asap*, otherwise if she did see it again and started examining it, writing down the registration *etcetera etcetera*, I'd be in big trouble. I searched around for her car keys – they were not in the drawer, and I had to sneak back upstairs into our bedroom and furtively go through Petra's cast-off clothing. Not there. She shifted in the bed, and opened one eye for a moment, before going back to sleep. I tried in her bag, which was looped over the headboard, but I couldn't find them, and Petra began to move again. I crept back downstairs and let myself out into the garden, and from underneath a pile of old newspapers in the shed retrieved the Transit keys. It was another risk, taking the van, but one I was going to have to take. I walked swiftly round to where it was parked up. At least I could leave it somewhere further afield when I got back so that Petra would be unlikely to see it again.

As carefully and calmly as I could I hit the familiar road leading over the M1 into Derbyshire. As I rolled into Coatstall, after the ruckus of the last week, the place seemed as if it had been hit by a neutron bomb. No people, but half-empty plastic glasses of beer parked on window ledges, half torn-down posters still hanging by one corner and flapping in the wind, lonely trails of snapped bunting dangling. Then I did see a few survivors as I got further into the town, a handful of folk dying of radiation sickness on corners of the market square as I drove past. The skeleton of the stage was still there, abandoned, bare of kit.

Outside the Grey Swan an ambulance was drawn up, and a policeman was guarding the door. I parked a discreet distance up the road and went back down to the pub. Having explained to the copper on the door who I was, he ushered me into the front bar. Maurice was sat on a stool, his face grey, whilst through the open living quarters door I could see Zurab's body on the hallway. Someone with their back to me seemed to be carrying out some kind of medical examination. A bloke with close cropped red hair and dressed in a polyester suit was sitting at the bar next to Mitch, drinking an orange juice. When he saw me he got up.

"Mr Silverthwaite?"

"That's right."

"Detective Inspector Leadbetter." He shook my hand, vigorously. "I understand that you ran the festival?"

"I did some of it. I booked Zurab." I gestured to the form on the floor.

The detective looked sharply at me. "You know about this then?"

"Of course. Mitch…" I gestured at Mitch. "He rang me."

"And why did he do that, sir?"

"Because, like I said, I book the acts. I got this guy to come over from Georgia, of course I need to know."

Leadbetter wrote something down. "You were here last night?"

"Of course. I was playing, with… With Zurab, and Mitch."

"I know," said Leadbetter. "I was here myself last night. I came out to see you. Great show."

"Thanks," I said. My mouth was dry. I wanted to ask Mitch for a drink, but I wasn't sure that that would be a good idea.

"Yes," went on the detective. "I was always a big fan of Zed's. I saw him lots of times, Nottingham, other places. And I saw you at that festival in York just before he died. Real shame that. Neck broken by a falling amp. Musical tragedy, as well as a human one." He looked straight at me, and I recalled what Joe Robotham had said "…Something odd about Zed's death…" What the fuck did this copper think he knew?

"It was a tragedy," I said, "But we kept the music going. So many fans wanted us to."

"They did. If it'd been me, I'd have done anything to keep the band going. Still, you've had a few changes of personnel, haven't you?"

I nodded. God, I needed a drink. Coffee. Black coffee with a bit of sugar.

"You had a good line-up last night," said Leadbetter. "Your drummer was bloody fantastic, as well. I didn't know him. What happened to… Erm… Whatsisname, the guy who'd been playing for years?"

Surely he knew the name? He was testing me. "Otto. Otto Anderson?"

"That's right."

"He cleared off," I said. I raised my voice a tad, so that Mitch, who was gazing miserably over at us, would be certain to hear. "He went off. Had some kind of row with you, didn't he, Mitch?"

Mitch nodded. Leadbetter was looking thoughtfully at him. "Anyway, the drummer chap?"

"He's from Côte D'Ivoire. Got permission to be here and all that. Refugee. Richard something or other. I can never remember his surname."

"Richard something or other, refugee," echoed Leadbetter slowly. He jotted something else down. "And where is he now?"

"I'm not sure." I looked across at Mitch, who raised his eyebrows, indicating the floor above.

Leadbetter saw this. "He's staying here as well, is he?"

"Yeah," I said. Holy fucking cowpoo, I suddenly realised what a trap we'd fallen into. I knew it had been *nbl* who pushed Zurab down the stairs but this copper was going to think it was Maurice. Judging by Mitch's expression he'd realised much the same thing. I couldn't believe that Leadbetter was smart enough to ever suss out who had really killed Zurab, but he was too tenacious to not find that Richard Lumuwu was not what he claimed to be. "He doesn't speak much English. You'd need an interpreter, if you want to talk to him. Unless you'd like me to do it..." I trailed off. I was saying too much.

"Okay,we'll see." said Leadbetter. "Tell me about Mr..." He spelt out the name from his black ringbinder. "Tuu...kuupishvili... How did you get him to play here?"

"It was all the fans, emailing me, or telling me at gigs about this video online, this bloke from Georgia, doing Zed songs. It went viral, everyone was asking when he was going to play at Zedstock, so I got hold of his manager in Tbilisi and booked him."

"Had Mr... Had the Georgian gentleman been drinking last night?"

"A lot," I said. "He was pretty paralytic by the time we left... The fans kept buying him drinks..." Anything to help along the impression that it was no more than a drunken accident.

Just as I was finishing my account the man with his back to me stood up and turned round. Erebus on an aeroplane, it was Doc Cridland, yet again. This time we could acknowledge each other. “Bill,” he said, his voice dropping in a leisurely fashion in tone on the single syllable of my name, as he grinned his shark grin, greeting me like a long-lost brother, pumping my hand. “I thought I recognise your dulcet tones.” He saw my puzzled expression. “I happened to be on duty, police surgeon. How’s Petra?”

“Fine,” I said. “She was out here last night, with our lad, but she was asleep when I left. She doesn’t know anything about this.”

“So I’d imagine. Quite a do last night, from all accounts. Not that I was here of course, not exactly my thing, you, know, *amplified* music...”

Leadbetter broke into the pleasantries. “You two know each other?”

Cridland grinned even more. “My dear Inspector, Bill Silverthwaite, as well as being a fine musician, is married to my ablest staff member, Dr van Rensburg, and I can vouch for his unimpeachable character.” Leadbetter looked sceptical, as well he might – he hadn’t actually starting impugning me yet, and Doc Cridland was being a bit previous. On purpose maybe? Fuck knew. Of course, he was probably still worried about my having spotted him at that dodgy Miss Nottinghamshire night, where poor old Arthur Mc had passed on. “Anyway, Inspector,” Cridland went on, “I’ve examined the body. Broken neck. As far as I can see, it was an accident, pure and simple. He had his shoes on, but not done up. I’ll test the blood alcohol level but I could smell it on the body. He must have got up to go to the toilet, tripped on his laces in an unfamiliar environment and fallen down the stairs. All the medical evidence, all the injuries point to that.”

Leadbetter snapped his notebook shut. Was there a trace of dissatisfaction there? “Okay, doc. Thank you Mr Silverthwaite. I think that’s enough.”

I wasn’t sure whether he still wanted to interview Maurice, but kept *shtumm*. Zurab’s body was wheeled out, Leadbetter and Doc Cridders following. “Will you be notifying the embassy?” I asked.

"I don't quite know whether I need to contact his family or whatever."

Leadbetter, whose smile was as foxy as Doc Cridders' was sharky, said: "We've already contacted the consulate in Leeds. Their man's coming down to take charge of the body and the repatriation. You needn't worry." He looked at me as if he knew damn' well that I had plenty to worry about. "Ivorian drummers, Georgian guitarists." He was no bloody fool, knowing the correct adjective for Cote d'Ivoire, and letting me know that he knew. "You wouldn't expect sleepy old Coatstall to be quite so cosmopolitan, would you?"

"No, you wouldn't," I said.

Out of Leadbetter's line of sight, Doc Cridland winked at me. "If you don't need me, I'll be getting back to do the full autopsy."

Leadbetter nodded. "Of course, doc. Thankyou."

"William. Give my regards to Petra." Doc Cridland shook my hand again. His nails dug into my palm. He was warning me.

Leadbetter smiled at me, his eyes as stony as a basilisk. "I want to show you something else, Mr Silverthwaite." He pulled a key out of his pocket and went over to the door which led through to the bandroom. Lordy, it was less than twenty four hours ago that Mitch and I had discovered the Dead Zed Band in here. We'd cleared everything up, well, at least I had, with Mitch slumped uselessly back at the bar with his drink, much as he was now, too strung out after burying the bodies to be able to do anything. I'd cleared the kit to the side of the stage, and got rid of the rope, and checked the floor and the tables minutely for anything overlooked. Leadbetter went through, and I followed him. "Yes?" I said, as innocently as I could. "What is it that…"

My voice trailed off. Standing in the middle of the stage, dressed in his porkpie hat, sunglasses and mohair suit, the cardboard Ida May in his immobile arms, a microphone on a stand poised before him, stood the dummy – the dummy I had stripped and carried upstairs the afternoon before.

Leadbetter was watching my reaction. "Interesting, don't you think?"

I laughed, casually, desperately trying to hold my nerve. "Yeah, forgotten about that. A bit of a joke. He... It was put up for gig a year or so back, and we've just left it on stage, ever since." I was desperately trying to see whether there was anything else out – had *nbl* managed to find Bogdan and Khaled's coats, which we'd realised we'd forgotten to put in the grave down below, and I had later taken upstairs? I couldn't see them.

But had I overlooked anything else? Could Leadbetter, with all his experience, see, detect, somehow perceive by some instinctive process what had happened here yesterday? Was there a stink, or an aura of death that his trained senses could pick up? Leadbetter's eyes came back to me, glittering with calculation. "Maybe not in the best of taste? I'll bid you good morning, gentlemen." He gestured to the constable to follow him and went out.

In the main bar Mitch drained his pint and drew off another. Without asking him I fetched out a couple of bottles of apple juice, opened them with my penknife and drained them one after another. The raging thirst was slaked for the moment. There was a coffee percolator on the shelves but it was empty. My phone said that it was half-past nine.

Mitch turned a bleary eye towards me. "That fucking rozzer's onto us."

"He's not. What does he know? The doc says it was an accident, and any shit about Zed's years ago. He can't prove tiddly squat." I was amazed at how calm I felt. The pills, I supposed. It was lucky that Baggins had given me those extras. "Anyway, if he had thought there was anything up, he'd have insisted on interviewing Maurice."

Mitch shrugged. I wanted out of there, away from him and this horrible, sterile place, back to my wife and child. "I'm off. Just don't say jack if that guy does come back." Out on the main road the ambulance was gone, but the police car was still there, the constable sat at the wheel. He nodded at me as I walked past to the van. I'd parked it the wrong way, the driver's door by the pavement. I was just about to climb in when a voice said: "Bill. The fans all call you Bill, so I suppose I can."

It was Leadbetter, leaning against the back of the van, looking round to the front. I pulled the key out of the lock. "If you want."

He strolled down to the cab, running his hand, along the metal panelling. He pointed down. "You need to get that tyre changed. That tread's illegal."

"I will. Thanks."

"Good thing that that's the only illegal thing I've spotted, eh?"

I smiled. "Superintendent, I may be a dissolute musician, but I'm still a law-abiding citizen."

"It's Inspector, but no matter. You know, I'm one of your biggest fans. I first saw Zed in, I don't know, seventy two, when he was still unknown. At the Swan. One of his first gigs, when he was still playing with Mitch. Must have been a bit tough on Mitch, actually, when Zed got famous and he got left behind, just the landlord of a miners' pub."

"He's reconciled to it."

"I guess so." Leadbetter scratched his neck for a moment. "You know, my dad was a miner too. We had a lot of problems during the strike. I'd just joined the force and he... Well, he used to drink there when I was a kid." He jerked his head down to where the pub sign hung over the pavement. He patted the side of the van. "And this is the very vehicle which the great Zed Beddington used to travel about in."

"Not this one. We got a new one after the crash, when Zed..."

Leadbetter smiled. "Yeah. That's right. Zed's neck broken by a falling amplifier. And Zurab, his neck broken fallen downstairs. Odd that, the way they both went."

"You could say that it was odd that they both had names beginning with the letter "z"."

"You could, but then Zed's name was really Brian. You know that of course. Funny how things are often not what they seem." He raised an eyebrow, still smiling, as if he expected a comment from me on his *aperçu*.

I put the key back into the lock. "Inspector, I have a wife and child at home. I need to get back to them."

"I know you do," said Leadbetter. "Must be hard, playing gigs everywhere and keeping a family life going. Police life's tough on marriage, too. A lot of divorces."

"It's not easy. But I love the music."

"So do I," said Leadbetter. "I play the harp, you know." He reached into a pocket, pulled out a harmonica, and, to my astonishment, put it to his mouth and played a plangent riff.

I laughed. "You want to audition?"

"You recruiting again, now that Zurab's dead?"

"No." I thought about what *nbl* had texted. "He was just playing at the festival, not becoming a permanent member."

"Permanent member, eh? Too many people who play with you seem to get into trouble." He put the mouth-organ away. "Zed dies in the van, Zurab falls downstairs, Matthew Barker falls out of a window, Otto disappears. And what happened to that other guitarist of yours? He vanished as well, didn't he?"

"Danny McPhee?"

"That's the one. Brilliant musician."

"Some might say. I don't know," I said. "He just upped sticks and left. Never heard from him again."

"Another one who went down to the crossroads at midnight, eh? You, know, I love the blues, and you guys are best blues outfit in England. Lot of folk think that, and they wouldn't want to look too hard into anything that might stop the music."

"I'm glad to hear it." I opened the door a fraction. Whatever he was getting at, it was making me uneasy.

"No, Bill. I love the blues. And do you know why?"

"Tell me."

"Because it's music reduced to its essence. There's no frills. It's stripped, down, pared away. Naked. That's why it never dies. Get that tyre fixed by tomorrow." He banged on the side of the van, walked past me, winked, and carried on to the squad car which was waiting outside the Grey Swan.

I drove back to Nottingham, left the van on a surburban avenue in Wilsthorpe, and caught a taxi home. Petra never asked me how I'd got out to Coatstall.

Twelfth Bar

Home Chord of A

beermonster37, harpmouth, and *bluesfiend666* are in the room

beermonster37: eni1 hurd about that crash after zeestok?

harpmouth: wot u on about?

beermonster37: u c that reely crap tribyute band on @ the blak horse?

harpmouth: those wanka's from dover?

bluesfiend666: yeah they woz totle rubish I couldnt c y bill had booked them

beermonster37: rite well they crashed on the m1 going home awl killed

harpmouth: wot hapened?

beermonster37: breaks failed and thay hit a lorry i red about it in paper

bluesfiend666: they desserved it i saw them 2 walked out

nakedblueslady has entered the room

nakedblueslady: they died like zee did true blue's death i am naked in there memory

bluesfiend666: u r man

I was reading this at the laptop in the kitchen at half-past midnight. I'd eventually managed to get Jimmy down, after he had screamed and screamed, wondering, poor little mite, what the fuck was going on, and where Mummy was that night. Yeah, *nbl* hadn't shown any scruples about making sure that the Ideal Platonic Zed Beddington band was safe – a truck had squashed three innocent guys, as well as Don Wankstaff to make sure that the latter never shot his mouth off to anyone. I should be grateful, I supposed.

wurzelman has entered the room

beermonster37: ani1 els c the lad's @ cheltnham yestrday?

harpmouth: i woz there drummer is shithot tommo ok but mitch fukin orful kept goin rong

bluesfiend666: they shoud sak him and go out as 3peice

wurzelman: I don't think that that would be a good idea. A lot of fans really like Mitch

bluesfiend666: oh look its lah de fukin dah wanka ☹ fuk off wurzeltossa evry1 h8's u

harpmouth: bill looked like he woz chewin a wosp awl nite

bluesfiend666: havnt u hurd? he has split from his missus

harpmouth: str8 up?

beermonster37: i reckon she is cing her boss now yeah wurd in hospital is that bills wife gave him ultimate tum

harpmouth: wot?

beermonster37: eether music with zee bee band or life with her

nakedblueslady: i am naked 4 bill that is not tru

bluesfiend666: fuk off nakedblueslady u r bloke

nakedblueslady: that is not tru eether bill and his missus split becos i am naked 4 him

beermonster37: anyway wurd @ hospital is that doc cridland bumped off his wife 2 go out with bills missus

harpmouth: mayb that xplane's the giglist

beermonster37: wot u mean? wot that got 2 do with doc cridland?

harpmouth: no u wanka i mean if u look @ giglist there r no gig's any tusday's or wensday's and no gig's evry other weekend xcept odd 1 near notingham

beermonster37: u mean thats wen bill haz his sun?

harpmouth: yeah but he can do gig's around notingham becos he can get babsitter and b bak urly enuff

bluewallace has entered the room

bluewallace: my wife coud babsit 4 bill if he want's 2 do gig's in dundee on tuesday or wensday

harpmouth: bill is our hero he put's keeping the music alive furst

bluesfiend666: u r rite harpmuth he is hero and he is our bruther we must support him i was in farther's 4 justis u mite hav seen me on tv drest as batman on crain in mackle'sfield

beermonster37: we r his famly

nakedblueslady: u r rite he is hero we all feel his pane

bluesfiend666: fuk off nakedblueslady how can u kno pane of seperated farther?

nakedblueslady: aha so u do think i am lady ☺☺☺

***

"*A Tribute to Zed Beddington*" On a wet Thursday evening in Rhyl I stood outside the Regency Theatre, looking at the four faces on the posters in their perspex cases; me, Mitch, Tommo (back from leave and proud father of three) and Dickie Lumuwe, former school-teacher and opposition activist from Abidjan, who had been granted political asylum in the good old U of K, complete with a house in the Nottingham suburb of Lady Bay which he shared with his sister Corinne and his niece Florence.

The others were inside in the band room, drinking, but I was too restless. We had forty minutes before we went on and despite the rain I wanted a breath of fresh air, so I walked up and down the pavement, glancing over at the nearby pub, wondering about a quick beer. I heard the sound of convivial laughter from within, and pushed open the door.

I sat at a table with a pint, and carefully fumbled in my pocket for a pill. I'd long since used up the free ones Baggins had given me at Zedstock, and what with the stress of the separation and all the rest it hadn't been long before I'd made another trip out to West Bridgeford. You weren't meant to take them with alcohol, Baggins had told me, but that was the least of my worries. My phone beeped. **r u okay for violin lesson 2mrw? x** It was Jasmine. I had to take any income source I could now, given that the band could only gig on the nights I didn't have Jimmy and I was back to paying the bills on my tod. The pills weren't cheap and neither were Jimmy's nappies. The others had groused about the time restrictions, but they didn't have the initiative between them to sack me and take on the organising themselves, which was just as well, as *nbl* would have had something to say about that.

I answered Jasmine with **yes 3pm** and went to the screensaver, a picture of Jimmy in his pyjamas playing with his giant Lego. His fat jolly face beamed at me. What was Petra doing right now? Presumably tucking Jimmy up in her flat. Did she have someone waiting downstairs? At least it wouldn't be Cridland, after the police had found that stuff on his computer. He'd protested his innocence, saying that the machine must have been hacked into and the material planted, but that hadn't helped. I'd enjoyed reading the articles in the local press with the lurid headlines. Petra had refused to talk to me about it.

In the warmth of the pub I sat surrounded by waves of Welsh conversation, of which I couldn't understand a word. Maurice and Clothilde had picked up the lingo pretty quickly once they were settled. I recalled Zurab's exiguous English, and he and Petra talking in German. There'd been a bit of a diplomatic kerfuffle about Zurab. The consul seemed to suspect that the Russian secret services had been instrumental in wiping out a star of the Georgian cultural scene and had insisted on re-interviewing Mitch and me, but we'd stuck to our stories. Then conflict had broken out again in South Ossetia and the consulate had had more important things to deal with. I hadn't realised that there were so many Caucasian exiles north of the Trent. I'd gone home after that morning in the Swan to find that Petra already knew about Zurab – she'd heard the breathless reports of his death on the radio. She too had joked about the life expectancy of members of A Tribute to Zed Beddington, and how great it was that last night had been my last ever, but the joke had turned pretty sour once she'd realised that I wasn't leaving. I had stood there, not able to tell her the real reasons, not able to say that somewhere out there was our greatest fan, the fanatic who would bump me or anyone else off without a twinge should the line-up of the band be endangered, and she had upped and gone to a rented flat in Rushcliffe, pending buying somewhere. She was disappointed in me, that was all she had said. And fucked-off, once she realised that I'd cleaned our savings account out. "Why the hell did you do that?" she'd asked. I couldn't tell her, of course. "Is it somebody else? Have you spent our money on them?"

"No." I'd shook my head miserably, unable to go any further, paralysed by her anger. "I just needed it. I can't explain."

There were other things I couldn't explain to her either – like why I never made any arrangements with her about Jimmy via email, and why I had carried on with the band. We played the canonical set list, as immutable and sacred as the Torah, and we were doing our best to keep the music alive. But Mitch was on the downhill, unable to hit the right chords or sing in tune. Alison had never come back and before every gig, and after, he'd empty beer after beer down his throat. The week before, in Norwich, he'd had to go off after three numbers, and me and Maurice and Tommo had had to finish the set without him. *beermonster* had been there, in the audience, and had given his thumbs up online, saying that the band was just as good, if not better, without Mitch. The fans had been baying in cyberspace for Mitch's head ever since.

Like I always say, it's all about the fans. We travel from town to town in our van, and *harpmouth* keeps adding shots to his website store every time we pass a camera. We'd even recorded a new CD album, and inside I'd insisted on a dedication to our biggest fans, *harpmouth*, *bluewallace*, *beermonster37*, *bluesfiend666*, and, so as not to cause suspicion, *whitecliffs* and *wurzelman* as well. That should keep them happy, I'd thought, and stop them blowing the gaff on us. Although I'd thought it unwise to publicly include *nakedblueslady* in the list, neither did I want fuck *nbl* off by leaving her/him/*wtf* out, so we'd also included a special secret track, one that you only find by pressing a code into your computer when you played it on the disc-drive, a track called *A Tribute to nakedblueslady*. The others, Mitch, Tommo and Maurice had thought that this was some special joke of mine, maybe a hidden message to a former lover or something, and had gone along with it. But for me it was insurance. I'd texted *nbl* with the code, to make sure that s/he, it, whatever, knew it was there.

Yeah, it's our job to keep the fans happy. Give them what they want. My phone beeped again. Another message. **good luk 2nite i am naked 4 u bill never stop bringing us the music**

I drank my ale, and stood up. I didn't have time for another one. I went out into the rainy street, crossed the road and pushed my way into the theatre by the stage door. In the green room the others were still relaxing, Tommo with his feet up reading the paper, Mitch and Maurice playing darts, pints on a nearby table. As I stepped through the door Mitch's arrow flew past my nose and buried itself in the wall four feet from the board. I jumped. "Fuck, Mitch, what are you playing at?"

The house manager appeared at the door. "Ready, lads?" I nodded, grabbing my bass, and the other three got to their feet, Mitch and Tommo taking hold of their guitars. Holding our instruments, the tools of our trade, we threaded our way out through the ropes and scenery and paraphernalia, onto the stage, where spots picked us out. Against the light I could see that the auditorium was maybe half full. A voice through the PA system announced: "Ladies and Gentlemen, please welcome A Tribute to Zed Beddington, still keeping the music alive!!!" A smattering of applause went round, and died away. I cast an anxious glance at Tommo, who nodded, then Maurice. He was ready too, twirling his sticks like a majorette. Mitch was fiddling about with his guitar lead, his hands shaking as he tried to push the jack-plug into the amp. He was taking too long, and we were looking like amateurs. I was, against my will, just about to step across and help him when he got the jack in. I heard a bang, the lights went out, and in the wide blue flash which came from his amp I saw Mitch throw his arms up in the air, his whole body extending as he danced a tarantella. Then, as screams came from the audience, everything was black.